A QUARTER PAST LOVE

A Censored Time Novel

Corinne Arrowood

This is a work of fiction. Names, characters, places, and incidents, either are the product of the author's imagination or are used fictitiously. Any resemblance to actual persons, living or dead, events, or locales, is entirely coincidental.

First Paperback Edition, 2021

Published by Corinne Arrowood
United States of America
www.corinnearrowood.com

ISBN: 978-1-7368189-0-9 (paperback)
ISBN: 978-1-7368189-1-6 (ebook)

Cover and Interior Design by Gene Mollica Studio, LLC

Contents

Preface	v
Let's Get It Started	1
Like a Rock	15
Hush	29
Changes	43
Dirty Little Secret	61
Tell It Like It Is	75
Killing Me Softly	93
The Other Side of Life	107
I Can See Clearly	123
Happy Together	131
Imagine	149
We've Only Just Begun	165
Country Roads	169
For Once in My Life	193
Like A Rolling Stone	207
We Are Family	221
Quick Peek	244
Many Thanks...	246
About the Author	247

PREFACE

I guess to get the full story, I have to begin at the very moment the cells split and what was to be one baby ended up being two. Rand and I were two peas in a pod, literally. It was always Rand and Rainie, kinda like peanut butter and jelly or red beans and rice.

Sometimes it felt like we shared the same brain or, at the very least, thought waves. We could hear each other's thoughts and have whole conversations without saying a word. I don't know if other twins have the same capacity, but they probably do. Developing simultaneously in such a small place, it only made sense.

Momma called us her beautiful reds and had all kinds of quippy momma-isms. I suppose everyone's parents have their quirks. Momma came across with wisdom like a sage combined with innocence or naivete that boggled the mind.

We were both Daddy's girls. Being such a big man, he could easily scoop us both up at the same time, one in each arm. We would belly laugh with a tickle from deep in our souls. Daddy was sharp as a tack and would hold comment, so you never knew what he was thinking—probably one of the reasons he was such an adept attorney.

Now that I've created the family landscape, the story requires more insight into those involved. Our best friend was Meredith; we were like the three musketeers. We became close friends back in kindergarten at the Academy of the Sacred Heart. We were the three tallest girls in our class, thus always at the end of the line together. She was a couple of inches taller than us throughout the years, but we united in our stature, unlike all the other petite pearls of Jesus in our class. In our close fourteen years, we made memories for a lifetime, thank God. It was the night of Mer's fourteenth birthday party that my life changed forever.

We were playing truth or dare when Rand told me she was feeling bad and had a pain in her abdomen. I remember rolling my eyes and telling her I had a pain in my butt. She laughed. As the night progressed, I could feel her trying to suck up the pain, and then, like a lightning bolt, my right side had me doubled over, and I was feeling Rand's pain, and it was bad, real bad. We often had phantom pain when the other was sick or injured, but this was the worst pain ever, and I knew there was something desperately wrong with Rand. I called Momma and Daddy, and we left in our flannel nighties and bunny slippers. Within minutes Momma had Daddy speeding to the hospital, and that's when my hell opened up. They whisked us into the emergency room, determined Rand had appendicitis, and off they took her to surgery. No one had to tell me what was going on. My pain increased, making it hard to breathe, and then suddenly, there was nothing. I had never felt nothingness before. I couldn't see her, hear her voice, or feel her presence. The pain in my heart and void in my soul was so great that I spun layers and cocooned both. While it isolated me, it also dulled the sorrow. It wasn't supposed to be this way. If one of us had to die, why not me? I hated God. There would be no forgiving Him.

While my parents tried to mourn the monumental loss, I managed to wreak havoc at home, school, and anywhere I went. My parents and the nuns at school coddled me way too much, at first. According to therapists and counselors, I was acting out, and, boy, was I. What I needed was a boot up the butt and to stop feeling sorry for myself.

I remember screaming at Momma and Daddy and running to my room, throwing myself on the bed like a wild animal, and then clear as a bell, I heard, "Stop being a jackass. You're acting like a spoiled brat. Wah-wah." It stopped me dead in my over the top hysteria.

"Rand? But where—"

"Uh-duh. Rainie, you gotta cut this crap out. You're torturing Momma and Daddy, and it's not fair."

Nobody could ignite my anger like Rand. She knew how to push all the right buttons. "Not fair? You're not fair. How could you leave me? Did you just give up and die? You left me. I woulda never left you." My stomach churned with anger, and I could feel the heat radiating from my probably bright red face. *How dare she?*

"How dare I, really Rainie? I didn't choose to die; it was my time. Pull yourself together. No more pity parties. It's half past time you get yourself together." Then she was gone; I felt her leave and knew she was right. I washed my face, went downstairs, and hugged my parents. Little did I know, at that time, the odd path my life would take and how much I would rely on Rand. The loneliness and insecurity were right below the surface, and it didn't take much for it to rear its ugly head.

Let's Get It Started

"I hate waiting; he knows I hate waiting." The thoughts ran rampant. *Why did I institute the no call or text rule? Oh yeah, my snotty need to feel somehow superior.* The flustered sigh of irritation and aggravation spoke volumes. Intolerance mounted to fucking pissed. *Where the hell is he?* Time ticked past midnight; the late hour was sticky with a blanket of humidity. It was suffocating. Most respectable people were asleep or bedding for the night, not galivanting for some twisted rendezvous. Talking aloud to herself – "I'm too freakin high to go home. This is one helluva shit show." She even heard herself growl.

Eleven was their appointed time. It was already midnight. "Fifteen more minutes, and that's it." Rattling around in her brain, she heard the words to leave. Rand was beginning another ranting reprimand, making her even edgier. Animated with impatience like the shiny silver ball of an arcade game, she went from one ding to another—sit, crouch, pace, finally glancing out the leaded glass door of the apartment foyer. Her respirations elevated, topped off by a racing heartbeat. Between sniffling remnants of her previous bump of coke and wiping her nose, her movements were non-stop. She didn't wreak junkie, so she thought, just way too fucking high.

The place was a crap hole, but the rent was cheap, luring tenants of questionable character or those starting out without a pot to piss in, but there she was, stuck in her better-than-them attitude. *What a joke,* she thought. She was no better than the likes of the boy she was waiting for, and yes, he was a boy, just legal. She was old enough to know better. Some shrink would have a field day with her palette of dysfunction. She was a story of two lives; a secret life of meaningless sex, a smorgasbord of drugs, and recklessness, and then path two, PTA mom from the upper echelon enjoying a platonic relationship with a successful surgeon who radiated sophistication and class. Michael had been a good friend, and toy boy Ryan served his purpose.

Why was she wasting her time? *Hell,* she thought, *my time? More like wasting my life when it could have been, should have been, so much more.* It was easier to watch the spider spin her web amidst the years of layered dust, cracked paint, and half-patched holes, than to contemplate the "should haves" or "would haves" of her existence. Lost in her sea of demons, she hardly noticed the door open.

In walked a man, muscular and obviously of Latin descent. Had she been in her right mind, she'd have found him unsettling. She had seen him a time or two coming in or out of the other downstairs apartment. Given the late hours, she was pretty sure he had something to do with drugs or some other nefarious activity.

He looked her up and down. "What you doin'?" He winked at her. "Waitin' for ya boy?" He nodded toward his neighbor's door. "I know I'd neva leave you waitin'. Ya know it can be dangerous around here this late at night." His smile sent chills down her spine, but she returned with a look that said, back off.

He put his hands in the air with a look of amusement. "No disrespect meant." He pulled out his key and unlocked his apartment. He looked back at the redhead beauty. "You wanna wait in here?"

"Don't think so." She flexed her attitude as her body stiffened and her shoulders pinned back in a pathetic stance of bravery. She slung the baddest tough girl mug she could pull off.

"Have it your way." He walked in and shut the door.

Impatiently looking out the glass door waiting, there was no avoiding the reflection glaring back at her. "Rand, let it go."

Fifteen minutes passed, and his door opened again. "Still there, I see – got a proposition. You take a ride with me; I give you a gram of some excellent coke."

She turned. Her 5-8 put her almost eye to eye with him. She started to reach for the doorknob, planning to ignore his overtures.

"Hey, hey, chica, I ain't no bad guy, jus' listen." He grabbed her arm, not forcefully, but enough to get her attention. She jerked her head around, staring him down, continuing the tough girl image with pursed lips, squared-off eyes, and set jaw. "I got this business transaction where havin' a lovely lady like yourself might be advantageous. Ya know?" It appeared he was trying his hand at classy conversation. Attempt failed.

She pulled from his grasp, opened the door, and started to walk away with calculated steps. Her heart pounded harder and faster with eyes straight ahead, denying his presence.

"Gonna pass on kickin' blow? All you got to do is walk in with me. I do my transaction, we split, an' you get yourself a gram."

She turned back around in curious disbelief, but the party girl in her started contemplating. "That's ballsy. You don't know me." She looked him up and down, trying to throw him off his game, sizing him up. If she had met him at a country club party, she might have found him rather handsome in a Latin lover kind of way, but his slick mannerisms and posture screamed of a low-class sleazeball. Adjusting his junk with a not-so-sexy wink served to accentuate the tacky toothpick he seemed to twirl from side to side in his mouth.

"With them pupils of yours, I know you're buzzing high. Now you can do this thing or wait here all night? Your choice, but I'm headin out."

"You bring me back here?"

With a curious look, he answered. "Yeah, where else I bring you?" He cocked his head, his chin tucked, and his eyebrows crinkled. He was perplexed by the question.

"Guess it can't hurt. If you wanted to hurt me, you would've already." Her shoulders lowered, her lips parted, and her demeanor chilled a little, but her stomach still churned. In a split second, she pondered, *was it the high, the want of more coke, or the lure of living on the edge?*

"Lady, there's a lot of things I'd like to do to you but hurt you ain't one of them." He continued toward his car. She followed behind, got into his tricked-out old Trans Am, and off they went.

He asked, "Your name?"

"Pass." She stared straight ahead, knowing she crossed a line that maybe had no return.

"Whateva. I'm Marco."

He drove through the streets going from Mid-City to a seedy, desolate area close to the river. Old warehouses with windows broken or blacked-out lined the street. Her skin felt clammy in a cold sweat. Trepidation passed over her body like the chill of a threatening winter's storm as he backed in alongside one of the warehouses. Her throat began to constrict, making it difficult to swallow as the fear mounted. Too late to change direction.

"This is it. Don't look at no one. Got it?" His movements were jerky, and he came across as nervous, not like the slick badass he'd portrayed before.

"Yes." Her voice was shaky. *What the hell all for the sake of a gram? No, it was the thrilling rush from taking risks; the gram was merely lagniappe.*

He knocked a couple of times. The door opened to a crack. "Marco?"

"Yeh." He moved her in quickly.

The guy took one look at her, asking, "Whatchoo bring dis bitch for?" Then the conversation went to Spanish. She was quite sure she was the topic of discussion from the few years she'd had of Spanish and the way they both kept looking at her. Beads of sweat formed on her forehead, and her lips felt glued to her teeth. Yeah, she was nervous.

Another guy came up and pushed her into a room with a few chairs, couches, and a gun, or two, or three. There was a mound of coke on the table. Her eyes focused down with thoughts of the morning headlines: *Debutante body found in dumpster near river.*

She tried to will away the trembling of her body. Wrapped in her arms, she fidgeted, staring straight down at the filthy floor. She attempted to slow her pulse from the bounding thump of a bass drum to a slower, steady beat with measured breaths. She kept swallowing hard, wishing she could click her heels and be home safe and sound. Marco appeared, grabbed her arm, and pulled. "C'mon!" She shot out the door behind him and into the car.

"It's Rainie."

Marco looked confused.

"My name — is Rainie." She wanted to cry but held back the tears and desperately tried to control her quivering bottom lip. The muscle car roared with great veracity as they pulled back up to the Mid-City apartment. When they entered the building, she could hear the Rolling Stones. It meant Ryan was home.

"Ever want a real man an' not a boy, you know where I live."

She lightly knocked on the door.

He answered with a boyish grin, grabbed her by the waist, and pulled her in. "Hey babe, I thought you were gonna be here earlier, but I'm glad you didn't have to wait. I know how you hate it. I was confused on accounta your car being here, but no you. Bummer." He was such a stoner and such a boy, and what the hell was she doing?

A divorced mom of two, she occasionally dated a respectable doctor, all the while screwing and drugging with this boy who was only legal by a couple of years. The life she was living wasn't what she, or anyone, had planned for her.

Despite her streams of promises to God, to get her home safely to her two sons, ne'er to snort another line of cocaine, she always dismissed them as impractical promises to a god that had probably given up on her years ago. She didn't blame Him. She understood. In her eyes, she hadn't been the girl everyone had hoped she'd be with the drugs, alcohol, sex, and web of lies. But she knew, and she knew God knew.

"C'mere, you." He pressed his young body against her, planting a deep kiss. He made her feel sexy and young—not that 33 was old, but it wasn't 20. His metamorphosis from boy to man was ramping up. It was part of the attraction. She smiled after the kiss as the tickle in her belly raced through her body, turning up her heat.

There was usually little conversation between them, and this rendezvous was no different. It was raw, serving one purpose. The way she wanted it. After the final hurrah, he drifted into slumber. While he slept, he looked younger, making her feel even more flawed, maybe even a bit perverse.

In the quiet, still moments, she would let her thoughts drift to the past with both happy and sad moments. Often she visited the memory that had shattered her and perhaps changed her forever.

☜☞

She was a daddy's girl, and he became even more protective after Rand died. The death took a toll on everyone, especially Rainie.

Their relationship, while different after Rand's death, still lived on. Sometimes looking in the mirror, she'd see more than her reflection as though Rand was gazing at her, trying to engage in an exchange. She'd talk to the mirror and imagined she'd hear her voice. It happened often when she was a teenager, like a kid with an imaginary friend. There were many times Rand's words warned her of impending disaster. It was as though she was Rainie's guardian angel. Rand had seen her through a lot of troubling times, but Rainie turned it off or ignored it when she veered off the path and embarked on her dubious journey. Those fleeting moments were becoming less when she stopped heeding Rand's warnings.

☜☞

Even though it had been almost twenty years, it still felt fresh. The pain her parents must have felt, she couldn't fathom. The thought of anything happening to either of her boys was more than she could bear.

Ryan sleepily whispered as he turned in the bed to look at her. "Hey babe, you okay?"

She looked over at him, her expression indistinguishable. Content, happy, sad, angry, it was anyone's guess? "Yeah, lost in thought. I gotta go. My kids will be getting up soon. Remember not tonight," she smiled and lightly kissed him. She never wanted to talk after sex, she surmised by some of the things he'd said before that he had no idea if he was a run-of-the-mill fuck, or was it good for her too? He shouldn't worry; she was the head case, not him.

"Sucks," he retorted, starting to get out of the bed.

She dressed, grabbed her purse, and was gone. Racing down Jeff

Davis Pkwy, she figured she could make it home in fifteen minutes, maybe even get a shower and a couple of hours sleep.

Morning came fast. *Good thing*, she thought, *I didn't open Marco's gram.* Volunteering at the kid's school had helped to curtail her decadent behavior. All the "what ifs" ran through her head: *What if someone at the school found out? Allie? Momma? Crap of craps, Dad? Shake it off.*

Her phone broke her berating roll of paranoia. "Good morning, Rai." Meredith's voice sounded chipper. They had been through everything together: high school, college roommates, sorority sisters and stood in each other's wedding.

Meredith was with her when she saw Tom hanging on the office girl. She also knew about the drinking, drugs, promiscuity, and knew Rainie was close to going over the edge.

More than once, Mer had ventured onto the subject of her lifestyle, but Rainie laughed it off.

"How long are you going to be at the kids' school? I got a call offering us a chance to bid on King's Court." Mer quizzed.

"Wow. I didn't realize the job was still up for grabs. Who gave the referral?" She fired question after question. "Mer, I gotta get dressed." The whole time she was rummaging through her drawers like a wild woman trying to find her look for the day.

"Get to the office soon, ya hear, Rai?"

"Ciao!"

"Rainie, no more than a couple of hours, okay?" Meredith pressed.

"I promise," she hung up, dressed quickly.

Through squeals like tire sounds, the boys raced in. "Hurry up, Mom!"

"Alright, guys, first one to the car—" They scampered to the car. "Buckle the belts. Did y'all have fun last night?"

As Thomas spoke, his head bobbed in a know-it-all boastful way. "Allie picked us up from school and brought us for sno-balls, that was fun, and then she brought me to practice. I don't know what she did with the little turd after that. He was with Daddy when he picked me up, but they didn't get there in time to see my perfect goal. You shoulda seen it." She could feel his foot as he kicked the back of her seat like striking the ball.

"Your goal sounds awesome." Her eyes sparkled as she smiled at him through the rearview mirror, then her expression changed to one of disapproval. "Um, 'little turd'? It's not nice talk."

"That's what Daddy called him."

"Doesn't matter, Thomas, it's not nice." She resented the hell out of Tom, and the thought of him cramped her stomach, sending a surge of acid up her throat. She knew she could never pay him back for the betrayal and insecurity he caused her, and it pissed her off, even more every time the memory popped in her head.

Henry blurted out, "that's not all he called me. He told me he was mad at you, and you were a bad mommy. I told him nuh-uh, and he called me a little shit."

"Oh, he did? Well, that's really not nice, is it?" She bit the inside of her lip, trying to hold back her loathing. Thoughts ran through her head. *Picking on a five-year-old, what an asshole!*

They pulled up to Stuart Hall. Both boys gave a quick kiss and jumped out of the car.

As she pulled off, heading to Mer's, she called Tom. His secretary du jour answered. Before the girl could say anything, she began with an unenthused tone, "Hi, this is Rainie Todd. I need to speak to Tom, and he's busy is not an option."

"Yes, ma'am."

He picked up. "He's busy is not an option? What if I had been too busy? Why do you have to intimidate my secretaries? You get off on that?"

"No, I believe you're the one getting off on your secretaries, but that's not why I'm calling. Firstly, calling Henry a little shit and a little turd? Really Tom? He's five years old. Plus, it's only causing even more of an issue with Thomas bullying him when he sees you do it. Oh, and not forgetting the bad mommy slamming. Tom, keep the kids out of this. You forget you were the one who started this whole damn thing. Couldn't keep it in your pants."

"You are a bad mom, Rainie. Try staying home with the kids sometimes and give the nanny a night off."

"Keep the kids out of this. It's hard enough on them. I sure as shit don't slam you to them. Cut the crap. That's all, Tom, stop it!" and she hit the end call button. A rising heat whipped with hurricane-force, painting her face red with anger. *How dare he judge me.*

She pulled into Mer's, got out, and went in. With her throaty laugh, she called out. "I'm here, darling, as promised." Mer was turned in her chair with the phone to her ear. She pointed to the pad and the notes, raising her eyebrows excitedly.

"Sounds good. I understand the setting you want to create. No problem. Tomorrow morning it is. Yes, bright and early. See you then, sir."

She hung up. She was gleaming; a huge smile formed budding expression lines where crow's feet would ultimately land. "You're never going to believe this. We're not bidding on the job. He wants us to do it, period. We'll be dealing with him and him alone. He wants to see fabric, paint, paper samples, furniture pics and said he knows our taste is 'exquisite darling' and will follow our lead."

Rainie picked up the notepad. She flipped through the pages furrowing her brow. "Who is this guy, and where'd he come from?"

Meredith took the pad back, pulled Rainie to her side of the desk, and went through the notes, pencil to paper, checking off the highlights. "Cyril Page recommended us. I guess it was worth the aggravation of dealing with his wife. Anyway, his name is Kevin Cramer. He will," using air quotes, " 'never use the decorator he's used in the past ever again.' It sounded personal, maybe an ex. I don't know."

"Oh, my gosh. What an opportunity, and it provides the perfect diversion for me today. Tom is such a jerk!" Plopping at her own desk, her animated hands punctuated her anger with Tom. She couldn't help but feel the burn of disgust in her stomach. She knew it was a combo thing— rage topped off with guilt, an all too familiar feeling.

"Always has been, Rai. I never understood why you didn't see it. Your dad sure as hell did and does. He'd say, 'Tom thought himself to be the big fish, only he didn't realize it was a tiny pond.'" She gave Rainie a told-you-so grin.

"Not the first time I've heard that line. Ya know, Tom can pick on me all day, but Henry? C'mon, he's five. Asshole." She dropped it and decided to clear her mind. "Project?"

Meredith went over everything she knew about the upcoming project, and the rub was they needed concepts complete with swatches and sketches for the next morning.

Rainie twisted her hair up with a pencil. "We need to get this kickin'. Remember I have that formal thing with Michael tonight, plus I need some quality time with the boys." She tightly closed her eyes in frustration. *Why did I say yes to Michael? Like I have time for this.*

She took her stash out, using a credit card, chopped the tiny mound, held her golden straw for two fat lines up the nose, wiping the remnants with her finger. Meredith raised her eyebrows. "What? I'm beat. Needed a pick me up."

Mer shot a disapproving look. She didn't have to say a word, her eyes intensified with a glare, and it said it all.

"Not today, okay? I had a hellish night with little sleep and on the go first thing. So, give me a break." Rainie adjusted the pencil in her hair, avoiding eye contact.

Meredith leaned her elbows on her desk, pensively. "What's the deal with you and Mike, and what about your toy, Ryan, is it? You need to pick one. I can't believe Mike hasn't a clue about your cavorting and the coke. He'd be devastated, Rainie. He adores you, and it's the stability you and the boys need." Mer's comment formed a knot inside her. *Guilt or truth, whatever?*

Rainie threw her arms in the air with her usual don't-give-a-shit attitude, "Ryan makes me feel young and is a total escape from the bullshit. There's something titillating about making time to the Stones. We don't have to talk, just listen to the music, do a little toot, and rock-n-roll under the sheets." *Why can't Mer understand? It's pretty simple.*

A bit more sternly, Meredith countered, "And Mike, you sleeping with him too, or just letting him take you to great dinners? How many clients has he sent us? Seven, eight?"

Her body stiffened, preparing for a battle. "It's not like that. We're friends, period. He's cute, he's nice, he's funny, but there's nothing there. Understand?" She rocked back in her chair for contemplation.

"He's the only plastic surgeon I know who doesn't think he walks on water, Rainie. Shit, you get free Botox. You need to ditch the kid and grow up. Mike's a gem." Meredith balled up a piece of paper and threw it at her.

Rainie managed to go through four swatch books and half a gram of cocaine. Meredith had a good start on the storyboard, and for every line Rainie snorted, Meredith shot her a glance of disapproval. After hours of intense scrutiny, they pulled it all together.

"Mer, I think we're ready for tomorrow. I know it's only the first round, but we're off to a good start." She had a look of contentment like a dog with his favorite bone.

"I do love you, Rainie, and because I do, I'm telling you to get a grip. What was once something you did for a thrill has become a survival tool. Tom will nail you with the coke if he can, and you know it. When it was occasional, that was one thing, but this is out of control."

"I hear ya. We'll meet here in the morning and ride together, okay?" Her thoughts echoed in her mind, *yeah, I get it, but I need an escape. Try on my life, friend.*

The entire ride home, she thought about the coke, the lifestyle, and Ryan. Rand would be disappointed in what she had made of her life. A sick hollow ached deep.

She looked in her rearview mirror, and for a split second, caught a glimpse, albeit fleeting, she saw it. She saw the love and sadness in the eyes. "You were more together than me, Rand. I miss you."

In her head, she heard, "You're messing up bad." *What? What if you were the one left alone?*

The shrill of the phone startled her. Her heart pounded in her throat, almost choking a swallow before answering the call.

It was Michael. "Rainie, we still good for tonight? All well with you and the boys? "

"Oh, Michael, I've meant to call you all day. Sorry. Yes, we're fine. The past week has been crazy with school winding down for the boys and completing your last referral. Pick me up at seven?" She mentioned the new account.

"Yes, seven. King's Court?" He was smooth and collected.

"It's the new boutique hotel on Gravier. I'll tell you all about it tonight; I'm in the car line—"

"And you can't be on the phone." She could hear his smile through the phone, which brought a smile to her face.

"You got it."

"Later."

Once the boys loaded in the car, Rainie ran through her list of how'd the day go questions. "Pizza and a movie tonight, guys, and it's Allie's turn to pick the movie. I'm going to a party with Doctor Mike, but we'll be together all day tomorrow," she hesitated. "Oh, no, poopers."

The boys started with tummy giggles.

Henry cracked up, "Poopers?"

Thomas, with his feet, pushed against the front seat, retorted, "She remembered she has to do something, and she's not gonna be with us all day." Thomas rolled his eyes. "What now?"

"Ouch, that hurt. Auntie M hooked a good job. We have to meet in the morning." She and Thomas exchanged glances. Tom's *"you're a bad mom"* tromped through her brain. Guilt.

"Mommy, you don't work on Saturday, and Thomas has a soccer game. Who's gonna be with us? And don't say, Daddy, because he's going to the islands with his friend."

"I'll be done in time to get Thomas to the game." She winked at him. *Am I being called out by my boys, guilt, guilt, guilt? The meeting is a must-do. Shit.*

They got home, and the boys went straight for snacks and video games. She poured a glass of wine, sat with them, and checked her messages. She heard Allie come in.

"We're in the den. How was school?"

Allie turned the corner. "The last exam was today. I'm officially a senior." Her eyes twinkled as she smiled with pride.

☙☙

Allie had been the boys' nanny for three years. Things came together like a perfectly tuned symphony: Academic scholarship, a nanny post from the Todd's with residence, food, and better than fair pay. It checked all the right boxes.

Mr. Todd's infidelity hit her hard. She was closer to Rainie and could feel the emotional strain after Mr. Todd moved out. She admired Rainie's strength. There were no ands or buts. He cheated, and that evening she packed all his things, put them on the front porch, and threw on the deadbolts. There was no hysterical crying or yelling or screaming. She seemed above it all.

Rainie moved over on the sofa and patted a place for Allie to sit. "Senior. It's hard to believe. It's your movie pick tonight, don't let them talk you into something you don't want to watch." She looked at the boys as they wrestled over the game controller.

"I'm choosing Peter Pan. I love Peter Pan. What time is Doctor Mike going to be here?"

"Seven," looking over to the clock, "yikes, I have thirty minutes."

She grabbed her wine glass and almost sprinted to her room. After an abbreviated shower, she pulled out her teal strapless with the slit up the side and whipped up her hair into a stylish twist. She slipped on her old faithful metallic slingbacks, put on some slinky earrings and a few bracelets. She stood back, checked herself front and back, did a quick spritz of perfume, touched up her makeup, and put the perfect frosty lipstick on her full puckers. *Yeah,* she thought, *that works,* just in time for the door chimes.

Coming down the stairs, she could see Michael's silhouette through the leaded glass. She was sure he'd be perfect. He didn't go for Botox or fillers. Just gave in gracefully to Father Time. He was handsome or maybe cute—either way, he was an awesome friend.

She knew he wanted more. Many women would give their eyeteeth to have him. He had a total look of sophistication, yet wholesome and healthy. She liked him a lot but didn't get the warm flush she got with boy toy Ryan, who could have stepped out of an Abercrombie ad with his no styled messy hair and casually wrinkled clothes to complete the look. "You look gorgeous. Rainie, great color on you. I miss seeing you." His smile was genuine. Warm, real, Mer was right, maybe she should let someone take care of her, but she didn't feel any sexual attraction.

"And as always, you, sir, are the perfect gentleman and certainly know how to make a girl feel special." She gave him a big hug. *Yep, no tickle, but was sexual attraction that important?*

The boys scrambling to the door sounded like a herd of wild animals. "Doctor Mike, Doctor Mike," Henry hugged his legs. While just as excited, Thomas refrained from the hugging, but the excitement was in his voice.

LIKE A ROCK

Michael drove a black Mercedes Sedan, nothing fast and sexy, but sophisticated and classy. He was into what she called Spa music. Immediately any hostility, anxiety, pensiveness was gone.

He made things easy, radiating confidence and an "I'm comfortable in my own skin" aura.

She likened him to an old soul. He had nothing to prove and didn't engage in pissing contests. She had seen him annoyed once, and it was with Tom. No surprise there, Tom could've annoyed Mother Teresa!

"I can't wait to hear about your new project." He opened her car door.

After walking around the car and sliding behind the wheel, he looked at her as though waiting for an answer.

She laughed, "Nothing to tell yet, Michael, but it's exciting."

"How's school going for the boys? They seemed rambunctious today. I love the energy." His eyes glistened with his smile. He reversed the car, and off they went.

"School is good, and I'm glad it's winding down." She smiled back. He asked because he wanted to know, not just bullshit conversation. It was refreshing.

They pulled up to an event facility in the French Quarter, overlooking the river. It was elegant. The flickering flames of gas lamps softened the darkness of the evening. Men were in black tie, and the ladies perfectly donned in evening gowns. This scene is what Mer and her parents wanted for her. The question was, what did she want for herself? Excitement and nerves bubbled from her stomach to her throat.

Upon entering the party, she immediately recognized several faces of girls from high school. The girls of Sacred Heart had been a close-knit group. There had been much kindness toward her and her family when Rand died.

"Last time I saw some of these people was high school graduation." She looked directly into his eyes, "This is nice. Thanks." The sincerity emanated from her eyes. He was the proverbial good guy. She was glad she had said yes, after all.

"Let's go over and say hello to your old school mates." He directed her with a soft touch to the middle of her back. His presence exuded confidence, his smile warm, charming, and completely real. His eyes were full of expression as he spoke, and he made a point to look people square in the eyes as if to read their souls while depositing a smidge of his self-confidence.

"Michael, this is your thing with your people. I'm with you." She turned her head and spoke over her shoulder.

"Rainie, you'll recognize some faces from my office. I want you to have fun and enjoy yourself. The night is young, and we have time to say hello to everyone. Can I get you a glass of wine?"

"I'd love it. Thanks. Ladies' room?" He pointed her to the Hostess, who directed her down the hall and second door on the left. Once in the stall, she took the opportunity to hit her stash a couple of times. Upon leaving, she checked her nose for any tell-tale signs, freshened her lipstick, and then started down the hall toward the party.

A slender man approached. She smiled at him and went to pass him. In a nasty tone, the man uttered an undistinguishable slur. It was unsettling.

Michael appeared, "Rainie, figured I'd come find you, rather than wait. He took her elbow and pulled her close, "That guy was odd. Are you okay?"

"Yes. What a creep. Your timing, Michael, couldn't have been better."

He offered the wine glass to her, which she gladly accepted, taking a few swallows. *Screw the sipping.*

"Do you want to leave? I'd understand." His eyes looked deep into hers.

"Hell no, I'm not going to let some creep ruin our night." She straightened up, grabbed back her poise, and gave him a determined smile.

He tipped her chin up and looked into her eyes. "Sure? Say the word, and we'll be out of here."

Their eyes locked, and she nodded. *Oh my,* she had a brief shiver. She thought maybe it was the drugs and the confrontation, but it seemed to happen when their eyes met.

The rest of the evening went without a hitch. They mingled, danced, drank, chatted, and had the occasional and purposeful touch, followed by a flirtatious look and smile. As the party was winding down, he had the valet call them a cab.

"Rainie, I think I've had a little too much vino tonight." By this time, he had his tie off and looked laid back.

"You're so sensible." She was trying to be complimentary, but it came out a bit sideways. The last thing she wanted to do was be insulting; she leaned up and kissed his cheek.

"Not quite. You give me too much credit," Michael helped her into the cab.

She remained a little quiet on the way to her house. *How is this going to work?* She thought.

He gently kissed her hand. "I don't want the cab to drop you and then take me home. It cheapens the night. See, I'm not always sensible."

"Michael, we've known each other for years, you can stay at my house. In fact, it might be a solution to my morning dilemma."

He looked curiously at her with a tilt of the head and a questioning brow.

"I have a meeting in the morning for King's Court, and I didn't want to ask Allie to work on the weekend. She will if I need her. No is always an okay answer, Michael."

"Are you kidding me?" His smile brightened, his eyes danced, and he was obviously eager. "I'd love it. After, you could take me to get my car?"

"Absolutely!" She melted into his side, wrapping her arm around his waist. He pulled her in tighter.

They arrived at her house.

She kicked off her shoes, dropped her evening bag, and plopped on the sofa in the den.

"My feet hurt. It's been a while since I've danced so much." She felt almost giddy. "Thank you, Michael. I had a blast."

"Here," he sat next to her and grabbed her feet, turning her to an almost lying down position. "You need a foot massage. It'll do the trick."

His hands were strong and practiced. He raised one of her legs, gently kissing each toe. "Getting better?" he looked up at her as he kissed the last toe.

"Yes, much better. Don't stop." She cooed.

He firmly grasped her foot, raising it even higher but gently bending her knee. "Maybe I better stop."

"Or maybe not." She seductively smiled. She felt her pulse quicken and knew there was probably dampness to her panties.

He always came across as the boy next door; this was a side of him she'd never seen. He continued to kiss her foot, slowly gliding his hand up her inner thigh, lightly touching her.

Her skin reacted with signs of arousal. Michael maneuvered up to about an inch of her panties. Inside her body, it felt like an acrobatic cascade of handsprings and cartwheels. Every nerve ending was aware of his touch. Her back arched, and her head tilted back. He slowly worked his way back down to her foot.

His sexual prowess was beyond any picture she ever had of him. *Wait, why is he stopping?* She waited for his next touch, his next magical move. The pause was growing longer and longer.

He placed her foot next to the other, then drew her closer to him. He whispered, "I think we better stop for the night. Don't you?"

"No. I think maybe we should take this to my room." She said with conviction, punctuating it with her ice-blue eyes. *Stop? Hell no!*

"Not tonight. Not with your boys here. I need to sleep on the sofa tonight, and you, beautiful lady, can play out the rest of the scenario any way you want in the privacy of your dreams. Maybe next weekend, when the boys are with Tom, we can plan a night to talk about a different ending to the night." He kissed her lips softly with a hint of his tongue. He increased the heat as the kiss deepened, then slowly, he let off. He kissed the tip of her nose and her forehead ever-so-lightly. "Sweet dreams."

"But—"

He put a finger over her lips. "Shh. Good night, Rainie. Sleep well."

She didn't know what to make of the encounter. She went up to her bedroom, taking with her thoughts of the evening, and what could've been a different outcome and what that might be like. She thought, *amazing, and yet, it was only a kiss.*

She felt Rand's presence, "alright already, he's got potential. From the vibes, I'm getting you approve? Good night, Rand."

Her peaceful sleep was disturbed by two young boys reeling in excitement, as though it were Christmas and Santa Claus had come.

"Mommy, Mommy, wake up! You're never gonna believe who's in the den. Doctor Mike's in the den."

They jumped on her bed, bouncing.

"I know, boys. I know. He's going to be with y'all while I go to the meeting this morning." She sat up, stretching the slumber from her body.

They went wild with excitement.

"I'm glad you guys are excited. Please, listen to him. Don't act up."

"I promise." Thomas put his hand over his heart.

Were they utterly starved for positive male attention? Since the separation, Tom resentfully took them on his weekends and was less than loving. He was not the diaper changing, up in the middle of the night kind of dad.

There were no stones for her to throw; she was hardly mom-of-the-year material. She couldn't remember a day in the past year and a half she hadn't been high, tipsy, or downright screwed up. When she found out about Tom's cheating, she went into self-destruct mode.

Her self-worth had taken a big hit when Rand died. Her shrink had helped her patch it, but it was always there, lying under the surface. Tom's infidelity sealed the deal and thus began the spiral. A glass of wine in her hand made her feel a little more sophisticated and was as essential as the right pair of shoes, while cocaine fostered a false sense of confidence.

She shooed the boys out so she could get in the shower and get ready for her meeting.

Regarding Michael after the oddly fabulous night— *Do I need to act like nothing happened? What's Michael gonna say? I wonder how he's gonna handle things.* Her mind ticked over and over as she washed, dried, and styled her hair. She did a couple lines of coke and finished her make-up. "Okay, here we go," and she exhaled.

Downstairs, Henry was showing Michael his new shoe-tying skill.

"Little man, good job. Tying your shoes was the ticket to first grade?"

"Yes!" Henry beamed.

"Good morning, guys!" her smile brightened the room as she entered.

"Good morning, yourself! You look lovely this morning." A tickle began from deep within like the beginning of an exquisite sunrise. "I thought we could drop you off at Meredith's, y'all could go to your meeting together, and the boys and I might get breakfast at Camelia Grill. They said they've never had a chocolate freeze." He looked at Thomas, smiling, "And I said whaaat?" With exaggeration, he threw his arms up in exclamation. Both boys giggled. "How's that sound to you, Rainie?"

"Works for me if it works for y'all." Thomas and Henry jumped and high-fived with the news of being with Michael.

They went to get in the car, Michael going to the passenger side.

"Want me to drive to Mer's, and we can switch over there?" She asked.

He opened the door, cleared his throat, and nodded his head, suggesting she get in the passenger seat. "I think I can manage to get you to Meredith's. If I start going the wrong way—"

The boys were already in the car, and as she positioned to get in the car, he lightly kissed behind her ear. "Sleep well?"

She felt a hot flush come over her body. She glanced at him. "Yes, I did. I hope the sofa wasn't too unbearable." She playfully batted her eyes.

As he walked around the car, he gave her a devilish grin, "It was fine." *The new Michael— most intriguing.*

He managed to navigate to Mer's with only a couple of prompts. "Good luck. Go get 'em."

She got out of the car and blew kisses to her boys. Mer was already coming out of her house. She hurried to the car with a big smile. "Hey, boys. Good to see you, Mike."

"Nice to see you, Meredith. Y'all break a leg. Rainie, call me when you're ready for us to come getcha." They waved as he drove away.

Mer looked over at her with questioning eyes. She raised her eyebrows with a shit-eatin' grin.

"I'll tell you all about it later. For right now, we have everything? Let's stay focused." They got in Mer's car and took off.

"Did Mike spend the night at your house? That's all the detail I'm going to ask for now." She grinned with a wicked glance.

"Yes, on the den couch. He thought he'd had too much wine, called a cab, spent the night, taking the boys to breakfast now, and then I'm bringing him to his car. Bah-da-boom. That's the story." Rainie had a brightness to her smile and seemed even more playful than usual.

"The hell it is, but we have to get the presentation done."

They parked about a half-block away from King's Court. The structural renovation of the building was near completion.

Walking up to the entrance, a short, roundish man, smartly dressed and impeccably coiffed, approached them with his hand out. "Cyril described you perfectly, tall blonde shoulder-length hair, making you Meredith James, and long auburn hair with unmistakable eyes, making you Rainie Todd."

He shook both the women's hands. "And I" He put his hand on his chest, "Am Kevin Cramer. Right this way, ladies."

"The decor you put together for Cyril was artful. It perfectly embraced the architecture of his home. I had to ask him who his decorator was, and he told me about you two. Thank you for agreeing to meet with me on such short notice. I can't wait to see your visions for King's Court."

After a thorough presentation, Kevin seemed elated. "Ladies, it's as though you saw the vision I had in my head. Exciting knowing we are on the same page. Loving everything, thus far."

Thirty more minutes of chatter back and forth addressed costs, billing procedure, timeline, and fee. Kevin wasted no time and pulled out the contract in record time, which fueled their excitement. Their energy sprouted from them like the Mardi Gras fountain.

Leaving the hotel, Mer looked over. "Okay, sista, spill the beans! You're beaming, and it's not just the meeting. Do tell." She put the storyboards in the car and turned with her hand on her hip. "Hm?"

Rainie got into Meredith's taupe-colored Jeep. She began the recitation of the prior evening's excitement. "The night was great. He looked more than good. I usually think he's cute and sweet, but there was more than cute and sweet last night. He took the reins and directed the night." Rainie was very matter-of-fact, but twinkling glints in her eyes told a different story.

"We danced all night. He's most engaging. He really listened to me. Like he wanted to know all about the plans for today's meeting. And as I told you, we both had too many glasses of wine and had to cab it back to my house. We didn't even think about his car until it was a moot point. Get this," she could feel her face flush thinking about the evening. "He thought it would cheapen the night to drop me and cab to his place. So, he stayed over." She gave a snarky smile.

"I can see it in your eyes; there's more. When have you ever held back? C'mon." Meredith wasn't about to let it go there. By this time, they were almost to the office.

In an "if you insist" tone Rainie began. "I told him my feet hurt. He massaged my feet." And then she began to giggle. "Oh, my gosh, he then started kissing my toes sweetly, but with some kind of sexy thing. Then he said," putting on a male-sounding voice. " 'I think this needs to stop.' I was like hell no."

"And?" Mer pushed.

"He continued to kiss my toes. Tongue was involved, then he tickled the inside of my leg as he kissed or whatever'd my toes, feet, ankles. Shit, he went all the way up, almost to my panties, and then was like, 'we need to stop here.' I was like, 'I don't think so. We need to take this to my room.'

"He said no because the boys were there, then lays this amazing kiss on me. I swear he didn't touch anything, but I sure as hell felt like he did. He told me to go to sleep and dream about alternate endings to the night.

"I have never before had someone take such control. It wasn't bad or mean or nasty or dirty feeling. It was amazing." Her voice took on an almost dreamy sound, surprising herself. "I'm not sure what to make of it or where it's gonna go."

"Wowza. You hit the bonanza." Mer's face lit up. "He's nice, funny, good looking, loves your kids, totally digs you, and from your description has sex skills. If you don't get on that, you're a fool. Hello! Plus, he's got great taste, no ex-wife baggage. I think you're the only woman he's ever loved."

"Now you're getting carried away. Loved?" She snickered. "He has had a serious girlfriend, Mer." She turned sideways in her seat.

"Only because you were gaga over Tom. Speaking of Tom, has he ever made you feel like that? Be honest. I bet it was all about him and his jollies." They pulled into the driveway.

She called Michael, "Where are y'all?" Her face beamed with a girly smile, and once again, she could feel the dance of butterflies in her stomach.

"We just finished kicking a soccer ball around in the park and figured you'd be done soon. We're now on our way to you."

"Perfect timing." She flirted.

Minutes later, he pulled up. On the way to get his car, the boys talked about how the three of them passed the ball. It was a dream come true having her boys play together and having Thomas compliment Henry.

Maybe there might be a place in her life for Michael. He seemed to have a positive influence on her boys. They pulled up to the valet, and he bid his farewell to the boys, wished Thomas luck in his game, and then gave her a quick wink and a smile.

"Call you Monday?" he asked. Her belly responded in flip-flops.

"Please." She said in a throaty voice, followed by a pucker of her lips and a wink. Inadvertently, he ran his tongue across his teeth, keeping his tongue on his eye tooth's tip with a huge smile. The valet pulled up. She felt a warm twinge between her legs. *Yeah, Mer*, she thought, *Wowza!*

When they got home, it was like a fire drill, everyone knowing their job. Thomas changed into his uniform and grabbed his sports bag. They were off to the field.

Thomas played his heart out, and even she could see he had a better understanding of the game and skills to match than his team members. Some of the dads high-fived him, which put him on top of the world.

The rest of the weekend went well. Sunday morning, straight up eleven, Rainie and the boys met her parents for Mass and then lunch at the Club.

"Suga, you had a nice time with Mike Friday night?" *Mer*, she thought. She made a mental note to scold Mer for blabbing.

"Did Mer tell you we won the bid for the renovation design of King's Court? That'll be quite a feather in our cap." She smiled and took a big sip of her wine.

No sooner had she put the glass down, one of the wait staff topped her off. She looked up to thank their server and almost choked. It was Ryan. "Thank you. That'll be good."

"My pleasure," he grinned with a twinkle in his eye.

Oh, crap, she thought, *this is going to be awkward*. She tried to avoid looking at Ryan but couldn't help herself. She'd steal glances at him, pretending to look at something or someone else.

She could tell he knew there was a cocky levity in his step. He was getting off on her watching him. Her heart was racing with fear of being outed. She was completely distracted.

"Are you all right, suga? Momma asked you a question."

"I'm sorry, I guess I'm preoccupied with the new project. What was it, Momma?"

"Just my point, do you think the project might be a bit much for the two of you girls to handle? I worry about you, Rainie."

"Momma, I'm fine, and of course, we can handle it. King's Court won't be our first commercial job. I promise I'm fine, but I need to use the little girl's room right now. If you would, please excuse me." All she could think about was Michael. Ryan was cute, but Michael left her smoldering.

She walked across the room in the direction of the restroom. She felt someone coming up alongside her.

"Hey, babe. I didn't know you came here, got hired last week. I hope it didn't freak you out. I tried to be cool, but I gotta say when I saw you walk in, I got a party in my pants. Gonna see you tonight?

Eight, maybe?" He peeled off from walking near her and headed to the bar.

She loudly whispered, "Eight-thirty, maybe nine."

When she got to the restroom, she had to gain composure, doubting her decision to see him. She looked in the mirror and stared back at her reflection, whispering aloud, "Okay, okay. I'll end it with him tonight. Why do you always have to argue with me?" Her voice was crystal clear, "Cuz you know I'm right, Rai." *Whatever, Rand.*

Moments later, a few ladies walked in, so ended their exchange.

The rest of the lunch was pleasant. Her dad had such a cool and calm demeanor, and when he looked at her, the love overflowed.

"Don't let Momma bother you. Y'all are more than capable of handling your business. I have full confidence in you. Meredith is a true friend to you, Rainie. I'm pleased you and Mike are friendly. From what I hear, he's stand up with a lot of character. Not like, you know who."

"Dad, not now, the boys." Her face was kind but determined.

She patted his hand and glanced in the direction of the boys who were spearing maraschino cherries on plastic cocktail swords. She didn't know what the boys would innocently say to their dad, and it was a headache she didn't need.

"Y'all, it's about time I need to get these two home. We've had a busy weekend, and with school coming to an end, we need to make the very best of it. Momma, talk to you tomorrow."

They walked out as a family, and her dad made sure she made it to her car, slipping her a couple of twenties.

"Not necessary, Dad, I'm doing well. One good thing about Tom is he's like clockwork with child support. He's good with the money but lousy with the attention and emotional support." She gave him a big hug. "Love you, Dad. You're my rock."

"You're my girl." Her heart filled. "We need some time together, and you need to go see your momma. She could use some time with you. Okay, suga?" He leaned in the car, putting his hand on her shoulder.

"I will. I promise." She waved goodbye, took in a deep breath. *Life feels good for a change.* The whole way home, she rehearsed in her mind how and what she was going to tell Ryan. Was she sure she wanted to end it? He was such fun, and it was simple with no expectations. There was something to be said for simple, after all.

Allie was asleep on the couch when they arrived home, but her slumber didn't last long with two rambunctious boys.

"Sorry, I tried to shush them. You've had a restful day?"

"I guess, but I miss y'all when you're gone. Things seem empty and too quiet when these two crazy guys aren't home." Rainie noticed how down Allie seemed.

All the while, Allie was thinking about her recent visions of Rainie's dead sister. Allie could see Rand looking at her, trying to get a response. Somebody had to do something before Rainie totally went down the tubes. Meredith's disapproving looks and comments were having no impact whatsoever.

The presence had begun soon after Tom's betrayal. There had been a time or two when it felt like someone was in the house, but the feeling was more like someone watching over the family. Not that she was one of those people who believed in ghosts, but there was no disputing; something was present in the house. It was there and was benevolent.

"We're here now, sweet girl." She leaned over and hugged her. "You're always welcome to come with us to Mass and lunch. Today was more than interesting. I got the third degree about my date from Mom and Dad. It's complicated. Do you mind if I head out for an hour or two?"

Allie couldn't hold back a smile. "No problem."

"What?" Rainie raised her eyebrows, bewildered.

"None of my business, but I know you're meeting someone, and I think it's good. I wish I could find someone that wasn't a jerk, a loser or lookin' for—"

"I don't know about good, but it's a distraction." Rainie rolled her eyes and shrugged.

"I get it. I can tell you like Doctor Mike, but that's more of a get serious kinda thing, I guess." Allie had a questioning look in her eye as though nit-picking some kind of truth or perhaps where the boundary lines were.

"Sounds like good reasoning to me. You seem down. All okay with you?" Rainie turned down the TV. "What's on your mind?"

"I'm fine. Talk about complicated. It'll last another day." Allie looked down but was nervously playing with the fringe on the blanket.

Wagging a finger in Allie's direction, "I'm going to hold you to it. Don't make me worry about you."

"It's all good." She reassured.

For the next few hours, they played with the boys, flipped through magazines, and chatted about nothing requiring thought. She checked the clock.

"Boys, get to bed and don't give Allie any slack, got it? Give me kisses." After a quick hug, she grabbed her purse and headed for Ryan's.

Much of the way there, she rehearsed what she would say to end it with him. She played devil's advocate aloud. There were pros and cons, but more cons. Rand's presence was strong, perhaps she was trying to give her the courage to break it off, or maybe she thought Ryan was hot, available, and casual. Her heart pounded in her chest from nerves like someone had turned the bass way up. "I feel you. Am I doing the right thing?" Not even the slightest whisper and then a brief – Grow up, Rainie! And just as fast, she felt Rand's spirit leave.

The thought of anything with Michael was a new concept stirred by his curious behavior and probably too many glasses of wine. *Maybe friends with a twist?* A wave of warmth rolled through her body.

As she pulled up to Ryan's, she could see light coming from a side window. She almost chickened out at the door, but he opened it before she could flee.

He pulled her close to him. "How weird was it seeing you today at my work, especially with your family? Man, you're like a real mom. I neva thought about it. It's not like you eva talk about them, ya know what I mean? I think of you like a chick I got major hots for." He squeezed her tighter with a bright smile. "All I been thinkin' about since I seen you is hookin' up." He backed her up to his bed, never letting go. He looked her straight in the eyes as he tugged on her clothes. "I wanted to follow you into the ladies' room, pull down your panties, and—"

"We have to talk, not play." She was serious, and it showed in her expressionless face.

His face went blank with confusion.

"Ryan, I can't come see you anymore. We always have a good time, and it's not you." She took his roving hand. She felt like crying and a lump formed in her throat, making it difficult to swallow. His bubbly Ryan-esque had vanished, and he was sad.

"Wow, I didn't see that coming. You're not like a lot of the other girls. You aren't looking for a boyfriend, and you don't make crazy demands. You're fun without drama shit. You're not diggin' me anymore?" He cocked his head to the side in question.

"Boo, firstly, you're right I'm not like the other girls. I'm not a girl. I'm a grown-ass woman with two children. Of course, I like being with you, but my ex is making things difficult for me. I don't need to give him anything to throw at me." She put her hand on his face.

"What a douchebag. Pisses me off." His eyes were sad and bewildered.

"I know it's out of the blue. It's not you, Ryan. Not you at all."

She could see his confusion. Her eyes teared up, knowing she had caused his sadness. She wasn't sure if it was what she wanted, but it was the best thing for now.

"Who knows what the future holds for either of us? I'm kinda freakin' out right now, that's all. It's not you. It's me." She emphasized again.

He tried to kiss her. "We got tonight, right?" He began to unbutton her shirt. She backed away and sat close to his side table.

She poured some coke on a magazine, chopped it with her credit card, made a bunch of lines, and handed him her gold straw.

"Ryan, you're precious. Our relationship isn't healthy for me and, sure as hell, not healthy for you." She was coming across more like a big sister than his hot lover.

She lightly kissed him. He wrapped his arms around her waist.

"I got it." He gently kissed her. "It's kinda weird to think I won't see you, but it's been real, babe."

Driving home, she felt sad. The whole thing was confusing, but ending the guilty pleasure was the best thing she could do for Ryan, as well as maybe starting to pull herself out of the destructive spiral.

HUSH

Allie stood facing the mirror in her bathroom and rehearsed. "Rainie, we have to talk. No." She put her head down, swept her hair back, and changed her expression, "Rainie, there's been, no, that's not right, either." She cleared her throat and smiled into the mirror, "Rainie, you know how you asked me what was wrong if I was okay? Yeah, that sounds better."

"Girl, please. Just tell her. Tell her all of it. Direct. You don't need to practice. Do it." Allie looked at the reflection of the young girl leaning against the wall behind her.

Allie turned to her, wringing her hands. "It's hard. You don't. No can't get it. She's your sister or was, or you know what I mean. What if she gets mad at me because you've talked to me instead of—" Allie sounded panicked.

Rand looked at her eye to eye. "I go to her a lot, but she doesn't want to hear me or talk to me. Rainie feels guilty and is on a collision course. She blames herself that I died, then she got better, and then stupid Tom." Rand boldly emphasized, "You have to tell her, and for crying out loud, don't tell her it's good she's messing around with the boy."

"I don't know who he is. I only know there's someone. I wanted to let Rainie know I knew some things, but who am I to say it's bad or she's wrong? You don't know how hurt—" she stopped. "Sorry, of course, you know. I'll try again."

"Don't try. Do it!" For once, she looked menacing.

Allie heard the front door open. She immediately collected herself, took a deep breath, and decided she would divulge all right then. She called out. "Glad you're home. I need to—" Allie met Rainie in the den.

Rainie warmly smiled, dropped her things on the coffee table, and sat on the sofa, patting the cushion next to her. "I told you anytime. What's going on?"

She sat facing her, gently smiling as a mother would to a saddened child. "I know I'm going to fumble through this, but I need you to listen and hear me."

Puzzled, she said, "Okay, I'm listening."

"I'm just going to say it. For some time, your sister has been talking to me, but I thought I was going crazy and ignored her." While Allie seemed calm and completely serious, Rainie couldn't comprehend the totality of what Allie was saying but continued to look her in the eyes.

"She's worried about you and thinks you're on some destructive course with the drinking, cocaine, and sleeping around. Rainie, it's not me saying this. She told me I had to tell you because she's been trying to talk to you, and she says you dismiss her. I don't know how else to tell you, and this is awkward and uncomfortable as hell. I'm not crazy, and I know it sounds crazy, and that's it." *You damn right it sounds crazy* was all Rainie could think.

There was utter silence as Rainie looked at her, stunned, squinting her eyes, and trying to process. She sat tall and almost standoffish. "Like how do you mean Rand has been coming to you? How do you know it's even Rand?"

In disbelief of the question, Allie answered in an impatient tone, "For starters, she looks like you, only younger. When I pretended not to see her, she got right in my face and said, 'I know you see me. I need you to do something for me. It's important, or I wouldn't be talking to you.' So, that's how I know." Bewildered, Rainie also felt perturbed and could feel her muscles tightening. All she kept thinking was, *really? I call bullshit.*

"She talks to me a lot. She tells me things I don't want to know about you. I look at you like a mom or a big sister. I don't want to know the crazy things you do. I just want to know what you want me to know. Do you understand? I'm not crazy, and I haven't told anyone else. You're looking at me like you think I'm crazy. I'm not. Say something."

Rainie sat still for a few seconds trying to collect herself, then softly, but with intent, said, "What am I supposed to say?" she looked her in the eyes. "This, Allie, is a lot to take in. I don't think you would outright make something up, but it sounds weird. I admit I can feel her presence and always have since, well, since her death. She speaks to me in my head. It was something we could do as kids. We could hold entire conversations, and no one would know it. Anytime I've started getting in trouble, I can feel her nudging me to do the right thing, but what I don't get is why you, why not Momma or Daddy, why you?" There was a blanket of confusion on her face as well as self-righteous indignation.

The room suddenly became noticeably cold as an outline of her sister approached.

"Holy shit!" Rainie tried to stay calm, but she was anything but calm. Her heart was pounding, and her body began to tremble. The situation was beyond any scope of reason she had ever had, and it defied everything she thought was possible. She could feel and hear her voice but never face to face and definitely not with an angry Rand.

The closer the apparition got, the more defined her features were, and there was no doubt.

She could tell Rand was pissed. She knew the look and knew she was about to be blasted like when they were kids. "Tell Momma, tell Daddy, are you kidding me? All their eggs are in one basket." The temperature dropped and the air got heavier as Rand's anger escalated.

Rainie dropped her head into her chest. Part of her didn't want to look at her, and perhaps, it was all some weird dream, but she knew the truth. Her heart was full of shame and sadness. She held Allie's hand.

"Rainie, it would tear them to bits. I've tried to talk to you in dreams, whispers in your ear, but you shut me down. I've tried with mirrors, but you turn your head. I had no choice. This girl listened, although she took forever to do anything."

There was no denying this occurrence; it was definitely her angry sister coming to her from beyond the grave. Even though Rand was mad at her, she could feel the love they shared, and she desperately missed it. The scolding continued. "You're lucky, and you don't even know it. Saying you feel guilty about me and it's your fault – What? You think you're all that? News flash, you're not! We go to God when He calls us. Period."

The room was noticeably colder, like the chill of December. She looked at Rainie. "Don't cha think I would have liked to drive, I mean legally with a driver's license and all, and not just in Audubon Park? Remember we talked about our sweet sixteen party, and you wouldn't even do that!"

Rand's eyes were sad. She shook her head in disappointment. It broke Rainie's heart, and all she could do was cry, "I'm sorry, Rand. I miss you so much." The tears were turning into sobs, but Rand didn't let up.

"You haven't even celebrated our birthday, not once, not even when those sweet babies of yours wanted to make it a big deal." She cocked her head to the side. "You can be infuriating. I knew if the girl told you about me, you'd let your guard down, feeling slighted, jealous, and maybe, just maybe, you'd be open to see me, hear me, and let me tell you how much you're screwing up. You're making a mess of something that should be beautiful. Tom's a jerk, I'll give you that, but he gave you two precious boys. Why is it you listen to me sometimes and ignore me when you shouldn't?"

With a longing look, she delivered her last words, as though it should be a mantra. "Rainie, please, live it fully. Live it happy. Live." And, as quick as she had appeared, she was gone. Rainie held her head in her hands and wept. Her breath hitched in her chest.

"You see? I'm not crazy, Rainie. Whatever you need." Allie was like a deer in the headlights, eyes wide open, staring blankly as the tears tumbled from her eyes.

Rainie gazed off into the empty space, a river of tears rolling down her face.

"Oh, God, Allie, I'm sorry. I'm sorry I put you in such a position." She continued to look into the emptiness. Then turned toward Allie, "I'm sorry I didn't believe you. Fuck, I trust you with the most precious things in life to me, my boys. Yet, I doubted you."

"I would've doubted me too. I know I sounded crazy, but I felt even crazier." Where would it go from there?

"If I go to my shrink and tell him Rand came and talked to me, he's going to put me in a nuthouse. And she was right; Momma and Daddy need to stay insulated from all this. The only one I think I can tell is Mer. She knows everything. I've been selfish and pathetic." She shook her head in disgust.

She looked up as though talking to the God who had stolen her sister. "I'm going to make this right. Please, God, help me." *Please. Please. Please,* she thought over and over.

They both leaned back on the couch, exhausted beyond words. Slowly Rainie muttered a word or two. It was nearing one in the morning, and wake-up time was going to come quickly. It was time to get some sleep.

In bed, she looked up at the ceiling. "Are you with me always? Can you even look into my heart, or is it like you're looking into a window and only see some things? If you can be a part of my life and maybe even live through me, we could be together always, like before."

There was silence, so much so she could hear the beating of her own heart. She was sad; the missing Rand pain was the worst. It started in the very pit of her gut and clawed through her heart and soul like a ravenous wild animal ripping apart everything in its way. She turned into her pillow and wept. She whispered, "I miss you. I've never been whole since I lost you."

She got out of bed, went to her stash, brought it to the bathroom, and flushed. "That's that."

She found herself at a loss for words when she went to bed but knew something needed to be said. "It's been a long time, God, and I don't know where to begin. I've made a mess of my life. Father, forgive me for my sins. I have acted terribly and have not been a good mother to my children. I pray for the strength to keep my life on the right path. Make me a better person. I guess that's it for now. Thank you. Amen." After her prayer, she dropped into a deep sleep. So deep was her slumber; she didn't feel the presence next to her.

Morning came, and with it, a new peace. Her emotions felt more real, more authentic. As she thought back on the revelation, it seemed a dream, although she knew it happened. The routine swung right into action like always, but somehow she felt a difference, and it was good.

"Any great plans for your day, Allie? If not, come play with Mer and me." They went down, grabbed a muffin, each with juice. "C'mon, boys gotta go. Oh, and empty your pockets. I saw you stash treasures." They got in the car and started heading to school.

Her phone rang, "Hi, Michael. The weekend was great, and the game went well. Early dinner? I'm not sure since —"

The boys screamed into the phone, "Yes, Doctor Mike. Yes."

"Michael, can I call you back in ten?" she said with frustration.

"Sure thing, I can't wait much later. I have back-to-back cases. Goodbye to the boys, talk to you in a few."

Thank Goodness, it's moving fast. There were no issues in the car line.

She dialed him back. "Hey, sorry, I know that was a bit awkward with the boys."

"Not at all. I understand it's a school night. I figured it would have to be an early dinner for them, and if Allie is there, she can come along. I have room for five in my car. It won't be anything fancy, maybe Houston's. Sound good to you? If so, I'll pick you up at five or five-thirty?"

"If you're sure." She couldn't help but smile.

"I'm sure. Later." He hung up.

It felt right. Going out with Michael and the boys was entirely innocent. They were friends, right? It was okay.

When she arrived at Mer's, the project was well underway.

"Didn't want to get started without you, but I hardly slept a wink, figured I'd get it going early." She caught Rainie up to speed, and both of them plowed through the details, the ordering and back and forth with Kevin, or as Meredith was calling him, Kev.

It was long past time for lunch. Meredith called for a break. It was quite noticeable Rainie wasn't high, but she wasn't going to call attention to it, merely count the blessing.

"Sorry you had a sucky night's sleep, Mer. I, on the other hand, had a great night's sleep. Best rest I've had in years. Up for salad?" Her body felt relaxed, and her usual manic movements were slower, calmer, and far more controlled. She wasn't tightly wound, like a top for a change.

"Don't have to ask me twice. You're driving, though. I'm beat." They got in the car and took off for a local café. Meredith seemed whipped. Her face was sullen, and she lacked her usual sparkle, which was out of character. It was like someone had blown out her candles.

☙☞

Driving down Carrollton, Mer asked, "So where did you sleep last night? Or should I ask, who did you sleep with last night?" Mer was acting snarky; she flipped her hair back and gave Rainie one of her but-you-love-me-anyway smiles.

"Really?" She turned and looked at her. Rainie looked like a taunting prize fighter standing in the corner of the ring preparing to trash talk the opponent. "Home and alone, and just for the cat swipe, I'm not going to tell you about my plans for this evening." She squinted her eyes, crinkling her nose, feigning a look of anger.

"Oh, come off it. You know I was playing, but maybe it hit too close? Food for thought, dearie." Mer shrugged her shoulders.

"Touché. The way I've been acting, the question is not completely off base. There is much I have to tell you. Hitting the highlights, I ended the thing with Ryan, the kids and I are going to dinner with Michael tonight, and I told Allie, who, by the way, already knew about the drugs and the thing with Ryan." Rainie's gestures were not as wild, but being animated was her way even as a child. When listing things or events, she held up fingers as though counting her list.

"W-w-wait, hold on. Not saying I'm not glad you ended the sordid perversion with the boy because it's about damn time, but something must have caused the decision. Maybe stronger feelings for Michael?" Meredith smiled with a look of hope.

Puzzled by how to answer the question regarding Michael, she held off until they were seated in the café. "No, well kinda, but not really."

"Clear as mud, Rai."

"Went to Mass, as usual, yesterday, then to the club with my parents and the boys—" fingers in the air.

"And?" Meredith shrugged.

"I'm halfway through a glass of wine when the server comes to top off my glass." She cleared her throat.

"I look up to thank him, and it was Ryan. I did everything in my power not to choke. I remained calm, and both of us continued as though we didn't know each other. Daddy went on about how happy he was to hear I had been out with Michael, and I thought to myself, how in the hell would he have known?" She raised an eyebrow at her friend.

"By this time, I excused myself to the ladies' room, and on the way there, Ryan chases me down. "Stop, Mer. Don't look at me that way. Anyway, lunch ended at about three-ish, then we went home.

"Allie was at the house and upset. She and I spoke for a while, then as I was broaching the subject of going out, she said she knew I was seeing someone, and she thought it was good. I needed some fun."

"Bet she didn't know she was probably older than the fun thing." Mer could be quick and cutting.

"Pull the claws back in, please. As I was saying, I went to Ryan's place. The way he sounded was like a kid with their feelings hurt."

"Sounded like a kid, Rainie, cuz he is a kid!" This time she flung her arms in the air.

"You want to hear what happened, or do I have to hear your ongoing commentary? I told him we had to cool it. He started with the 'what do you mean, when will I see you again.' He was confused. I allayed any fears about him and his boudoir abilities, but I had to cool it because of Tom and the divorce."

"Quite true. Tom would nail your ass." Meredith said pointedly.

"That was it. I drove home." She looked across the table at her and smiled.

"And that's why you had such a great night's sleep?" Mer questioned like a teacher quizzing a schoolgirl.

"No, it's what happened after I got home. Weird shit, unbelievably strange."

"I'm listening, growing impatient but listening."

Very quickly, she brushed fast over the fact Allie had communicated with Rand.

There was complete silence for nearly a minute, which felt like ten.

"How did she mean, communicated? I dream about Rand occasionally, but y'all were my besties; I sometimes do, but Allie? In a dream? Nevermind, continue with the story. What did Rand supposedly say?"

"No, supposed, it happened." Mer sat mesmerized, holding onto every word. Her expression was blank, absolutely void of any emotion, maybe disbelief.

Tears rolled down Rainie's cheeks. "I saw her, and I talked to her; however, she was angry with me. I wish we could have gotten past the angry disappointing part, but you know Rand."

The server brought the food to the table, and in between bites, the conversation pursued.

Mer was full of tears, but it was more in a befuddled manner. "Don't get mad at me, but I have to ask how high were you last night? Sorry, wait, I didn't mean that. I don't know what to say. I don't have words. Rainie, do I say yay, or I'm sorry? Help me here." She took a few more bites.

"You don't have to say anything, Mer. I wanted to share this with you. You've been by my side through it all, and I had to tell you. One thing's for sure—I'm going to be a better mother, a better friend, a better daughter, and a better me."

People in the café were gawking at them as both were tearful. Rainie signaled for the check and took the last bite of her lunch. The server quickly brought it, and they got out of there. She drove to the park, and they sat there for another hour, crying, laughing, and remembering.

"You know, you remember your sister a lot different than I do. You paint her memory as sweet, angelic, the good sister. Don't get me wrong, she was precious, but you two were equally as sweet. If anything, because of her total jock mentality, she came across as stronger rather than sweet. You, on the other hand, were the artsy one, not that you didn't do well in sports—" they were sitting face to face with their backs against the car doors.

"But I was no Rand. She was badass at volleyball and basketball. I don't think about the real her and paint some fantasy picture. I wonder why. You're the first one to point it out. None of the shrinks, nuns, or counselors at school, even my parents, ever told me. They let me keep this almost helpless, wimpy victim image of her.

"She was very strong, far more outspoken than me. Out of the two of us, she was stronger." She turned her head slightly and stared out of the windshield, contemplating the revelation.

They sat quietly listening to sounds in the park. It was a mixture of cars, bikes, squeals from kids, a real cacophony.

*

It had been a strange but most productive day; even with the emotional craziness, they managed to get everything done.

"Allie's picking the kids up from school. Just as well, it's four o'clock. I gotta get everyone ready for our family date with Michael." She picked up her purse and headed to the door.

"Have fun tonight. Behave, please. See you in the a.m." Mer blew her a kiss.

Rainie turned around with an ear to ear smile. "Good day, today, my friend, good day. Love ya."

She had it on an oldie station trying to stay upbeat, but she couldn't help wondering when this merry-go-round life was going to settle down and feel real and right. It had been one big ordeal after another.

Traffic was a nightmare, and by the time she made it home, Michael had already arrived.

"Sorry, y'all traffic was a beast. I'll be ready in a few." She gave the boys each a kiss and nodded in Michael's direction. "Promise a few minutes."

He smiled. "Relax, take your time, no need to rush. We won't leave without you." The boys giggled.

"Is Allie going? I didn't have a chance to ask her yet," and up the stairs she went.

"Yes, she'll be going, too." He could hear her muffled, "oh good."

Light chatter commenced as they drove down St. Charles. Traffic was heavy, but not the routine stop and roll. Michael asked about everyone's day and commented his day was good as well, but it was even better because he knew they'd be having dinner together.

Allie mentioned making calls about internships but did a lot of napping and soaps. She was all about summer but commented it was too easy to be lazy and non-productive.

The conversation continued at the dinner table with Doctor Mike. "What field do you want to explore?"

"I think law, but then I think what Rainie does is interesting. I can see myself in a lot of places. It's hard to pick one."

"Try a few. See what you like." He turned to the boys, "How many more days left in school?"

Henry excitedly answered, "ten."

"No," Thomas bossed, "nine now because today is over, which makes it eight and a half. The last day is a half-day."

"It sounds like it's going to fly by fast." Michael gave his full attention.

"Hi boys," Tom towered over the table. "Hello Mike, I see it didn't take you much time."

Mike stood up, they were roughly the same height, but Michael had a more solid build. He offered his hand to Tom. Reluctantly, Tom shook it and, under his breath, said, "You fuckin' my wife?" It was loud enough for only Mike to hear, but Rainie saw Tom make the quiet remark to Michael and knew his asshole look. Despite the possible snideness on Tom's part, both men remained with a poised smile.

Keeping total composure, Michael asked, "How were the islands, Tom? It looks like you got a bit of a tan. The Bahamas, right? Good of you to stop by. Boys, give your dad some sugar. I know they look forward to seeing you Friday after school." Then he sat down, dismissing him, and sure enough, Tom walked off and out of the restaurant.

"I'm sorry. That was awkward, Michael." Rainie apologized with a pout.

"Rainie, why are you sorry? Tom saw the boys and wanted a hug. There's nothing wrong with that, is there?" He winked at her. He was definitely in control.

She relaxed and eased up. It could have been ugly, of course, she hadn't heard Tom's remark.

There was an underlying tension for a few seconds, but it quickly dissipated, and the laughter and cheer returned to the table. It was a lovely evening, and Michael couldn't have been more attentive to the boys and Allie. His flirty smiles encouraged a blush or two from Rainie.

He managed to divert Thomas' digs at Henry quickly and painlessly, and in a snap, the snide remarks were over, and the night was fabulous.

When he pulled up to the house, they all bailed out of the car.

"I've got the boys, and we'll get ready for bed if you and Doctor Mike want to visit." Allie winked at Rainie.

"A nightcap, perhaps, Michael?" Rainie asked in a flirty tone.

He checked his watch. "I guess I can manage a half hour. I have a full book tomorrow with the first surgery at six." He followed her into the house and then the kitchen.

She reached up for a glass. Michael beat her to it, standing more than close. The heat radiated from his body; his breath whispered on the back of her neck. It caused tickling throughout her body and an involuntary body shiver, almost like the first wisps of autumn.

"Pour you a glass of wine?" he asked.

"No, thank you, no wine tonight, but I will grab a bottle of water. Want me to pour you a glass of wine?"

By this time, she had turned and was facing him. "Water will be good for me, too. I very well couldn't tell you earlier how beautiful you look." His gaze was pure.

He brushed away a lock of her hair, keeping his hand on her cheek, framing her face. "I've done nothing but think about you since you dropped me at my car Saturday. Those eyes of yours are hypnotic."

She could feel the blood flow to her face and course her body. "Are you blushing again? What a compliment." His smile was honest as his eyes darted back and forth between hers as though looking into her soul. "The other night when we were together, I know I confused you. I wanted you then, and I want you now. I've thought about us together a lot, but we have to wait for the right time. Agreed?"

He picked her up and sat her on the counter. He traced the details of her face with his right hand and pulled her closer to him with the left. Michael moved his hand up to the nape of her neck, grabbed a handful of hair, and pulled down. Her head tilted back. He ran his tongue up her neck. Then he kissed her lips.

Michael's every move was calculated, planned to perfection, leaving her wanting more. She could feel the passion burning inside him, which ignited her, yet he commanded his temptation.

She looked deep into his eyes, trying to solve the mystery of him.

"How do you do this to me, Michael? I've never experienced this sensation before. All you've done is kiss me, and yet I feel like we've—"

"It's what you do to me when I'm with you. I don't want to push you away or say the wrong thing, but you have no idea. Rainie, I'm electrified talking to you on the phone, sitting in a noisy restaurant, or dancing with you amidst a crowd of people." His eyes glittered, making her pulse race with excitement. "Connecting with you makes me feel like I've never felt before. When we're alone together, it takes everything I have not to show you or tell you how I feel. When the time is right, and I know it will be soon, there will be no more secrets, Rainie."

CHANGES

No more secrets, hmm, she thought, *sounds kinda crazy Sounds mysterious. Is it good curious or?*

Between ball practices and end of school parties, the week was drawing quickly to a close. She had spoken to Michael almost every day, nothing but "Hey, how are you?" She didn't know what to expect from him. He was proving to be most puzzling.

When he called in the evening, she was waiting for the "What are you wearing" line, but his calls were always mannered, pleasant, and interested in the day, the job, the boys, and refreshing.

The end of the year awards program was Friday evening at seven. She figured it would last about an hour, and then the plans were to go to Michael's. It was Tom's weekend.

In all the years she had known Michael, she had never needed to go to his place. She and Tom had many parties and get-togethers at their house during their married years, and Michael had attended some, but she had some idea where he lived.

Since the separation, she and Michael had gone out fifteen times, but it was someone's party, an event, or just dinner. It was out in the open, and for all to see, they were only friends. Until the night of his office event, there hadn't even been a kiss. He may have held her hand crossing a street, but that was it.

Little did he or anyone know, other than Mer, she was seeing Ryan, but they always stayed in his apartment. They'd order pizza, lay naked in bed, get high, and screw all to the rocking sounds of the Rolling Stones, but it was never any serious intellectual conversation. It was always behind closed doors and raw. Michael was a different relationship. Everything was above board, like two old friends, nothing more. There was a sophistication to their relationship – easily defined as being grown-up. Their divorce was yet to be finalized, so she wanted to keep an air of propriety.

Tom, on the other hand, had been flagrant in his dating and fooling around. He'd been seen all over a few women, usually some dumb kid from his office, pawing them like a dog in heat.

Years ago, Tom had swept her off her feet. She was but a mere freshman pledge, and he was president of his fraternity, getting ready to sit for the LSAT.

He stood about six foot two with a thin runner's build, dark frat hair, and dreamy dark eyes. He had a winning smile, but she knew it was like the cat who caught the canary. The voice inside tried to raise the red flags, but, as usual, she ignored Rand's subtle warnings. He had given her the two most precious people in her life, her boys, and there she could say, thank you, Tom.

Tom hadn't always been such a jerk, but he always perceived himself as God's gift to women, which ultimately translated into cheater. He could switch his charm off and on like a light switch.

All in all, the world saw a good-looking happy couple, but on the inside was a completely different story.

She started to get some of her self-worth back when she and Mer opened the interior decorating firm. Along came her pregnancy with Thomas and, two years later, Henry. Every day Mer would come to her house. They would put proposal after proposal together, and then as fate would have it, they landed a big job with one of New Orleans' well-known families. Rainie didn't question how or why they got it.

Their little business suddenly felt legitimate. Rainie and Meredith went from helping people pick out the right fabrics for an upholstery project or decorating a single room to full-fledged inspiration and design. They were in the big time. This total transformation was the whole enchilada, a sixteen thousand square foot home on St. Charles Avenue. Quite posh.

The project was massive and full of minute details. Rainie decided it was time to advertise for a nanny. Allie applied and was perfect for the position. After the hire of a nanny, Rainie and Meredith decided it was time to move the office to Mer's downstairs spare room. It now resembled a proper office without noisy kids.

The job earned them a cover story and exposure in the most popular city magazine, which was better than any advertisement they could have purchased.

Rather than congratulating Rainie on the success, Tom went another route, guilting her with the "bad mommy" thing. More and more, he stayed later at the office or went for drinks with co-workers.

It wasn't until a year later, when she and Mer had an evening appointment at the Windsor Court, her perception of life changed.

The meeting regarded their first commercial project. The client waved to someone across the room, and when Rainie looked up, there was Tom and his newest secretary. They were standing way too close together for it to be professional. Rainie waved, Mer blanched, and the client asked if she knew Tom. Very clearly and without pause, she said he was her ex-husband and smiled.

She could tell the man felt uncomfortable, but she reassured him it was all amicable, and she moved on to the project.

Following the meeting, she went home, packed all his things, and put them on the front porch. She bolted all the doors, so his keys were useless.

Two or three hours passed, and she heard him trying to get in, then his ranting and raving started in the front yard. She turned up the television volume and ignored the commotion until it began to disturb the children. She called the police.

A few months later, she realized Tom kept an apartment or love nest. Just as well, because after that night, he was no longer welcome in the house.

She merely explained to the boys; Daddy had a different home. And that was that. The boys were young and didn't understand. All they knew from her was Daddy no longer lived at home.

Rainie answered they decided to be friends when asked why, and there was nothing wrong with friends. It meant they had two homes.

Tom's family didn't seem to hold anything against her. Nobody broached the subject of why they separated, but she figured they probably knew way before she did, which seemed unfortunate.

Why was it, she wondered, *nobody ever told the wife?* If she knew Paul was stepping out on Mer, she'd be the first one to kick his ass and tell Mer exactly why she had. She would help her pack his things, but the thing with Paul, he adored Meredith and was a fabulous husband. He gave her space to be who she was, and she did the same. They supported each other completely. Why couldn't she find someone like that?

⁂

The Great Hall at the boys' school was packed. She wanted to be on the aisle, allowing her to see as the boys passed. Across and down, three rows sat Tom with someone attached to his arm.

All in all, it hadn't been as bad as other split-ups she'd seen. Tom had been extremely generous in monthly child support, even though it hadn't been dictated by the courts yet. Her children wanted for nothing, but quality time with him, which was becoming rarer and rarer.

He always had an excuse as to why his weekend needed to be cut short or why he couldn't take them. It was okay with Rainie because without saying one single bad thing about him to the boys, his actions were allowing them to develop their opinions for themselves.

It was more than obvious the boys were starving for a daddy figure. They had latched onto Michael fast. She questioned if this was a good thing or not.

She could hear the rustling and shushing as the kids were all lining up to make their formal entrance. Henry's class was the first to come down the aisle. She waited, and then he appeared. Eyes welling with tears, she felt her chest expand with emotion. She was proud of her guys.

After an hour and a nice end of the year program, it was time to leave. Rainie walked to Henry's class, first scooped him and his folder of many projects up, then made her way to get Thomas. She and Tom met in the hall, he with Thomas and she had Henry. The girl on the arm was nowhere in sight.

She held a pleasant smile on her face, as did he for the sake of the boys, but the body language was something else. She reached up to fiddle with her necklace, which she had learned from her shrink was a subconscious move to cover her heart, one of her many defensive mechanisms. "If you want, I can take their folders home, Tom. I have their bags in the car. You can grab them on the way out. I'm parked close." The four of them walked to her car.

Tom was obnoxiously cavalier with a loud voice and grand animated gestures as though he were on stage. However, she could hear his nervous laugh, the tone he used to connive. " I'm going to bring them back to you tomorrow afternoon. I know how much your parents like having them for Mass and lunch on Sunday."

Like hell, she thought and spun around sharply. "Actually, you can drop them at church on Sunday in time for Mass. I'll wait outside." She smiled defiantly at him as he tried to wiggle out of his weekend. *No, she thought, not this time*, she had plans.

"Not sure that's gonna work, Rainie, but I'll get back with you." He took the bags from her, and with a smirk on his face, he commented, "Really Rainie, Mike? I always knew there was something there."

She kept the fake smile glued on her face and found she was standing just a bit straighter and taller with poise and confidence, ignoring his snide comment, "See you Sunday, Tom." She hugged and kissed the boys, shut the trunk, got in her car, and pulled off. "Bastard."

She dialed Michael. He answered immediately. "Program good?"

She found herself with an ear to ear smile and feeling happy. She had a warm glow in her heart that shone in her much more relaxed demeanor. "Yes, I'm on my way to your place now. Still the plan?"

"You bet. Drive carefully, and I'll see you in a few." She knew she could be there in fifteen minutes. "You know where I live?"

"I think so. You're still in the Quarter near Jackson Square?" She had heard someone mention once that he lived near the square.

"Yes. Four doors down from St. Ann. Park in the Place d'Armes. Tell them you're a guest of mine. Better yet, I'll be there waiting for you."

"See you in a few." Her heart began to beat faster, and she could feel a flush in her face. She wasn't sure what to expect. *What was he going to be like in his place, and what did he mean by secrets?*

She had butterflies in her stomach like some schoolgirl on a first date. Exciting but scary. What she wouldn't give for a bump of coke, it had given her a false sense of security when she had been nervous, but it was a thing of the past. She swallowed the lump in her throat and ignored the tremble in her stomach.

All kinds of random thoughts swirled in her mind. Michael did live in the French Quarter, he hadn't been married, he was so sweet, but he didn't give off gay vibes, especially during their recent encounters. She was now a block away, and crapola could see him standing almost in the street directing her into the parking garage. She swallowed hard and tried to get control of her racing heart. There was no backing out. Then the voice whispered in her ear, "get a grip, Rai, he's just a boy."

His faded jeans and snug tee-shirt enhanced his physique. The sight was more than pleasing to the eye. All she could think was, *what a body*. He opened her door, leaned in, and gave her a soft hello peck. He took her hand as she got out of the car. He said something to the garage guy. The beat of her heart was in a full drum roll. He looked delicious, and she felt sure there would be a lot more than talking ahead. He was nothing short of eye candy.

"You have a bag or something you need to get out of the trunk." He walked to the back of the car, expecting the trunk to open.

"Crap, no, I didn't want to seem presumptuous." She stood there statue still, face flushed with embarrassment.

He smiled, "No worries. In the future, you can be as presumptuous as you want." He took her hand but stood back, admiring her.

"You're gorgeous. I'm happy to see you and want to hear all about your day and the program, but first things first. I should have asked before, but are you okay with dogs?" He hadn't taken his eyes off of her. Hand in hand, he led the way.

"Yes." Her nerves made her body tighten. No matter how hard she tried to mimic his calm persona, she was stiff as a board.

"Good because I have a pair of black labs, Bonnie and Clyde." His eyes twinkled, "Wanna know the backstory there?" Her shoulders started to release, each muscle giving into his utter calm, it was intoxicating, and she couldn't help but smile. "When they were pups, if you left anything lying around, they'd steal it and then stash it. Every time I cleaned their kennels, I would find all kinds of things in the back amidst their blankets and cushions. I think my dogs are the only dogs who have security blankets. They're four now and quite laid back." He stopped, "Mi casa." He ran his hand through his hair.

He opened the door. "Make yourself at home." Whatever he was cooking filled the air with a mouth-watering aroma. Two humongous black dogs greeted them. They were friendly but not obnoxious and followed his commands to perfection.

"Are you cooking?" She turned to look at him, eyes wide open with intrigue.

"Yes, I hope you like pesto. I've got some trout topped with pesto and a garden salad. You look surprised. I love to cook, and, for the most part, everything has been edible." He kicked off his shoes.

"I love pesto, and I don't mean to insult you, but I never pictured you as someone that cooked. I don't know what I thought or if I even thought about it. Like any other New Orleans girl, I love food, but I have to admit, I'm not very good in the kitchen." She started to take a few steps further into the living room.

"I'm an excellent teacher if you want to learn." There seemed to be multiple layers to the statement, or maybe her mind was still on the secrets. Okay, *secret number one, he liked to cook. Secret two he liked to teach.*

"Please take off your shoes, relax. I have scrubs you could change into if you want." He turned and pulled her into him. Looking down so their eyes could meet, he spoke softly with sincerity, "I want you to throw away all the cares of the world and just breathe. This weekend is all about you decompressing. That's something I'm also pretty good at, relaxation techniques." *Secret three*, she thought. "You still have your shoes on. Take them off," he spoke sweetly, yet with command. He put a hand out to take the shoes.

"Better yet," he picked her up, threw her over his shoulder with one hand holding her legs and the other on her butt. Michael led her down a hallway, past the kitchen, into an open den, and placed her on the couch. He covered a lot of space quickly.

"Is this standard for your house tour? None of your guests have found it strange? Quite unconventional, I'd say," she was amused with a slight laugh and a batt of the eyes, "But, I'd like to get a look at the place. From what I could see, which wasn't much, it's different. I like it, but gotta say, not at all what I expected."

He took off her shoes and placed them on a side table. "I've never given anyone a tour because I've never had anyone here." He watched for her expression.

"Why not?" She asked with a look of disbelief.

"This is my, I guess, sanctuary, my personal space where I let it all go. There's no stress here." Michael walked over to the French doors leading out to a courtyard. She came up behind him and wrapped her arms around his waist.

Rainie looked out at the idyllic setting with beautiful flowering plants and a lovely dipping pool. An old carriage house framed the far side.

"This is excellent. I love your design. Did you do all this, the garden?" She could feel the ripple of muscle through his shirt.

"No, I have a guy who does all the garden work. He's great. I come out here in the morning for Tai Chi. It's usually dark, and the flames from the gas lamps create interesting images on the wall."

"Are you going to give me the dollar tour or not? A girl's got to know where the potty is, ya know." She let go and put her hands on her hips. She had gotten her cocky on.

He laughed. "This is the den and the kitchen." He started from the back of the house and moved forward.

He could tell she was looking with a designing eye. "You did a lot of work in here. I've never seen any French Quarter homes with an open floorplan."

"I know. I did it myself, no permits, or it wouldn't have happened. There's a lot of bullshit red tape you have to go through. I have a couple of people who help me with projects."

He took her hand and led her up the hallway toward the front door. They stopped at the first door, "This is the potty." He laughed. Next door, "My bedroom, it had been two rooms." He walked her into his room and opened a door. "This is my bathroom." It was gorgeous. His use of stone and wood was interesting from a design standpoint. His bedroom was unequivocally masculine. He pulled her into the hall.

"Then the parlor, which I have no idea what to do with except put a sofa and coffee table."

He was right. The room, compared to the rest of his place, was dull and traditional. Anyone looking from the outside, should they see in, would expect nothing less. *Smart*, she thought, he had broken many of the Vieux Carre rules throughout the rest of the place.

"You've now had the tour! Whaddya think?" He was totally at ease in his place. It was relaxing. He spread his arms wide to receive her comments.

"I love it. What do you use the carriage house for?" She had started walking toward the back, still looking at the details.

He touched her shoulder, sending an almost electric pulse through her body. "We better get ready to eat. Do you want those scrubs I offered?"

"Sure. Thanks." Still savoring the feel of his touch. Why had it never happened before? He had seemed so sexually stale, and then bam, he turned it on like abracadabra.

He brought her into his bedroom and opened a drawer filled with hospital scrubs. "Turn around." He unzipped her dress then gave a light tap on her butt. "Change, and I'll get everything ready in the kitchen. Perrier?"

"Please." He left the room, closing the door behind him. She quickly changed. She looked for photographs, but there were none. She hadn't seen any anywhere. She looked around the room, sat on the bed, and nosed in his closet – immaculate and organized. She hurried out to the kitchen, where the table was ready to sit and eat.

The conversation at the table was easy. "This is delicious. Who'da thunk the good doc is also handy in the kitchen." He tapped his bottle of Perrier with hers and thanked her for the compliment. They talked about the boys.

She started to bring up Tom. "Nope, not this weekend," he said, shaking his head as he set the rules sealed by his determined stare.

"Okay, boss." She playfully retorted. "It was a part of my day." Her eyebrows raised with a touch of sarcasm in her voice.

"Yes, but not a nice part, right? Erase it." He punctuated his statement with a smile and swig from his bottle, never once taking his eyes off her.

She laughed. "Tell me about your day."

For the next half-hour, he talked about all the pleasantries of his day, successful surgeries, of course, no names, his fabulous staff, and then things he heard on the radio. He got up to take their plates.

"No," she said as she stood reaching for the plates. "You cooked; I clean."

"Okay. Now, who's being bossy? How about together since I know where everything goes?" He followed behind her.

"Makes sense, I guess."

It took all of five minutes to do the dishes and put them away. "Dishes are done all tucked away, and the night is still very young." He smiled at her as he shut the last cabinet and walked up to her.

"Any suggestions?" She asked. "Watch a movie, play cards, or..." and he leaned in to kiss her. She kissed him back, but between kisses, she said, "Let's talk." She had questions.

"Questions?" his expression was one of amusement. "Okay. Outside or sofa?"

"Too humid outside. Don't want bad hair," Rainie said as she fluffed her mane.

"What do you want to know?" He relaxed on the sofa.

"Secrets? No more secrets. Do tell?" She lounged next to him, almost melting into him.

"I had planned on this conversation somewhere around lunch tomorrow. I'd have a better feel for any reactions you may have. Promise me you'll stay for the night." He brought his arm around her with a squeeze. She turned to face him, backing up against the armrest, then put her feet in his lap. She raised her eyebrows, and flirty smirked. "Okay, lady, fire away. One thing you'll learn about me should this go where I hope it goes. I'm a man of my word."

"Go on, Doc." She watched as he began.

"When I was in med school, and you were but a cute freshman sorority pledge, I fell in love with you at first sight. Corny, I know, but true." More out of quirk, he ran his tongue across his teeth, stopping at the eyetooth. "I had my share of relationships and then some." He closed his eyes as though remembering. "You were in a blue print sundress and laughing at something someone said. Some, if not most, of the other girls were far more dressed up, but you didn't seem to care. My God, that laugh." He opened his eyes and grinned at her. "It was from the deepest part of you. You ready to run out of here thinking this man is psycho?"

She cocked her head to the side and held up her hand, touching her thumb to each finger as she began her barrage. "Am I running? No. Do I plan on running? Not so far. How 'bout I'll tell you if I start feeling like I need to put on running shoes?"

He smiled. "Okay. I'll continue. I watched you as you made your way around the room. I thought this is one ballsy freshman. She's not intimidated by anyone in the room, or so it appeared. That was a bit daunting. I mustered the courage to talk to you. I said hi, you said hi. I asked if you knew what you wanted to study; you laughed and said, 'hell no.' Then you asked me. I told you I was in med school. You said, 'wow,' I could see it register in your face. You didn't think we had anything in common. We continued small talk."

She put up her hand, butterflies still fluttering in her stomach. "Pause button here. I remember the night vividly. Do you know what I was thinking? 'Holy shit, med school, this guy is too smart to be talking to me.' I was going to look like some dumb freshman. I was more awestruck. You were somebody that knew what they wanted to do. Especially after I had brilliantly said, 'hell no.' I thought you were together then, and I believe you're together today. That, my friend, has not changed, and I'm still sorta awestruck, FYI."

"No need. Back to it," Michael continued, still enveloped in her eyes, "So, we were talking. Me, knowing it wasn't going anywhere, then in walks studly Tom Todd. You would've thought he was the second coming the way everyone reacted, guys and girls alike. I thought he was a pompous, arrogant snake in the grass, and my opinion remains." He looked away, running his hand through his hair, and then with a look of amusement, zeroed back in on her eyes. "He saw you, yeah, he most definitely saw you. He grabbed a beer from one of the younger fraternity brothers and slithered up to you. He nodded at me then says something to you like—"

She interrupted, " 'is he asking you to play doctor? Don't fall for that lame line. It's a typical med school tactic, right, Mike?' See,

Michael, I remember too." She nudged him with her foot. Her breath hitched in her throat, and she wanted to pinch herself to make sure she wasn't dreaming.

"Yep. Then the whole conversation came to an abrupt halt when a friend of yours, Meredith, who I didn't know at the time, came up to you and said she felt sick. And poof, y'all were gone. I saw you a few more times, but school required a lot of book time, and I missed out on much of the fun. Mind you, I've more than had my share.

"But," he held up his hand, "I digress. On the other hand, Tom made the most of it all and had you in his snare by mid-term. You were his and very cool, almost cold to any other guy that might want to talk to you. I lost track of the world with internship and residency, but I never stopped thinking about the redhead with the big laugh. Didn't have much time, so followed the three F rule to the point where it was anything goes."

Her hand went up again. "Three F rule?"

"Crude. Very crude." His face came close to a blush. "Find'em, fuck 'em, forget 'em. I know crude and heartless, and here I was, at that time, thinking I made a mistake wanting to be a surgeon; my true calling was to be a psychiatrist. Hypocrite, I know.

"I've always been interested in why people behave the way they do, thought processes, feelings, anyway, it wasn't until the last year that I settled down some. I started dating a girl with some major issues, which then became my issues, unfortunately. Want more or want a shoulder massage?"

"I want more, but the massage sounds good, too. Maybe some more after the massage," Rainie responded with a chuckle. "You're thinking 'get a load of Miss Thing, wants her cake and eat it too.'"

He pointed at her. "Exactly, my thoughts, behind your back, I always refer to you as Miss Thing." It felt like there was magic in the moment. Too good to be true. "C'mon, either sit between my legs or lie down in my bed."

She got up, turned, and looked at him. "Shirt on or shirt off?"

"Up to you." He followed her into the bedroom. She peeled off her top, undid the strings, stepped out of the bottoms, and was standing there with nothing on but a smile. She laid on her stomach, waiting.

"Hm, this is almost like at the spa. I'm ready." She flirted.

"Hold tight for a sec." She could hear him go into his bathroom and come right out. "Tell me if this is too hot." He straddled her hips; she could tell he was naked, too. He put droplets of warm, almost hot oil or cream on her back and began to massage. "Do you like it deep?"

"Yes," she purred.

The pressure got firmer as he kneaded her shoulders and traps. He stroked and massaged her back for at least twenty minutes. Then he slid his hands down her back, grabbed her hips, and lifted them. He let go as he adjusted his position on the bed. She started to lower her hips.

"No, keep them raised." He slid his finger inside of her moving it slowly in and out, touching every nook and cranny, then started tracing his movements with his tongue; her body was responding, her breathing became faster. His movements became more purposeful, and she was right at the point where her body was about to release. "Not yet."

He flipped her over, grabbed both her hands in one of his, and held them over her head tightly against the pillow. He kissed her neck and felt her back arching. Her breasts were perfect for her build. He traced her nipples with his tongue, giving a slight nip. His free hand moved over her body; she was asking for more. He placed himself as to slide inside her easily. He pushed deep, and she could feel all of him. His movements were well orchestrated and timed perfectly – slow and methodical but then upped his pace. He placed her right ankle on his shoulder. He looked intensely in her eyes with a look of satisfaction. She couldn't help wondering what he was thinking. The pleasure consumed her.

The moment seemed surreal, and together they were in complete harmony. The pace got faster and more intense. Again, and again, until neither could hold anything back. She felt the tremendous swell and release as she watched him watching her. There was nothing quite as erotic.

Timing, it was all about the timing. He kissed her ever so wonderfully, and she soaked in the state of total relaxation.

Neither one spoke for well over five minutes savoring the experience. Then Michael said, "You're everything I've wanted, needed, and you make me feel complete. I hope it doesn't wig you." He ran his fingertips along her curves as he gently smiled, looking into the depths of her eyes. "What are you thinking, pretty lady?"

"Total contentment, unlike any I've ever known. Being with you isn't just a roll in the sack. There's far more depth and intensity almost spiritual." *What in the hell am I going on about? He doesn't need to know my thoughts. Danger, danger leaving myself way too open.*

She watched as he slowly got out of bed. *Great ass!*

The sound of bathwater beckoned her to him. The light coming from the bathroom was dim, almost teasing her senses. He took her hand and led her to the bath. Sitting behind her with his legs on either side provided a natural lounge. "I've waited a long time for this moment," he whispered, moving her hair to the side followed by a soft kiss to her neck.

"I hope it was worth the wait." She held his hands.

"And then some. You're magnificent, spectacular, more than I could've imagined. What more can I say?"

A few moments passed. She didn't want to ruin the atmosphere, but curiosity and her sharp tongue got the best of her. "You've imagined this, you say. Was it as good for you as it was for me?" She coyly giggled.

"You are a sassy lady." He whispered. "I don't want this moment to end, but there is a bed calling us back. I want some Rainie pillow talk. You come across as a 'what you see is what you get' kinda girl, but your river runs much deeper, and I want to explore."

He helped her out of the bath and wrapped her in a slightly warm towel. "Towel warmer, I'm impressed." She handed him the towel to dry her back. "You're so tender and gentle with me. I don't break, you know."

"You wish I were rougher?" He paused. "That, my dear, can easily be arranged."

They got in the bed facing each other. Twirling his hair, she asked, "What were the girl's issues? The ones you said became yours, Michael?" She gazed into his eyes with wonder.

"Switching gears, I see. Cocaine. The girl had a problem with cocaine. We would party together. She was into a lot of things. It certainly wasn't uncommon, but the partying lifestyle, after about ten months, grew old. No judgment. I just enjoyed sleeping and eating way too much. We parted ways. I learned many things along the journey." He lightly touched the tip of her nose.

"Since it's true confessions, I feel compelled to tell you I used to do cocaine too but quit." She had a dead serious look in her eyes, waiting for his disappointment or a "shame on you" response.

"When? Two days ago?" He chuckled.

"What?" Her eyebrows instantly arched in shock. *He knew. He knew all the time, holy shit.*

"Rainie, once you've been around a person high on cocaine, it's easy to spot. I've known you were using, but I figured Tom had done a number on you, and you were looking for self-confidence. Of course, the wrong place. Cocaine feeds the self-doubt beast, ultimately."

"Wow, you knew and still wanted to be with me."

"I'm glad you felt comfortable enough to disclose, and I'm overjoyed it's a thing of the past." He stroked her hair.

"Okay, Michael, you ditch the girl."

"No, we parted ways. That's different. I joined a practice with a group of surgeons from Baton Rouge. I was with them a few years but wanted to move to New Orleans. I had started dating—"

"Julia?"

"Yes, Julia. Did I tell you she encouraged me to buy this house even though it was an architectural nightmare? I lived upstairs in the carriage house, which I donned the name, Pandora, while I made my home livable.

"As serious as we were, and I do think I loved her, there was something not right. I know she was hurt when I broke it off." She could tell from his expression he truly felt bad, maybe even guilty. "From then on, I've pretty much been a loner, had dates when I needed them, but nothing more."

"Sounds reasonable. Did you ever figure out what the missing element was?"

"Yes, I was in love with someone else." He paused and started to speak a couple of times, hesitating each time. "Rainie, I love you. I have loved you, like I said, from the moment I saw you, and nothing could fill the void. Tom's carousing was common knowledge, and I figured you'd finally get your fill, and then I would—"

"Make your move." She laughed but could tell instantly he felt awkward. "And I'm glad you did!"

His demeanor lightened. "I know this is a one-sided thing, and I'm prepared to wait; in the hope, it won't be one-sided forever." He brushed a lock of hair from her face causing a flutter in her belly that rose to her throat.

"Since we're spilling the beans, I've always thought you were a great guy and would make some woman a very lucky lady. You're a stellar catch. Then after the shit with Tom, it felt good to have the support of a male friend. One without expectations—" her voice drifted off as she looked away from his eyes.

"I have no expectations. Rainie, look me in the eyes. Just because I have these feelings for you doesn't mean I expect—"

"I know. I know you don't. I love our relationship, and I don't know what it's changing into, but I know it's changing, and," Rainie rolled her eyes, "I'm loving this change. I think we're on a special journey, and whether you and I are meant to be together, I don't know. I'm too scared to even go there, but this, what we have, is nice. It's real. Was that the revelation?"

"In part, but the rest will be more of a show and tell experience if you will." With the backside of his hand, he stroked the side of her face.

"Are you bi or a crossdresser, or what could you show and tell?" She was ever questioning behind her smile.

"No, I'm not bi or whatever. We'll have a show and tell tomorrow after lunch."

"I'm curious now. You can't do that to me."

His eyes took on a devilish twinkle. "But I can do this to you." He pulled the covers down and kissed her stomach, then started with the roving hands more playful than sexual.

Through laughter, she asked. "You want to play doctor?" playfully fending off his tickling hands.

His face brightened as he cracked up. "You're too much. And for your cockiness, you need a good spanking."

She raised her eyebrows but grinned. Surely he wasn't going to spank her.

"You're in for an awakening." He tossed her over his lap as though there wasn't a pound to her. I'll only do it three times, but you need to count. I might lose track."

"Are you kidding?" Thinking, *this is crazy.*

"Say one," he instructed.

"One." He slapped her butt. "Youch," she laughed, "What if I don't say two?" Swat again. She started giggling.

"You said two, and for all that giggling," Swat.

"But I didn't say three, Michael" Swat. Then he kissed each perfectly pink side.

"Sweet, sexy, and sassy." He lay facing her as she arched her back, resting her chin in her hands.

"I guess I'm the three S girl. Not the three F."

"Hell no, you're anything but a three F." He pulled her close, spooning her. He lifted his head, kissed her neck, "I love you." It wasn't uncomfortable or awkward. All the muscles in her body relaxed. She was content like there wasn't a care in the world.

DIRTY LITTLE SECRET

She woke to the sound of music emanating from the direction of the kitchen accompanied by heavenly aromas. He slightly turned his head as she approached him. "Hope you slept well." *Could he sound any sexier?*

"Slept well? That's an understatement. I think I passed out. Whatever you're cooking smells delish." Arms around his waist, she peered into the skillet.

"A very light scramble with fresh peppers, we need to keep it light. You'll need room for lunch but enough to keep you with energy to burn."

"Oh, are we doing yoga or something of the sort because frankly, that's not what I was shooting for this weekend?" She stepped to the side of him.

"What were you shooting for?" With a sassy twinkle in his eye, he grinned as he stirred the eggs.

"I don't know, but not yoga, I can promise," she laughed as she put her hand on her hip. "I'll be happy to watch and cheer you on if it's part of your morning ritual."

"You like to watch, hm, interesting. I figured you more of a do-er." The corners of his mouth turned up with a wry smile.

She straightened at attention, feeling challenged. "I like to do; I'm a do-er. I don't watch well. I'm a total participant. No yoga, okay with you?"

He found the conversation funny. "Who mentioned yoga anyway? I recollect it was you, not me, and it's Tai Chi. I wanted to make sure you aren't hungry. I thought you might like to walk to the French Market." He put his hands up in surrender. "But, we'll do whatever you want to do."

"Really?" She teased. *I know just what I'd like to do,* she thought.

"Really." One eyebrow raised, he taunted.

"Hm." Her hug became tighter.

"Rainie, what do you want to do, may I ask?" She stared into his eyes with a half-smile on her face as she slid her hands down to his butt and pulled him even closer. "Should we have breakfast in bed?" he asked.

She gave him a slight pat on the butt. His eyes widened as he grinned from ear to ear. "So, doc, have I found a sweet spot on you?"

He took her hand and put it on his erection. "That is my sweet spot." In one fluid motion, he had the stove off, his pants untied, and her against the fridge. He lifted her, and instinctively she wrapped her legs around him. He fulfilled her desires right then, right there, and to perfection.

She gasped. "I thought wall sex only existed in the movies. I tell you, you've got some moves, Michael. The surprises keep coming. No pun intended." She raised one of her eyebrows as he had just before.

"In the movies? I don't think I've ever heard that before." He mused.

"Yeah, you know, you always see the guy hike up the girl's skirt and bang against the wall hot and heavy. I'm still spinning, it was a first for me, but I see not for you. No complaints here." She held up her hands.

Back on her feet, she began looking in drawers. Michael touched her arm. "Need something?"

"I'm starving. Fork please?" she said with a guffaw. He handed her one.

She took a bite from the skillet. "Rainie, want a plate?"

"No need. All I need is a fork, and you might want one for yourself, too. All we'll have is a pan and two forks to clean. Then we can take a morning nap. I'd take a walk to the French Market, but, oops, I have no clothes."

"I took care of the clothing situation before you woke." He went to the front and came back with a hanging bag. "Here, I'm pretty sure these will fit."

Jeans and a nice flowing top made for a funky but fabulous look. She pulled the jeans on. "These fit great. I love this look. But how—"

"I have connections. It's amazing what a little free Botox can do. All I did was make a call to one of my neighbors who owns a boutique a few streets over."

They scooted out of his place and walked to the French Market, stopping at different bays examining the fruit and vegetables, then headed to Royal Street for window shopping.

It hadn't felt like three hours, the time seemed to slip away, but it was already time to start walking back to his place for lunch and more answers. It was fun and, indeed, an adventure beyond her wildest thoughts.

The churning of hunger in her stomach made loud gurgles. Maybe desire, maybe nerves, perhaps both. They kicked off their shoes as they entered the house, and she could hear someone coming in and out of the back door.

"Who's here?" She showed puzzlement in her furrowed brow.

"A friend doing me a favor." He smiled at her continuing down the hall.

The short round man called out, "So sorry, thought I'd be finished by now, but everything is to perfection, doc," and he kissed his fingertips. "Voila!" he held the door open. Their lunch was set in the courtyard with champagne and the mystery meal under silver domes.

She peered under one of the silver domes. "Yum, shrimp, veggies, and angel hair. Lemon, rosemary, but what else? Whatever, it's exquisite. Don't tell me, Botox again?" She said sarcastically.

He escaped back into the kitchen with the man and then re-appeared. "Now, it's only the two of us."

"And answers," she prompted with a slow bat of her eyes.

The breeze was slight. Just enough to make it pleasant. "Here, taste," as Michael lifted off the dome and took a seat.

She lifted her champagne flute. "To a wonderful weekend." She went through the motions but didn't sip it.

He leaned in. "Yes, to a wonderful weekend. FYI, it's sparkling ginger."

"This has been storybook, Michael," she commented as they carried dishes into the kitchen. Taking her hand, he led her toward the quarters in the back.

"Remember I told you I lived back here during renovation, and I had done a good bit of the work myself?' He unlocked the door. "Enter." He had a fully functional workshop, one a real cabinet maker would gladly call his.

"Wow, this is impressive, commercial machinery. " Rainie looked around at all the machines.

"Yep, the real deal." He lifted her onto one of the tables, stood between her legs, then tilted her head back to look into her eyes. Her pulse began to race again as she gasped. She felt her face begin to flush. "Remember I told you about the young lady with the issues? I don't know if it was the drugs or my state of mind at the time, but I was in a dark place and found few outlets for my frustration. She introduced me to an alternate lifestyle, which I indulged even after the split. I bought this house and built my ultimate playpen. I had fun building and stocking it, and I found it was my only pleasure and fulfillment. It took a while, but I moved through it and came out on a much brighter side.

"I'm telling you this because I want you to know about my past and to have no question." She sat silently with a quizzical look. *What the hell?*

He took her hand. "I lived upstairs. You'll see. Although the relationship with the troubled girl was long over, and I was dating Julia, she encouraged me to buy this place. Anyway, my predilection remained."

He unlocked the apartment door. "Keep an open mind, and it's not necessarily me anymore, but you need to know. I don't want any secrets between us, even as friends." He pushed the door open.

Holy shit! She walked in, totally unprepared for what she saw. There was a massive bed with four ornate posts, a wall filled with leathery straps, riding-crops, and an assortment of odd paraphernalia. She wasn't sure, but one of the things looked like an old wooden stockade. In one corner were a few wooden boards and hardware laying on the ground in a heap.

"This looks like something out of a book I read once. Bondage, erotica, I get the drift. Have to admit, I've never used anything like—" Rainie cleared her throat. "I get you used to play these kinds of games, but with who, I can't imagine the one-night dates would agree to be strapped to a bed and whipped."

He watched her almost bemused.

"Alright, everyone has a past. I get it, Michael." Her hand went up, "The question is, what is your pleasure now? I liked the way we played in your bedroom and your kitchen. The thought of being tied seems like medieval torture."

"They had a lot of fun back then." His tongue swept across his teeth, once again stopping on the eyetooth. *Sweetness, could this man get any hotter?* "This is a place for pleasure, but to answer your questions. My friend with a problem introduced me to bondage, dominance, and submissiveness. There are clubs for people with this palate. I learned a lot about it and found it stimulating, strictly self-gratifying. It was private and exclusive. No one developed relationships, per se. She and I had a relationship outside of the club, but not once inside.

"I told you I was in a dark place. You would probably be surprised by the people who live the lifestyle." He watched her as she walked around, looking at the array of paraphernalia.

"Do I still feel comfortable in this setting?" He followed behind her. "Put it this way. It's not my thing anymore. Some things can be fun, but the rest, been there, done that. I have started taking it apart." Pointing to the boards in the corner. "Now, sweet Rainie, you know all my dirty little secrets."

He put his arms around her but paused, waiting to see her response. She wrapped her arms tightly around him, looking up into his eyes. "We all have pasts. It's what we do with the here and now that counts, right?"

"Right. I was afraid you were going to hit the road and never want to see me again."

"I thought about it, just kidding." She smiled softly at him. "You're a good man, Michael, the real deal. There are things about me I'm sure you wouldn't approve of, like about the same time I stopped the coke—"

"You mean a few days ago." He winked at her.

"Smartass, I was having a physical relationship with a twenty-year-old boy, but I ended it. His name's Ryan, and he's a sweet kid, but it's over."

"Twenty? You're what thirty-three, right? You know I'm thirty-eight. I'm glad I didn't know about your young friend before, talk about create some insecurity. Baby skin, no wrinkles, toned muscles—" He kept his arms around her waist.

"And inexperienced and lackluster in the boudoir. I think it was more ego-stroking for me since Tom—"

He put his finger over her lips, "No Tom, remember?" He moved her hair from her face.

"Right, no Tom, no insecurities, no more questions, how's that?" She put her hand to his face and kissed him. She felt a gentle flutter in her chest.

He looked in her eyes with warmth. "With all secrets revealed now and neither of us scathed, we can take each day as it comes."

"Michael, there are so many things I don't even remember. I've given you all the broad strokes, but I had many demons." She felt a shameful sadness causing her head to drop.

"I get it." He tipped her chin upward. "You have no idea how happy I am you want to share time with me, even if it's only friends. Just FYI, I'm not seeing anyone. I wanted to be clear, and I'm not saying I'm expecting anything from you. That's just me."

She went back to looking around, running her hands over the leather. She held up a feather and looked at Michael.

"Get on the bed," he prompted. Rainie raised an eyebrow. "No, get on the bed. If what I do bothers you, say stop. She got on the bed and reclined; he pulled her shirt up to below her breasts and delicately swept the feather up her stomach.

Her reflex was to wiggle away from it, but she held back the temptation. "That tickles."

"Under different circumstances, you would be restrained. The whispered touch of a feather while restrained can be arousing. See, it's not about the pain. It's about controlling pleasure, and I no longer feel the need to have control, for the most part." He pulled her to him.

"You don't say? When I think back to the night of your party, was it a control move to run your fingertips up my leg and stop before?" She tilted her head with a smirk.

"No, maybe a little. Point being, nothing was going to go further because your boys were home, and it wasn't time."

"Do you realize it was only last week? It seems much longer, at least to me."

"Bearing in mind this story has been played and re-played in my mind over the years, it has seemed much longer and far more rewarding." *You can say that again*, she thought.

She felt comfortable, safe, and protected. "If we were to ever play in this room, where would we start?" Although the tickling had stopped with the feather, she was feeling a wild tickling inside.

"We aren't. I wanted to be forthright." He looked serious.

"But, if I wanted to, just sayin'? I've never been around any of these types of things, and I might be curious. Hm? I guess if you don't demonstrate them, maybe I need to go to one of those clubs," she threw her head back and laughed.

"Like hell you do, wild woman. Besides, you can't just saunter in there. It's very elitist. Admittedly, I was uncomfortable at first. It was awkward, but I got past it fast." He laid on the bed, pulling her to rest next to him.

"I'm not easily distracted, Dr. Landry. Where would you start with a beginner?"

"I already did when I held your hands above your head. I still have a tendency for control at times. It keeps me focused, and it makes it far more pleasurable for you. It's difficult sometimes keeping it all together when I'm with you."

He changed the subject. "Where do you want to dine tonight? Galetoire's is one of my favorites. If I can get a table for a late reservation, would you be good or somewhere else?" He took her hand, leading her off of the bed, but she wouldn't budge; she pulled back.

"Let's play with the feather." She batted her eyes at him.

"You're insatiable. You sure you wouldn't rather wait? The

anticipation can be an aphrodisiac in itself, ya know?" He pulled her hand again.

"Alright, we can wait and, yes, I will dine with you anywhere. Remember it's Saturday night," she taunted. "After dinner, I'll have to go home in case Tom drops the boys early in the morning." Tom's name conjured an emptiness inside, a lonely void.

"He's supposed to meet you at church. It was the deal. Stick to your guns." He held her hand as they walked toward the door.

They left, and he locked up Pandora.

Sure enough, he was able to get reservations for a late dinner. Rainie put on the dress she'd worn to his house. So much had happened yet; it had only been from the night before.

Things were comfortable. He was easy-going and had been honest with no expectations. After a short cab ride, they arrived and were seated with no waiting, smooth as silk. They talked about everything from her business, his practice, politics, and even religion.

"Usually, I go to the Cathedral. It's so close. My life turned around when I embraced my faith and let go with God in control; what was there to worry about—nothing. It hasn't always been. I was in a dark, dark place." The way he looked into her eyes, she felt like he was pouring himself into her soul.

"You had a great business, well thought of in the community, and you were in a relationship?" He nodded. "So, with having everything, what brought you to a low point?"

She couldn't even fathom him at a low point. He seemed self-assured, but she knew low points all too well, and her heart hurt for him.

"I had all the accomplishments one could strive for at the time." He paused in thought. "But then, I stepped back and looked at me, my life. In many cases, the patients who generally came to see me were unhappy, insecure, and lacked self-worth. It bothered me to see so many people down.

"Society has created this false ideology of what is beautiful and what isn't. Whether it's clothing or make-up, this false sense impacts everyone from retailers to restaurants, everything, Rainie, everything." He sipped on his water, but she could tell he was on a roll.

"I wasn't going to buy into it, yet I started thinking about what I made my living from—frankly, people's insecurities. I wanted my work to be more to have more meaning.

"The straw that broke this camel's back was when a mother brought her fifteen, almost sixteen, year old daughter in for a consult. Get this. Her mother wanted a breast aug for the girl as a gift for her sixteenth birthday. I thought it was a bit over the top, but then in the discussion, I couldn't help but notice the sadness on the girl's face." She noticed his hands flexing then balling tightly. His neck was getting pinkish, as was his face. She watched him getting upset all over again, remembering the situation. "I stopped the conversation and asked because I had to know who wanted the augmentation, the daughter, or the mother? It was the mother. Do you know what horrible message the mother was giving her daughter?

"The girl was clearly embarrassed and sad. She was only fifteen years old. So, whether unprofessional or not, I told the mother I would not perform the surgery; perhaps she needed to look more into what was important in her life.

"Boy, she was pissed." He shook his head and started biting the inside of his cheek. "She called me a self-righteous asshole and was going to tell all her friends, ruining my business.

"All I could say was I was sorry she felt that way, but 'no' was my final answer. She stormed out of my office, and I could hear her yelling at my staff, screaming in the waiting room, and telling my patients they should leave. The screaming finally stopped.

"The three patients following went out of their way to express their confidence in me, which helped, but I gotta say, I was jarred by the whole encounter.

"Rather than destroy my business, it more than doubled. I heard the woman went to two or three other doctors who said the same thing I had said. She finally got some hack to do the surgery, but I questioned myself as a person and felt I was part of the problem.

"It bothered me so much I started seeing a therapist. I didn't know at the time; he was a Christian therapist. After many sessions and lots of prayer, I turned to religion." His clenched fists relaxed, and the pinkness faded; he was Michael again, cool, calm, and without a worry.

"Oh, and the girl after turning eighteen came in for a consult. She wanted the implants removed and whatever it would take to make her look like herself again. So, while I do cosmetic work, I have definite stipulations. I have a doctor on call for psych evals. The majority of my work now is reconstruction due to illness or injury, and it feels right. I feel as though I'm serving people." He leaned against the back of his chair as if to say The End.

He had been animated and committed as he spoke.

Tears welled in her eyes. "It leaves me with little to say other than you're most remarkable. It took balls and conviction to turn her down. I know it's gotta be big bucks. I've never understood the desire to have huge breasts. Clothes fit much better without huge ta-tas." While being serious, the conversation did not exhaust her; instead, she felt captivated and learned more about him. The more she discovered, the more she liked him.

"I like your ta-tas just the way they are." It was the perfect segue from serious to silly.

"Well, I'm glad you do." She could feel her own eyes twinkling, maybe with happy tears or tears of contentment, but the smile she felt in her heart.

They hailed a cab and went back to his place. Standing at the door, Michael put his arms around her. "Thanks for a great night," he leaned down and kissed her.

"You're the one who took me. Thank you for dinner."

He had hoped she had put Pandora out of her mind, and they could relax and go to sleep. He figured maybe one day they'd explore Pandora together, but he didn't want anything to turn her away. She did, however, seem interested. While his predilections had tamed, there were still a few aspects he found arousing and figured one day she might too, but not until then.

She went straight to the bedroom, kicked off her shoes, slipped out of her clothes, and then, to his surprise, back into his shirt and into the bed.

"I'm beat, how 'bout you? I feel like our time together has been longer. Perhaps it's been all the newfound info. You know, Michael, the more I learn about you, the better I feel about myself as a person.

I know it sounds strange, but I'm starting to make healthy, happy choices, which has evaded me most of my life. Rand would've liked you a lot," she smiled. "Yeah, a lot."

"I wish I could've known her. If she were anything like you, it would've been tough figuring out who I was in love with, but everything in life happens for a reason. I don't believe in coincidences. It's all part of the plan." His eyes fixed on hers in a mesmerizing dreamy trance.

He turned the lamp out and crawled into bed next to her. "Sweet dreams, pretty lady." He spooned close.

Morning came, and it was time to get to church.

"I hate to snack and run, but I can't be late for the boys. This has been the most wonderful weekend. Talk to you later, maybe?" She gave him a quick kiss.

"Relax, your car will be here any second. Breathe. Here's some juice for the road." He handed her a cup.

Her car pulled up. *Just breathe*, she said to herself. There was no need to rush. She had visions of sprinting to the parking lot, having to wait for her car, and then speeding to church as not to be late.

She made it to church with time to spare. While she waited outside for Tom to drop off the boys, her mind flashed back to the wild and wonderful weekend. She couldn't help but smile.

"I see you haven't changed since I saw you on Friday. Pulled a weekender; wow, that's even a bit much for you." Tom was such a jerk.

She felt like she needed some quick comeback, and then she heard Michael's voice in her head 'breathe.' She ignored his demeaning comment and focused on what was important, her boys. She hugged them tightly. "I missed you guys this weekend. Come quickly to get a seat. Kiss, Daddy."

Tom grabbed her arm tightly, "You'll be getting the papers served tomorrow. Just sign the fuckin' papers and get them back to me ASAP! Don't make this difficult."

Her dad walked up, took a sharp glance at the tight hold Tom had on Rainie's arm, and instantly his face went from jovial to intense. In a deep, barely personal tone, he nodded, "Tom." Then turned to Rainie, "C'mon, boo, we need to get a seat." She ushered the boys in and took a seat by her mom.

"Honey, everything okay?" she had a knowing look with all the earmarks saying it didn't look as though things were all right.

"Momma, for the first time in quite a while, things are better than okay. Apparently, I'll be getting papers tomorrow, and I'm glad. We can talk later out of earshot." She tipped her head in the direction of the boys.

It had been fifteen minutes, and her dad had not come in. She thought she needed to check on him. Then she heard him say, "Look who I met coming into church." She turned toward the voice and saw Michael with her dad. He winked at her as she gave him a quizzical look – head tipped, eyebrows raised, and a twitchy upward curve to her mouth.

"Doctor Mike," the boys squealed, "What are you doing here?"

"The same thing you're doing here, going to Mass." His smile was genuine, and his voice gentle. He seemed pleased to see them.

"Good morning, Mrs. Williams," he walked down the pew in front of them, "Nice to see you."

Her Mom smiled broadly. "It's good to see you. I trust all is well with you?"

"Yes, ma'am, couldn't be better," he nodded in affirmation, "I'm going to move on and grab a seat while I still can."

"Sit with us, Mike," she looked to Rainie, "You have plenty of room. Make space. Dad can sit down here with me." She shot a look at her husband and smiled.

Under her breath, Rainie whispered, " When did you decide to come here instead of the Cathedral?" She could feel her heart beginning to race.

He quietly answered, "Am I taking too many liberties? I crossed the line?"

"Heavens no, that's not at all what I meant. It's surprising, in a good kind of way." She held his hand, looked straight ahead, and smiled. In her peripheral vision, she could see her mom nudge her dad regarding the hand holding. The cat was going to get out of the bag eventually, and with the divorce papers being delivered the following day, she threw caution to the wind.

As the priest said to go in peace, her dad asked, "Mike, we're going to the club for lunch. Please join us?"

Michael looked to Rainie for the right answer; it was said in her smile, which sparkled and twinkled as her eyes glistened brightly. She squeezed his hand. "I'd love to, sir."

"Doctor Mike," Thomas spoke with exuberance, "What are you doing for summer vacation?" They loaded in Rainie's car. "We're going to horseback riding camp, soccer camp, the camp at the club, oh, and a vacation with my dad to Disneyworld."

"Thomas, I think I'll probably visit my mom and dad. Maybe see my sister, but unfortunately, I don't get a full summer vacation like you guys, but it sounds like yours is going to be packed full of fun."

Tom had not consulted her, but it might prove to be beneficial with the big job at hand.

They parked and waited for her parents at the front door. The boys were horsing around. She heard laughter in them she hadn't heard in a long time. A peaceful warmth blossomed inside her like the first taste of a cup of hot chocolate, yummy and delicious.

Her parents arrived. They took their seat at the table, and he excused himself to go wash off. The boys wanted to join him.

Once out of earshot, her dad said, "Looks like Mike might be interested in my little girl."

"Yes, Dad, he is interested in me, and I'm most interested in him. I spent Friday and Saturday night at his home." She raised her eyebrows at him.

"Rainie, more information than I needed," his face blushed. "He seems like a nice fellow."

"He's nice, and he's kind and smart and funny and thoughtful. He's the whole package. He doesn't have an arrogant bone in his body, which is refreshing. Most of the men out there are jerks." She nodded. "He's the proverbial good guy."

Her Mom chimed in, "oh my, I've never seen you this, I can't put a finger on the word, but it's good." The boys came barreling to the table.

They ordered their food, and then Rainie excused herself. Once again walking to the ladies' room, Ryan approached her. "I wuz hopin y'all would be here today since it's Sunday. Babe, we have to talk." He had a look of concern.

She started to interrupt, but he went on, "Hey, I get it, you got a man, that's cool, and if you're happy, I'm glad. You deserve happy,

Rainie, but there's a real situation you need to know about. The dude that lives next to me got sliced and diced, and of course, they come to me asking if I heard anything or knew anything, an' I guess they asked the people upstairs. Someone said they seen him with a redhead a week ago, an' I figured it had to be you cuz I haven't seen any other redheads comin' roun'. Tell me you weren't messed up with that dude, Rainie. He even creeped me out."

A lump developed in her throat. "Oh shit! Yep, it was me. While I waited for you the other night, I took a ride with him in exchange for a gram." She put her hand to her mouth.

"Oh, fuck, babe. They've been dusting the doors and the stairs. Your fingerprints have to be all over there, but they probably don't have your fingerprints, anyway, right? I mean, I had nothing against the guy. He just creeped me out. I can't believe you got in a car with him. You musta been really fucked up, huh?"

"Yes. This can't be happening. The police do have my fingerprints from a long time ago. I'll come see you. I don't know when but—"

"No, you gotta stay away. I don't want no one pointing you out. I miss seein' ya, an' not just for the sex, but what can I say, it was great, true. I like you a lot, Rainie, but stay away."

"Thanks, Ryan, for the head's up," she hugged him. She felt like she was about to throw up. Her hands were shaking slightly, and she knew she'd paled. "Thanks. I'm getting my life in order, for a change." After using the restroom, she sat back down at the table. Her mom looked startled, "Good Lord, Rainie, what on earth is wrong? You look upset."

"No, Momma, my stomach went queasy, and I got a little sick, but I'm fine now."

"You sure, suga?" Her dad's brow furrowed with concern.

Michael suggested she have a little ginger ale. After all the drama of her feeling sickly, things at the table returned to normal. She tried to take any look of concern off her face, but her gestures and laughs were hollow.

TELL IT LIKE IT IS

Maybe her parents might buy the not feeling well, but she knew Michael didn't. Following lunch, she drove him to his car. "We'll talk later?" he asked.

"Mom, can Dr. Mike come over, please?" Henry's sweet little voice was almost undeniable. Almost.

"Guys, I'm sure Michael has plans, and it's already been a long day, maybe another day. Besides, I haven't had any time with you this weekend, and I want my boy time." She looked longingly at Michael, as if to say, throw in an objection and back me up.

"Boys, I would love to come over, but I have a few things I need to get done today. I promise I'll come by one night this week, maybe order some pizza? How's that sound? You need to be with Mom."

They were not happy with his answer but knew not to beg. It was something Rainie had instilled in them.

"Tomorrow night, maybe?" Thomas asked.

"Maybe guys, we'll see what tomorrow brings. Rainie, call me when you get a moment this evening. Please thank your parents again for me. And I mean it, call me." It came out strong, like forgetting to call him was not okay.

She reached out the window and grabbed his hand. "I'll most definitely call you. The boys go to bed about eight or eight-thirty. Expect my call around then." She mirrored his intensity.

He bent over and kissed her hand. "Yes, ma'am."

They pulled off. "Mom, I like Doctor Mike. Do you like him?" Thomas seemed a bit more than curious, staring at her through the rearview mirror.

"Of course, I do, Thomas. We've been friends since I was in college."

"I know, Daddy told us, and he said, he didn't like him then, and he doesn't like him now. He called him a buttinski. He needed to mind his own business and leave us alone; we're his sons." She saw the bottom lip jut out, and his forehead crinkled. *Tom pissed him off*, she thought.

"Interesting. I always thought your dad and Michael got along. He's been a good friend to both your dad and me, and I like having him as a friend." Her eyes darted from mirror to road.

"I do too. Dad asked me a lot of questions about him. He asked Henry, too. He told us we shouldn't like him either, but I told him I liked Doctor Mike. He got mad at me, but I do like him, and Henry likes him too."

"Good, I'm glad you do."

Henry chimed in, "but who I don't like," his eyes rounded big as saucers. "Is Daddy's special friend, Miss Diane – she's mean. All Miss Diane wants to do is talk to Daddy, and anytime we talk, she says, 'that's nice,'" he mimicked a high-pitched voice. "She even said 'that's nice' when Thomas pooted. There's nothing nice about Thomas' poots." Their laughter was contagious.

They imitated the woman saying, "What do you think my big Tom-Tom? Momma, she calls Daddy Tom-Tom, and she baby talks to him." Their laughter began again. She shook her head, holding back a giggle.

Allie was happy to see them, "I missed you guys. Y'all have fun this weekend?" She took the boys' bags. "It's too quiet here when y'all are gone." She gave Henry a side hug.

As they walked upstairs, he continued. "Daddy's taking us to Disneyworld for a whole week with you know who. You wanna come?"

"Oh, no. I have too much I have to do. Besides, who would be here with your mom? I know she's going to miss you two. I can't leave her too, but it sounds fun."

Rainie retired to her room and drew her bath. Looking closely in the mirror, she examined her budding wrinkles. It was time to get some more Botox, which made her think of Michael. She felt loved, and it may have been for the first time. Tom had never made her feel that secure, that happy, that loved.

Why had it taken so long for her to see Michael for who he was? She knew he had been fonder of her than she was of him but had no idea of the extent of his feelings until the weekend. He had never attempted any sexual anything, not even a good night kiss; it was as though he purposefully kept his hands off. She pondered the thought.

There was a hollow whisper of affirmation. With closed eyes, Rainie felt Rand's presence and absorbed the approval.

The phone rang, she checked her watch as she picked up the phone it was only five. "Hey, Mer." The call pertained to her absence and lack of phone calls for the entire weekend.

"I was with Michael, and there's much to tell. I don't know where to start; he's amazing. Oh my gosh, he thinks ahead and anticipates everything. It's been real, no pretense, and completely honest. I don't know what I feel, but it's good. He came to Mass and lunch with my family. Ryan approached me at the club."

"Don't tell me—"

"No, I wish it had been a flirt, but it had to do with his neighbor's murder. He was worried for me because I had been seen with him and identified. It's only a matter of time before the police knock on my door. They'll have my fingerprints from the buzzed driving thing."

"Crap. I thought it went away. No?"

"No, Mer, don't you remember my parents wanted to make a statement, so it didn't happen again. They're still freaky protective, and before you say it—no, I can't blame them. I get it, but it doesn't make it any better with my fingerprints being in the foyer and all over the stairs at his place. After running the prints, they'll take one look at my picture, and ba-da-boom, they'll have me. Everything's turning around in my life, and then this happens." She checked her bathwater.

"Okay, they'll know who you are; obviously, you didn't have anything to do with the guy getting killed. Rainie, it's gonna be okay, but dang, you get into more crap than anyone I know. Talk about wrong place, wrong time. What was Mike's read on the whole thing?"

"Haven't had a chance to tell him, and I'm not sure I want to either."

"Are you kidding me?" she asked. "Mike's going to know something's up with you, but whatever, it's your decision." She heard Mer's heavy sigh.

"I can't wait to see you tomorrow to tell you about the weekend. Lemme say everyone has skeletons and secrets."

"Mike?"

"Wait until you hear. He's fantastic in every way. For him, it's all about my pleasure. Talk about a novelty. Oh, which reminds me, I'll be getting served with divorce papers tomorrow. Couldn't come at a better time, agree?"

"Agree, but you seem too casual about it. You do know there's going to be some grieving over the loss of the marriage."

Stripping off her clothes, she responded. "Friend, I have grieved long, been angry, and gone through the whole dang grief cycle. I think I'm over and done."

"All right, Miss Over and Done, normal time tomorrow?"

"What do you think about Allie doing some work with us?"

"Sure. We can't pay her much." Mer was quick to point out.

"I don't think she'll care. She's out of school and bored, and until the boys are out, she doesn't have much to do, and I think she's lonely. Besides, I pay well for the nanny gig. Tom, while a total asshole, is good on the money. I think she'd love doing it between watching the boys. She doesn't have friends and never goes out."

"I'm elated about Mike and look forward to some spellbinding story. Now take your bath. See you in the a.m."

The boys were deep into a movie with Allie. Henry was sitting in her lap, and Thomas sprawled on the couch. Rainie scooted him over. "Can I get some couch time with you?" He popped up for her to sit, then snuggled next to her.

He whispered, "We missed you, Mom." He wrapped his arm around her waist. She kissed the top of his head. Sometimes he could be sweet and other times too Tom, but the precious, gentle times seemed to be getting more frequent. Perhaps some of the anger from the separation was fading. Henry climbed out of Allie's lap, came over to her, and snuggled on the other side.

When the movie ended, it was time for the boys to go to bed. "Allie put whatever you want on TV. I have a call to make, and then I'll be back. I have an idea I want to throw at you."

"I'll be here."

Once in her room, she picked up the phone and dialed him. "I'm glad you called. I was beginning to think it should be time; I didn't want to have to spank you." She could hear his smile through the phone. "The sick stomach, you couldn't come up with something better? They may have bought it, but you were lyin' like a rug. What's wrong?"

"It's convoluted and difficult to explain." She knew what he was going to say. *Crap!*

"After this weekend and my complicated stuff, hey, I came clean. If our friendship is going to be real, it has to be open and honest. I get not wanting to upset your parents, but it's truth time, Rainie."

"Remember I told you about Ryan?" She propped the pillows up in her bed and got comfy for the conversation.

"Yes, I do, smooth skin, toned body, yes, I remember, and I know he was working today. I couldn't help but notice him. He was obvious, looking at you and sizing me up, but that's okay. He looked like a decent kid, and I can't blame him. You're one hot lady but continue."

"He approached me, and I thought he was going to hit on me or make some 'come see me' comment, but he didn't. His neighbor, a kinda creepy guy, was killed. While that's horrible, this next part casts a new shadow on the situation. Here goes." She sighed.

"One night, I was waiting for Ryan. I was high as a kite. Anyway, Ryan was late, and I was waiting, which I don't do well. While waiting, this guy, the neighbor, comes in the door. It's one of those old houses divided into four apartments. I'm embarrassed, Michael."

"Go on. The creepy guy comes in and?"

She took in a deep breath. "Creepy guy talked to me. I pretty much ignored him, he went into his apartment, and then fifteen or twenty minutes later, he comes out and asks me if I can do a favor for him, and he'll pay me with a gram of coke. Against better judgment."

"You were too impaired; you couldn't have made a good decision but go on."

"He asks me to take a ride with him. He said he wouldn't look as suspicious. I don't get it, but he has some deal he's gotta do. I went with him." She closed her eyes, took another deep breath, and continued. "We get to this place near the river, and he knocks on the door. An even scarier man opens the door, then they start speaking in Spanish, and I knew it was about me.

"He put me in this room with a lot of nasty looking people with big guns all over and a mound of cocaine on a table. I kept trying to focus my eyes on the ground. Marco, the guy's name, hurries in, grabs my arm, and we bolt, like really bolted. He kept checking his mirrors."

"Yeah, Rainie, I'd say they mentioned you in the conversation. I'm willing to bet Marco's friend wanted you as part of the negotiation," he sighed, "go on."

"We got back to the apartment, and Ryan was home. The guy gave me the gram, and it was over, so I thought. Now he's been killed. One of the neighbors saw me leave with him, told the police, shit, my fingerprints are all over the entry and the front door. The police have a record of my fingerprints from when I was eighteen or nineteen and picked up for driving under the influence. I told you I'm screwed. I feel like my life might be coming together, and I can be the person Rand would be proud of, and this happens." Her breath hitched, and the tears began to flow.

"Don't cry. It's all going to work out. I gotta give it to you, that was dangerous, not to mention a boneheaded thing to do, but it'll all work out. I can't promise you it won't be in the newspaper, but not on page one, okay? I'm not going anywhere, and I'll support you throughout the whole ordeal. I wish I were there to hold you right now."

"When will the bad stuff stop?"

"Baby, you've only begun the better part of your journey. Get some sleep tonight. I'll come by tomorrow night to see you. I love you, Rainie. It took courage to confess aloud. It'll get easier each time and put distance between you and your past. You'll get through this, and so will we. Get some sleep. I'll see you tomorrow. If you need to, you can call me, no matter the time. Got it?"

"Yes. Good night, Michael."

Downstairs she joined Allie on the couch. "Think you'd like to work with us while the boys are in school and then camp. We can't pay much."

"Absolutely. It'll be fun."

Sleep was anything but restful. It was filled with nightmares sending Rainie into a full-blown panic attack. Her heart was pounding, and the anxiety raged – dream or no dream.

She dressed, got the kids to school, headed for the office, and looked forward to seeing Mer. Perhaps she could help her shake the anxiety. Mer was her cool head of reason.

"Good morning," she didn't even look up; she had her head down intently reading some documents. "Kev sent over the info about the florist. I don't recognize the name." She looked up. "God, you look like hell."

"Thanks. I'll make sure to say something nice to you today," Rainie sarcastically responded.

"I know you said you had a good weekend, but did you get any sleep?"

"The weekend was awesome, and I had great sex and sleep, but because of the new situation, I had nightmares all night and woke up in a freakin' panic attack." She dropped her purse on the credenza behind her desk.

"You have worked yourself up. Look at you. Things okay when you told Mike?"

"Yep, he's awesome." She wiped her eyes and blew her nose. "You're the best, and I feel like a blubbering problem child."

"Get a grip, problem child? We can talk about the weekend over lunch, but for now, do you know this florist?" she handed a proposal to her.

"Nope."

After a few hours and a growling gut, Rainie asked, "I'm famished, you?"

"Yep, I have leftovers from the weekend in the fridge. It'll give us plenty of time for you to tell me about your weekend."

She hopped up on the counter and watched as Mer pulled containers out of the fridge.

"What's his place like?"

"It's a small French Quarter cottage with a courtyard and carriage house in back. It's a smashing place, blew my socks off." She went through a detailed description.

"Sounds great. What did y'all do besides—" Mer heated her leftovers for them.

"I didn't have any clothes, other than what I wore to the kids' program. I hadn't planned on spending the night. Luckily he had scrubs and tee shirts of his to lounge in; it was a truth-telling adventure. We both let our skeletons out of the closet. He ordered an outfit for me from some boutique, which got delivered. We talked a lot, went to the French Market. He's straightforward, Mer, simple, and easy-going. He said he had plans for us for lunch. We get back to his place; he has a chef friend who prepared a fabulous dish under silver domes. Michael spared no expense, and everything was the bomb. Then he takes me on a tour of the back quarters. His workshop was downstairs, unbelievable, and then upstairs was the apartment. It's a studio. He then suggests a late dinner at Galetoire's.

"I'm thinking good luck, big guy, but he got us in, to my surprise. When I tell you we ate, I mean it. We were exhausted from the day and crashed when we got back to his place. I slept the entire night in his arms. A first for me."

Meredith brought the food down and relaxed back in her chair, "Best I remember, legs flailing and arms smack across my head. I dreaded sharing a bed with you. What was the secret?"

Amidst a mouthful, she continued. "Michael gave me his life history, and it hasn't always been roses for him. He told me he had been in love with me since college and was the reason no other relationship worked. It made me feel great and horrible at the same time."

"I wondered if he was going to tell you."

"Why didn't you tell me?"

"I did the other day. Besides, at the time, you were up Tom Todd's ass. No, my lovely, you were going to have to discover on your own. There have been a few occasions where he and I ended up at the same place over the years. Having one too many, he'd lay his heart out and ask me how to get your attention. I told him to be patient, I could see the writing on the wall with Tom, and he'd get another chance.

"When you ended up pregnant with Thomas, I thought things might change with Tom. If you hadn't seen it with your own eyes, you would never have believed Tom was a cheater. It's all come full circle. You've sewn your wild oats, I should think, and have grown a bit wiser.

He knows what it's like to appreciate what he's longed for, you. I'm hardly surprised he is, as you put it, amazing."

Rainie plucked another grape. "You're not gonna ask about the sex?"

"No need to; it's written all over your face. Maybe you don't know it yet, but I think you're in love with him."

"Whatever. I'll say I'm 'in like' and that'll have to do for now."

The rest of the day zoomed by, and before she knew it, the workday had passed, and it was time to get home to her boys. As she was leaving work, the mailman brought her divorce papers. It wasn't bittersweet. It was delightfully sweet.

My new life has officially begun! On paper, she was now single. Michael called. "How was your day?"

"It was good, but I'm exhausted, didn't sleep well, nightmares, and stuff. How 'bout you, did you sleep well?"

"I feel bad saying this, but yes. Unlike you, I had great dreams reliving the weekend."

"Oh, those kinds of dreams!" She teased.

"Guilty as charged, but it was all beyond my control. All I could think about was your body, those eyes, and your smile. I can recall your laugh on command. Woman, what you do to me is near sinful. Before I run off the road thinking of you naked, what kind of pizza should I pick up? I know the boys are cheese and pepperoni fans, but what about you and Allie? Anything more adventurous?"

"Surprise me. It's your specialty." She giggled.

"Surprise is my specialty? I thought you said—"

"Michael, now I'm going to run off the road if we don't stop this. I'm blushing and getting flush. Before I get picked up for reckless driving, I'll end this conversation. I'll see you at my house in what, an hour?"

"As fast as I can."

"Later." She checked her face in the rear-view mirror. Besides an ear, to ear smile, she was blushing like a schoolgirl.

She pulled into the driveway. "Mommy," Henry exclaimed as he ran out to greet her. Getting out of the car, she crouched down and hugged him.

"Glad to be home with you guys. Gotta get ready for company."

"Company?" Henry asked.

"Surprise guest." She jogged up the steps, jumped in the shower.

She heard the doorbell ring as she was getting out of the shower. He was faster than she thought he'd be with the pizza. Allie called to her. "There in a sec," the tickle she felt ran from her belly south. She purposely put on a fitted shirt, leaving one extra button undone and half-tucked into her jeans, scrunched her hair, did a quick spray of perfume, a touch of gloss, and went to greet her suitor.

To her surprise, it wasn't Michael, but two official-looking men waiting for her, "Mrs. Todd?"

"Yes?" Her body stiffened.

They presented badges and introduced themselves. "Can we speak privately?"

"Sure. Right this way." She ushered them to the formal parlor. The last time she'd used the parlor was Christmas. "Please take a seat. Can I get you some water or ice tea?"

"No, ma'am." The older man spoke while the other sat with pad in hand. "Do you know Marco Goncalez?"

"Yes, I've met him once." She sat across from the men with eyes wide like a trapped animal. Her heart was thumping so hard she felt for sure the detectives could hear it where they sat.

"Are you aware he was murdered this past Thursday night?"

"How awful." *Shit. Breathe*

"You met him once?" The detective clarified, looking straight through her.

"Yes." The walls were going up fast.

"And you got into his vehicle with him?"

"Yes, I did." *Nosy neighbors.* She nodded as though it was no big deal.

"Are you aware he was a known drug dealer? What was the nature of your encounter?"

"Nature of the encounter?" she asked, stalling for the right words to say. "It was late, and I was waiting for a friend to come home, and I met Marco during that time. We spoke while I waited. He said he had to take a ride, and rather than sit and wait, did I want to take the ride. As I said, it was late, and now, in hindsight, it was foolish. At the time,

I thought it would help pass the time while I waited." It sounded like a reasonable answer to her.

"Did you know you were getting in the vehicle with a known drug dealer?"

"No, sir."

"What is the name of the friend were you waiting for?"

"Ryan" *crap*, she thought. She didn't remember his last name. *Did I ever know his last name?* "He lives in apartment 1A next to—"

"And what is your relationship with Mr. Thibeaux?" She looked puzzled. *Ah, that was his last name. Friends with a twist?*

"We're casual friends." She kept a pan face.

"And you went to this casual friend's house late at night, and for what purpose?" The voice went off in her head. "Yeah, Rainie, for what purpose? You better hope Momma and Daddy don't find out." *Not now, Rand!*

"That's personal. I don't know I should answer because it is personal, and what does it have to do with this horrible crime?"

"Mrs. Todd, you were the last person seen with the deceased."

Just then, she heard the side door open and the kids squealing to her, "Mommy, Doctor Mike is here with pizza."

"I'll be a moment, boys, y'all go ahead and get started." She paused. "I'm sorry, sir, where were we?"

Michael walked into the room. He leaned over and kissed her. "Hi you," she said. "Officers, this is my boyfriend, Michael Landry." He shook their hands.

"What's all this about, Rainie?" He stood next to the chair she was sitting in.

"I'm not sure."

"Mr. Landry,"

"Doctor," he corrected them.

"Dr. Landry, perhaps it best you go back to your food. We have a few more questions for Mrs. Todd."

"And perhaps it's best I not."

"We were asking about her relationship with Ryan Thibeaux, a young man who lives in Mid-City." The detective had a smug look on his face like he knew something unexpected.

"Yes, Ryan is the waiter from the club, nice kid. He has a fondness for Rainie, like a big sister, if you will. I would say her relationship is like a surrogate big sister." He looked at Rainie. "The other night when he called you late?"

"Yes."

"And the night you," almost in a scolding tone, "Rode in a car with a perfect stranger?" he shook his head as he looked at her.

"Yes. The man was murdered. I was the last person the police can identify with him."

Michael shook his head. "Tragic, but what's even more tragic is it shows perhaps Ryan's neighbor wasn't someone to go with on a joy ride, agree?"

The detectives did not appear amused by the charade. "Where did you go with the now-deceased?"

"To his friend's place close to downtown by the river. He lives in an abandoned-looking warehouse."

"You know why he went there?"

"No, we didn't talk about it. I realized I had made an awful mistake getting in the car with him when he started asking me personal questions. It was a bad mistake. He had a sweet smile. I don't know how I can be of help."

"Could you take us to the warehouse? Or point it out?" Detective Marse asked.

"I could get you in the vicinity, but it was late and dark, and I don't know exactly where, but I'll do what I can."

"Any chance his friend saw you? Because, if so, you could be in danger if this person had anything to do with the homicide."

"I doubt it." She lied.

"If you can think of anything else, please give me a call." He handed her his card and underlined his cell number. "Thank you, folks. Good night Mrs. Todd, Dr. Landry."

They walked the officers to the door.

As soon as they had pulled away, she threw her arms around his neck. "Thank you. You made it easier."

"Didn't I tell you it was going to be all right?"

"I do, and yes, you were right. But I kinda lied."

"Kinda, ya think?" He did a double-take.

"Yes, I know the guy knows what I look like. Do you really think I could be in danger?"

"You have to be on your toes, keep aware of your surroundings, and don't go anywhere alone, or alone with your boys. Stay away from the river and the warehouses. Now let's go eat and put this to bed for the night."

Walking into the kitchen, she nudged him with her hip and a sassy smile. "By the way, I got my papers today."

"Mommy, who were those men," Thomas questioned.

"They're police detectives." She quickly answered.

"Why did they come here to see you?" He was half sitting and kneeling on the chair. He had Rainie's boundless energy.

Michael jumped in, "They needed your mom's help."

"Wow, cool."

"No, my sweet, not cool, it was scary. How many pieces have you eaten?"

"Four, and I'm full."

"Y'all go play." That was all the nudging they needed.

Allie was deep into a novel, looking up every so often to watch the boys.

"Allie, you gonna be in here for a while?"

"Yes, ma'am."

"I need a few grown-up moments with Michael."

After having police at the house, she figured they probably did need some time to talk without little ears. "It's all good."

Rainie grabbed Michael's hand, led him to her room, shut the door, and flipped the lock. "Thank you for handling everything tonight. I was nervous."

"You were doing fine. I was there for moral support, and sometimes it's good to have a man involved in a conversation with another man, but you were handling it fine without me."

She sat on the bed at first, and he sat back in one of her side chairs. She went over to him, knelt in front of him, and looked at him with purpose. She began to undo his jeans.

"Rainie, the boys, and Allie," but she had already taken hold of him.

She gently stroked him. "Just returning a favor," and she took him deep into her mouth. She devoured him thinking all the while how he had satisfied her. It was her turn to change the tide, and she did. It took everything he had not to moan. He ran his hands into her hair and grabbed hold at the peaking moment. She could feel every muscle in his body tighten in preparation for a powerful release.

He pulled her up to him locking his lips on hers. She climbed on his lap.

"You like? I've always doubted my—"

"Don't. Like hardly comes close to a description. More like ecstasy. There's a strong current running between us. Can you feel it, or is it me, savoring the gratification?" he asked.

Yes, she thought. Her body tingled at the thought of Michael, and she could feel her face pinking. "I've felt it for some time now. Being close to you, I feel drawn. If that's what you're talking about. It's raw yet loving, intense yet peaceful, sound about right?"

He stood up, holding her wrapped around him, turned, and pushed her against the wall. How convenient it was she wore a mere thong it presented little if any kind of barrier.

"Here's to the movies," and he guided himself inside her. He went hard and deep; he pushed her further down on him.

She gasped. A heatwave ignited her body like a spark to tinder. His rhythm mounted faster, deeper, and more forceful. She felt as though her body couldn't take any more. Sex with him was beyond description. He carried her to the bed, gently laying her down. She smiled up at him.

"So that's all you got?" She teased.

"Woman, you're impossible, absolutely deplorable, and so gorgeous. Tonight you're with me. In my world, it doesn't get any better." His eyes twinkled as he spoke. He watched her face from her eyes to her lips and back again. "Kiss me. Sorry, it had to be quick. Kids."

Once appropriate for the boys and Allie, they headed downstairs. "I know you said no to the house. I'd say this was extraordinary circumstances." She batted her eyes at him.

"You're right, but not again." He seemed in a fog. They joined everyone in the den.

"Doctor Mike, you look like you're sleeping with your eyes open. Did you hear me talking to you?"

"I'm sorry, Thomas, my mind was a million miles away. You said?"

"Do you like my Mom?" he asked, standing right in front of him.

"Do I like your Mom? I love your Mom. She and I have been friends for a long time."

"Yeah, I know, but is she your girlfriend?" Thomas had a pensive, straight in the eyes kind of look.

"Hm. Never thought about it." Michael smiled.

"I heard her tell the policeman you were her boyfriend; wouldn't that make her your girlfriend? It makes sense to me. We want you to be her boyfriend. My dad has what he calls a special friend, but we know she's his girlfriend. He thinks we're stupid." Still, with his head cocked, he awaited an answer.

"I haven't put a name to our relationship, but I suppose she's my girlfriend. She's the only one I have dinner with or visit at home. I don't have many friends and feel like I'm one lucky guy to have you, Henry, Allie, and your mom as my friends. I work a lot and don't get out often. You're my friend, right?"

His chest puffed up. "Yes, Doctor Mike, I'm your friend. Do you take care of people with fever and coughs or broken arms or take out 'pendixes? My friend at school had his 'pendix taken out. My Aunt Rand, Mom's twin, she's in heaven, had a sick 'pendix. Want to see a picture of her?" He jumped up and grabbed a frame with a picture of two smiling redheads. "Betcha can't tell which one's Mom."

Michael studied the picture carefully. They were identical, no doubt about it, but one of them had a little more confidence in her smile while the other had a more playful smile. "I think that is your mom, but they look like the same person, don't they?"

Thomas lifted his eyebrows and gave a devilish grin. "Mom, Doctor Mike picked right in the guessing picture."

"Hm, why am I not surprised?" she looked over Michael's way. "I can't recall anyone getting it right, can you?"

"No, ma'am. What kind of doctor are you?" Thomas was giving the third degree.

"Thomas, you have bugged Michael long enough. It's late, and you two," she pointed at each of the boys, "need to get ready for bed and get to sleep—tomorrow's school. Only three and a half days left, mind you. Get a wiggle on."

She grabbed the frame from him and plopped next to him, resting one of her legs across his. "What made you pick me in the picture? I love that photo because it reflects how close we were. Not a day goes by I don't think of her. I know you're going to think I'm crazy, but she comes to me in my dreams, and sometimes I can hear her in my head. She actually scolded me harshly one night about my lifestyle."

"That's what brought on the big change." It was more of a statement than a question.

"Yes, but I knew something had to give. Rand pointed out how reckless and neglectful I had become. The thought of letting her down was more than I could take. She even referred to you. She knows everything I do." With her index finger, she stroked Rand's face in the photo.

"How's that make you feel? Do you feel like someone is always watching you?" He cupped her foot.

"More like watching over me. Do I think Rand's hanging out in the corner while we're, um, playing? No, I wouldn't think she'd get so up close and personal, but I don't know, to tell you the truth. Maybe she watches everything, but the fact I'm happy, and it's all healthy, I think she's cool. It doesn't freak me usually. Last time—"

Michael sat listening attentively. He had known people to have the gift, as his mother would call it. Rainie continued, "was different. It felt more intense. You think I'm a whack job." Changing the subject, "How did you know to pick me, anyway?"

"Your smile looks a little more playful. I don't think you're a whack job. I think more people would communicate with deceased loved ones if they were open to it. No one knows where heaven is, people tend to point up, but it could easily be a different dimension they can move in and out of." When he spoke, he looked deep into her eyes like straight to her soul. "We don't know, and I don't think we're intended to know. I think it's beyond our comprehension, but Jesus said a place had been made for us with Him, and that's what I believe." He kissed her toes.

"I love it; you're so spiritual and yet bad at the same time." She touched his cheek, turning his face toward hers.

Glancing at her lips, he whispered. "Bad? How am I bad?"

"You know," she tilted her head to the side, grinning.

"Rainie, He made us with all our parts and creative minds. I don't think He thinks we're bad. I know premarital fooling around should be off-limits, but I'm pretty sure He gets it. If it makes you uncomfortable, it can always stop."

"I didn't say I was uncomfortable!" she playfully slapped his arm.

"I was pretty sure there had been no objections thus far. It's getting late, and while I hate to leave, I have a big day tomorrow. My life feels," he thought for a moment, "complete. Scare you?" They were walking to the door, but he stopped. "Does it?"

"Not at all, Michael, I love it, can I see you tomorrow night?"

"Probably. I know I'm booked solid and might be exhausted. You do tend to wear me out." He gave her a quick kiss and a big hug, "I love it."

KILLING ME SOFTLY

Morning came with a bang, and the race was on—brushing teeth, dressing for school, and work with a quick not-so-healthy breakfast. Out the door, they flew. She yelled back to Allie. "See you at the office?"

"Yes, ma'am."

The phone rang. It was Tom. "Good morning, Tom. The papers have been signed and are on the way back to you."

"Great," he said, "Thank you." *Really? Where's Tom, and who is this impostor?* "Any chance I can have the boys tonight? I need to talk to them, but before I do, I wanted to let you know I'm getting married." She couldn't help but think, *Wow!*

She wasn't sure how she felt about it. She had some kind of wrenching inside. Could it be she was angry, or was she sad, or was she jealous? The boys had earbuds in, which made it easy for her to talk freely on the phone. "I guess congrats are in order, and of course, the boys can be with you. What time do you want them? Tom, I haven't interjected my opinion, but since you're tying the knot, I think Diane has to work harder to get along with the boys. She needs to accept them. They've been candid with me about some of the things she's said, and if it's too uncomfortable for you, I don't mind having a word with her."

He said he'd pick them up from school, and he would talk to Diane about her interaction with the boys.

"We're getting married at Disney during the vacation. It'll make an awkward situation for the boys a little easier."

"Maybe so," *what gives? The last time we spoke, he nearly yanked my arm off and was a total dick.* She wondered what had changed. He was pleasant and had a very different tone in his voice. "I'll let the boys know you'll be picking them up, and then I suppose you'll be bringing them to school in the morning?" He answered, yes.

As she dropped the boys off and told them their dad was picking them up. Their response was less than thrilled. She cautioned they needed to be respectful and no more making fun of or being ugly to Diane. They started with the "that's nice." "Boys, that's what I'm talking about; stop being rude. I do not expect you to be disrespectful or rude, got it? I think you'll find things different. If not, I want to know, okay?"

"Got it," Thomas snickered. She gave him the look, eyes squared, and jaw set, "Yes, ma'am, I got it."

"I'll see you after school tomorrow. Now give me kisses. Have a good day, and be good!" Thomas saluted her, and they ran off. She couldn't help but reflect on the strangeness of the conversation. Then it occurred to her. He must have done something questionable, or he got caught with his pants down. She'd heard stories about the law firm. She held it as a speculative rumor. If true, he worked with a bunch of sleazeballs, but the firm had always had a good reputation, at least until they took on Grayson Smith as a partner.

Rainie couldn't wait to get to Mer's; she would be the only one to find the irony of the whole thing. Tom was outraged when Rainie told him they were expecting Thomas. The discovery of Henry bought on Tom's abusive behavior. If Diane was pregnant, she didn't envy the woman. Or if he did do something iffy, she must be threatening him. Either way, he was screwed.

Rainie could barely contain herself as she entered the office. "You beat me here, I see. Tom called with the great news he's getting married." She watched the expressions on their faces. Both had jaws dropped and eyes wide open in disbelief.

"Hell, Rainie, the ink isn't even dry on the divorce papers." Mer always straight to the point.

"Tom was nice and friendly and asked if the boys could be with him tonight. I thought it was odd at the time, but when he told me he was getting married, it started to make sense. I bet the asshole got caught with his pants down, or he's in some deep shit, and she has him by the balls." Rainie threw her arms up dramatically, almost giggling.

Meredith and Allie were both in a stupor. Allie was concerned. Sitting among stacks of papers, she had a look of both surprise and dread. "He's going to tell the boys tonight? I hope they're okay. You know they don't like her. The marriage is going to be hard for them."

Mer didn't hedge bets. "He's such a jackass. If I were to bet, I'd say he has a few fish on the line and got unlucky with this one. I agree. It's gotta be something of magnitude. When's the big day, did he say?"

"Disney World wedding, for the boys," Rainie smirked.

Meredith shook her head with closed eyes. "What a cheesedick. If he thinks the boys won't see through the charade, he's mistaken. Your boys are perceptive, Rai."

"Enough of this; how far did you get after I left yesterday?" She had already wasted way too much time on Tom.

They agreed Meredith would meet with the florist, Rainie would pick up odds and ends, and Allie would hold down the fort taking calls.

Meredith and Rainie went their separate ways.

Rainie perused Oak Street, finding a few chachkies, but not what she had hoped for, and Magazine was the next stop. She dodged in and out of shops returning to her car with each bag of treasures. She was so absorbed she didn't notice the man scoping her out across the street.

He was in a black Navigator, watching her every move. Back and forth, she would go from shop to car to shop again. She called Mer. "How done are you?"

"Meet me at the hotel. We need you for a tiebreaker. How'd the shopping go?"

She pulled off, "Pretty good. I have a trunk full of junk," and laughed. She didn't notice the car following her. She arrived at King's Court, found Mer, and met the florist to her colossal surprise. He was the guy from Michael's party, the weirdo who freaked her out. Kevin walked into the room.

"Hello, I wasn't expecting you today," Kevin seemed taken aback, maybe even startled.

"I bet you weren't. Perhaps we could have a private conversation if you don't mind."

The florist piped in, "I know what you're going to say, Mrs. Todd, and I'm embarrassed by the whole ordeal at the party. I wasn't myself, and I give you my word. There will not be one harsh or ugly word. I'll be quiet as a kitten. I thought you were bidding on the floral, but it doesn't matter anyway now, does it? Please forgive me."

Mer was confused, and the embarrassment on Kevin's face was revealing. This man was, from all appearances, a close friend.

"It has nothing to do with forgiveness. I believe it would fall more into the appropriate and inappropriate realm. You know what, Kevin, this is your circus, and if this is who you want for floral, it's your business. We're merely providing you with our service. I can play well with anyone, but let's get it clear there'll be no nastiness from this man to my partner or me. Are we clear?"

When they exited the hotel, Mer turned to her. "You blew me away. I had no idea he was the creep from the party. What if you hadn't come downtown today?"

Rainie couldn't have been more blasé. "I would've been none the wiser. It's over and done with. I think he's going to work out fine for the opening. His contract will be with Kevin, and we'll have gotten our payment and out of the picture. He's going to be a thorn in Kevin's side, but not our problem."

The Navigator parked outside the hotel. Rainie got in her car to get back to Allie and check on her progress.

She called Michael's office. He hadn't returned from the surgery center, and they didn't know when to expect him. They would let him know she had called. She hoped she could get him to let him know the kids were not going to be home. He could stay over.

A small familiar voice whispered in her ear. "Watch out. There's a bad guy out to get you."

Speaking aloud, "Rand, what do you mean? Who's out to get me? You know your whispers and fleeting moments in the mirror watching me make me feel crazy. I know it's you, or maybe I am fucking nuts. Who knows?"

When she returned to the office, Allie had everything organized.

It wasn't long before Meredith returned, and they went over the project. It was apparent Allie was excited and had taken to the job well.

The black Navigator waited at the end of the block. As predicted, Meredith was over the moon with the job Allie had done. "How 'bout call it a day and resume in the morning?"

"Allie, if you want, you can head home now. I'll be a few minutes behind you."

Mer had seemed upset when they left the meeting. She turned and faced her, brow furrowed with a look of concern. "Are you okay?"

"I feel awful about the man being the one from the party." She turned to sit at her desk. Mer's whole demeanor was out of sync.

"For crying out loud, Mer, I'm a big girl and can handle myself. Besides, the florist is Kevin's problem, and we'll be long done with the project when the shit starts hitting the fan."

Rainie was concerned. Mer wasn't an overly emotional person usually. "What's wrong with you?" She sat on the edge of Mer's desk. "Are you sick or something?"

"No, I don't know what's wrong with me. I'm just emotional. Tears and anger for no apparent reason. I'm high then low." Mer looked like someone had just sucked all the wind out of her sails.

"Doesn't sound like you, my steady Eddie. How long has this been going on? If it doesn't straighten out in a week, I'd see your doc. Maybe you need some antidepressants. Don't make me worry or I'm gonna have to call your hubs. All okay there?"

"Yes, of course, but I've got him twisted. He doesn't know if he's coming or going. He's walking on eggshells, and I hate it." She grabbed a Kleenex, wiped her eyes. "Get going. I'm okay. I'll see you and Allie in the morning. She impressed me, by the way."

Rainie hugged her. "You worry me. I've never seen you like this. If the job is too weighty, let me take point. Kev'll have to get over dealing with me."

"No silly, I'm okay, really. I'm just emotional."

"See you in the morning, my friend." She walked to her car and, for the first time, took note of the Navigator. The way it was parked felt ominous. She dismissed her feelings, got in her car, and drove home.

All this new info about Tom was weird. She called Michael's office again. "Hey, this is Rainie. Is he back yet?"

The receptionist said no, not yet, but she had given him the message. "Thanks and I promise not to bother you again." The receptionist laughed and said she could call as many times as she wanted.

Her mind drifted to the past weekend and what life may hold for her or them in the future. She could see their relationship growing, but she could also see where he may get over the novelty of conquering what he desired. Either way, she was enjoying the ride.

She pulled into her driveway. Allie had already gotten home. "I'm home," she called out. No answer.

Rainie went to change her clothes. She heard the ding of the side door, followed by a scream. She dropped everything and ran toward the scream.

Allie was lying on the floor with a stream of blood running down her face. She quickly looked around and caught a glimpse of a dark-haired man running down the driveway. She thought she saw the same big black car.

She shook Allie hard. Groggily, she responded. Rainie dialed 911.

In minutes the police and the paramedics were entering her door. Her phone rang – it was Michael. "Hello, gor—" but stopped when he heard the chaos.

"What's going on? Are you okay?" His voice had a quiver of concern.

"Someone broke in. The police and paramedics are here."

"I'll be there in less than five."

The police asked Rainie what had happened, but she didn't know, only to tell them she heard the side door, then the scream, and caught a glimpse of a man running maybe to a black car. She mentioned a big black car down the street from her work, which seemed out of place.

Allie told the police she had come down from her room into the kitchen when she saw a man coming through the side door. She screamed and hit him with the closest thing she could, but he slammed her to the floor. It was all Allie could remember. She had hit her head on a chair on the way down. The police looked around. They found half a bat seemingly flung across the room.

Paramedics were tending to a cut on Allie's head as Michael came in through the door. He went straight to Rainie; she was shaken but not hurt. He checked out Allie's wound. "I can fix that, and no one will ever notice a thing. You'll be good as ever."

He encouraged her to go to the hospital in the ambulance with Rainie, and he would follow. "Tell the ER that I'll be doing the suturing. To wait." He followed and had already parked as they were moving her out of the ambulance.

The police waited and filled out the appropriate report as Michael stitched her up. He ordered a CT scan.

As he and Rainie waited, he started with the questions. "Do you think it could be the guy from your trip with Ryan's neighbor?" His face had an intense look, with eyes darting into images of what-ifs in his mind. Unlike his usual laid back demeanor, he looked like some pensive primal animal from a documentary. She'd never seen him as anxious.

"I have no idea. What if my boys had been there, Michael? Oh, God, I can't bear the thought." Her body was rigid, making her gestures appear jerky. She paced.

"Good thing they were gone. Where are the boys?" Michael asked, grabbing her hand and pulling her into him. "We have to breathe." He was calming himself down as well as helping her.

"I called you earlier today to tell you about my strange morning, not saying this evening hasn't been strange." Her eyes had a desperate pleading, her expression grave. "Tom wanted the boys to stay the night with him because he wanted to tell them he was getting married."

"Whoa, I didn't know he had a particular girlfriend. I've seen him with several different ones, but who knew. Good for him." Michael tried to be upbeat.

"I think the marriage thing was a bit of a surprise to him maybe, but I don't know for sure. Either he's in some trouble, or Diane's pregnant. They're getting married at Disney World so that it won't be as hard on the boys."

"Whatever, he's a strange duck." Michael put his hand on her shoulder, leaning in to listen.

Her breathing slowed. "Went to work as usual. Allie started this morning. Mer met with the florist, and I did the chachkies."

"What?" he asked.

"Extra odds and ends."

"Oh," like he got it.

"Then I finished early met Mer at King's Court. Of all things, the florist is the creepy guy from your office party. Remember?"

"Yeah, the office party, I remember and fondly, may I add?" His touch and the tenor of his voice were soothing.

"I left Mer's. Down her street, I saw an old black SUV. It was out of place, and I thought it was weird, but I put it out of my mind. Got home, and you know the rest."

He pulled out his wallet and found the card from the detective. "I think we need to call Detective Marse. It's gotta be one of the guys from your joy ride. Who else would it be? If he is following you and comes into your home, I'm pretty sure he's part of the cast of characters from the drug house." She shook her head, no. "Humor me, Rainie. The whole truth has to come out this time."

He dialed the number, "Detective Marse, Mike Landry here. We met at Rainie Todd's house regarding the murder—"

The detective cut him off, telling him he remembered him, and asked was everything okay."

"Rainie had a strange occurrence at her house this evening, and I believe there may be some connection. She called 911, but I thought you might want to know. She saw a black SUV on the street down from her office – It seemed out of place, but she blew it off and went home. Soon after, a man entered her home, attacked her nanny, and fled. I wanted to pass the information along. It may be nothing."

He held the phone so that she could hear as well. "I'm assuming you already have officers at the house? I'm glad you called. They've more than likely passed this to another detective; you did the right thing calling me. I'll handle it on my end. Stay where you are. I'll come to you. The break-in is hardly a coincidence. Where are you?"

"Baptist ER."

"Any officers there at the hospital with you?"

"Yes, sir," Michael was quick to answer.

"Have them call me."

Rainie looked at him. "Really? He's going to think I lied to him."

"You did. The group of thugs saw your face, and you know it."

"I don't want to get involved," she pleaded.

"You already are, but it's gonna be okay. Trust me? Rainie, the more you acknowledge the bad stuff, the better you'll feel, I promise." He kissed her hand.

The radiologist approached them, "Dr. Landry, she has a hairline fracture left parietal. I advise admitting tonight to make sure there isn't an incident of intracranial pressure. She took a hard blow, but so far, there aren't any indications suggesting swelling. She's asking for Mrs. Todd."

"Absolutely, overnight observation." Michael nodded.

"Where is she?" Baptist Hospital brought back painful memories for Rainie.

"We're bringing her out soon," the nurse answered. "We'll transfer her to a room."

Rainie was apprehensive until she saw her. "Oh, God, Allie. Do you want me to call your mom?"

"I'll call in a couple of days. I'm sorry I didn't stop the bad guy, but I did hit him. I broke the boys' bat."

"I thought he hit you with the bat."

"They're going to make me stay here for the night."

"I know," she stroked Allie's hand.

"I don't want you going home. I'm worried the monster will come back."

"You worry about you, okay? Let me worry about me. Get some rest." Rainie, like a worried parent, instructed.

Detective Marse showed up. He looked bigger and older than she had remembered. He was perhaps in his early fifties and had a no-nonsense appearance to his stoic face.

"Mrs. Todd, what would make you think this man has anything to do with the case we spoke of the other night? You seemed confident nobody saw you. Did you perhaps leave some detail out of your story? Any information left out could be important to the case and the apprehension of the responsible party." It was as though he was looking straight through her with his bullshit-o-meter on high alert.

She looked down at the ground and began to fidget. "I may have been mistaken about not being seen."

"Mistaken, Mrs. Todd, is that akin to omission of fact?" the detective asked.

"I wanted to stay out of it. Can you blame me? I have two small children, a well-respected family, and a prominent boyfriend. I don't want to be involved." She looked like the kid caught sneaking back in the house through the bedroom window.

"But, you are, ma'am. If you're so worried, start telling the truth. Do I make myself clear?"

"Yes. I didn't sit in the car while Marco went inside. I got out with him. It's a pretty rough area around there, and, of course, I knew I had made a poor decision."

"It's safe to say the people in the house saw your face?" He looked down into her face.

"I didn't look at anyone and didn't look up, but could someone perhaps recognize me? The answer is yes, but I certainly don't travel in the same circles as any of the people there. It's not like I gave my name and address."

"Maybe not, but you don't know who these people are or where they go, and someone saw you somewhere and followed you, right?"

No point in arguing. Obviously, the criminals had seen her, followed her, and because of poor decisions and fucked up life, now everyone she loved was in danger.

"Describe these people as best you can. Did you hear any names? Do you think you could recognize any of them? You said you could get us in the vicinity of the building?"

"Yes, the vicinity, not the actual street or place. They were Hispanic, I think, dark hair, dark features. They were about my height, at least the men were. The ladies didn't stand up. I went in with Marco, and the guy in charge, or seemed in charge, threw me into a room with a couple of women and men while he talked with Marco in the other room. There were guns, and I'm assuming a pile of dope on the table. It was clear they were drug dealers, and I was pretty freakin' scared. I thought I was going to end up dead in some dumpster. That's the story, okay?"

He stood there looking at her. "It will never cease to amaze me when it comes to people and the dumb shit they do. I don't know what the hell you were thinking, and you're lucky you didn't end up raped, sold, or dead in some empty warehouse, but they are looking for you now. You need to sharpen your memory and help us identify these people before you end up dead. We have an extensive database of known dope dealers. I'll need you to come down to the station tonight."

"Can I at least wait until they get Allie in a room?" she pleaded.

"Crime lab is at your house, and they're dusting for prints or anything that could give us information. By chance, you don't have some hidden surveillance system we didn't see?"

She shook her head, no.

Detective Marse left the hospital, and as he left, Michael said they'd meet him soon.

"God, Michael, you don't have to," she looked despondent.

He took her face in his hands. "I'm not going anywhere, do you understand? Who knows, something good may come from this. Maybe you can help them get some goon off the streets. Rainie, you need to start looking at things from a more positive perspective. I get it; you fucked up and did it quite royally."

Like a child throwing a tantrum, she said with a pout, "You're right, okay? You're Mr. Perfect."

From his expression, Rainie might as well have stabbed him in the heart. She saw the pain in his eyes.

He spoke softly, "Rainie, I'm in no way perfect, my love, sorry, but I'm as flawed as they come. My only advantage is, I have surrendered to God. Not to be a dick, but you need to examine your heart."

"That's what I mean, Michael. Right there, could you be more perfect? You should be angry with me, hate me for dragging you into this shit." She watched as his eyes glossed over.

"Don't cha get it?" His eyes squinted with anger. "Right, wrong, or indifferent, I love you. I know where your pain is coming from, and we can get through this. I know we can. I'm going to take you down to the station, and while I can't help you identify anyone, I can get you coffee or tea and be there for whatever you need. Don't shut me out. Rainie, you need to start speaking out about your past demons."

He was open and raw and vulnerable. She could take him down in one sharp blow, but he trusted her with his heart. He had faith in her when she couldn't even have faith in herself.

"I'm sorry. I'll try, Michael. I'm freaked out."

After a few minutes, once Allie settled in, Rainie told her they were going to the police station to look at mugshots.

She seemed confused. "I saw the guy. He had a gray mechanics shirt on with the name Santa above the pocket. If he's in their system, I'm sure I could point him out."

Rainie asked. "Santa? Are you sure?"

"Absolutely, you don't see that name every day." She gave her an are-you-kidding-me look.

Rainie kissed her cheek. "I'm sorry this happened, Allie."

"I'm fine. You and Doctor Mike get some sleep. I know I'm going to try if they ever leave me alone." She glanced toward the door as it began to open.

Rainie and Michael left the room as a few nurses entered to complete all the transfer paperwork and take vitals. "Michael, you think she saw the name correctly? Santa?"

They moved with haste to the car. "Who knows, but we're certainly going to throw it out there, and maybe they'll send a sketch artist to see her. I didn't realize she saw the guy, did you?"

"No. If Allie told me, I'm sure I woulda remembered, especially the name."

Detective Marse was waiting for them at the police station.

After quick greetings, Rainie went straight to the point. "I talked to Allie, my nanny. She saw the guy. She said he was in a gray mechanic's shirt with the name Santa above the pocket." She and Michael sat in the chairs in front of his desk.

The detective's face paled. "Santa? Shit. His name is Santana Hernandez. He's not a big name, but he's an underling in the Moreno family business. Mateo Moreno is a major player in the cartel world. Maybe we'll get lucky, and forensics can find something to place him at Marco's, so it sticks. We can get him from your place, Mrs. Todd, but Grayson Smith will have him out in record time. A light went off in her head. She thought, *Grayson from Tom's office? What the hell?*

Marse made notes on a pad, all the while glancing at them. "At the same time, this just got easier and harder. Santa isn't someone to mess with. He's gonna come back; the bastard is off the wall crazy, a real psychopath. You have somewhere you can stay until this settles down and we get him off the street?"

"Maybe my parents. How long are we talking, a few days, a few weeks?"

"Anyone's guess. A lot of this depends on Crime Lab, and it can take a couple of weeks depending on how backed up they are, but I'll try to push it faster. No promises."

Her blank expression reflected her innermost being, and it all spelled failure in her mind, which triggered Rand, "Rainie, get over yourself. Poor pitiful Pearl. You made this mess. Now you have to clean it up. Dang lucky Momma and Daddy don't know about you and your drugs and screwing around, and for the record, don't blame me. You always play the my-sister-died card. Not this time. It's all you." The voice was loud as it echoed inside her head. Certainly, others could hear it.

"Hello? What's got you captivated? I was saying, for tonight, Rai; we'll stay at my place." Michael took her hand. "Free to leave?" He looked at Marse.

"Yeah, y'all go. I got your numbers if I need you. I wish I'd have known it was Santa. Coulda saved y'all a trip."

They walked out of the police station. "Trust me yet?" Michael asked.

The voice started up again. "Trust your man yet? Good question, sir. Think dang it, think." Rainie stopped mid-step and held her head.

"Would you stop?" she said aloud.

Michael looked surprised, "Stop what?"

"Not you, Michael." Most bewildered, he glanced at her with a pondering expression.

THE OTHER SIDE OF LIFE

"I'm gonna kill that fuckin' bitch." He held a dirty rag to his head. "I don' know where she came from, but smack. I think she broke the fuckin' bat."

"You whiny little bitch. I tol' you to leave it. She don' know nothing, she's jus' some uptown piece bangin' Marco for coke. She don' know nothin', I tell you. Leave her the fuck alone. She's gonna be trouble. You aks me, Santa, you got what you deserved goin up in her place." He flicked a cigarette butt out the window of the Lincoln Navigator. "Uptown people got cameras an' all. I ain't goin' down cause you got some hard-on for this bitch."

"Fuck you, Tomas. I tol' you. She saw it all, Bro,' you were there an' Angel, an' Delores, an' Paco. You should be watchin – who knows what she tells. I don' want no one comin' down on me cuz I didn't tie up loose ends." He nervously checked his rearview.

It was seven, not even dark. How many people could have seen him? With all those big trees up and down the street, there was a pretty good shadow. All was cool. He was looking out for them all.

Tomas tried to take charge, "Marco got what was comin' to him. He stole, he lied, he fucked with Mateo's money. He knew what the score was. Leave the bitch alone. She don't know nothing, for the last fuckin time. Man, jus' get me back to the shop, I don't want nothing to do with this shit – all's I wanted was another boost."

"I think I'm gonna need stitches. Look at this shit." He continued to glance in the rearview mirror at a patch of blood-soaked black hair. He turned onto Coliseum and headed toward the river.

Going through a series of one-way streets, they ended up at the warehouse. Santa hit the horn a couple of times, and the warehouse door began to roll up. He pulled in. Two of the guys were sitting at the table, and Delores was walking from the entrance after she closed the warehouse door.

Tomas got out from the back seat and started talking to one of the guys sitting at the table. "Ya boy here, got his whiny ass beat trying to go after Marco's redhead bitch. My ass ain't going nowhere wit him again, that's for fuckin sure." He looked at Santa, "You too fuckin crazy for me."

The woman walked over to Santa to examine his head. "You got it good it's about this long," she held her dagger-long fingernails about an inch and a half apart. " I guess I got to take your punk ass to the clinic."

"I don't wanna go to no clinic. Get ya friend, the nurse, to come over. She can stitch it up. Tell her to bring what she needs to do the job. I'll pay her with some blow. She'll do it."

The woman called her friend and asked her to come over and explained why.

"Angel said she'd be here after work, so you gotta wait an hour, an' she said ya better have some product cuz it's pay before play." She came right up to his face. "She said ya already owe her. You stiffed her last time she did ya a favor. You're a real piece of work, Santa."

"Fuck you, Delores." He sat and kicked his feet up on the table.

"Yeah, no, it's fuck you, Santa. You're one stupid motherfucker. You better leave that bitch alone. Listen to Tomas."

A couple of hours later and a half a gram up the nose, Angel had him stitched up and got her blow. It was almost eleven. Santa was tired of the ragging; it'd been going on since he got back from the redhead's place. They were the crazy ones; he was the only one who got it. Jorge and Angel sauntered out as though there wasn't a care in the world. What the hell were they thinkin?

Paco's place was the upstairs office, and he called it a night. Delores and Diego left with Tomas, so he sat there alone, stewing about how they all disrespected him. Before long, the drug-induced paranoia began.

He was gonna show them all. He'd send out a message not to fuck with him. He waited for another hour, grabbed a bag, loaded it with the clothes he had lying around, stole a couple of thousand dollars, an ounce of the blow, keys to an older Tahoe, and slithered out.

Santa thought that if he were running the place, the money, product, and keys woulda been locked up. It was their fault they were sloppy. He thought he'd get moved up in the organization once he told Mateo it was him that cleaned the mess.

Santa rode around for an hour, and the more he drove, the more pissed he got, and the more crazy bravado entered his head.

"Who the fuck are those motherfuckers to judge me? Nobody gonna disrespect me like that an' get away with it. No fuckin way." He cruised down Orleans, turning down one of the side streets where he saw a couple brothers on the corner.

They glared at him as he rolled up. He nodded. One of the guys walked up to his car, flashing a peek of his piece. "Lookin' for some big firepower. The word is you got it all."

"Maybe, maybe not."

Santana held up five crisp hundred-dollar bills fanned. "Come back in an hour, an' I'll gotcha big bang."

For the next hour, Santa planned his retribution. Marco had been small potatoes with a big mouth. The longer the night went, the crazier he got.

"Why the fuck he brought the bitch, who knows. I ain't takin no chances. He did what he had to. There's not one of them that would walk away an' then, to dis me like I was a dog. Ain't no way I'm gonna let it go."

The hour passed, and when he turned the corner, he could see a whole group hangin'. "Look at dis shit. They betta not pull anything." He had his own piece next to him on the seat. For his plans, he needed something more Rambo.

The man he had talked to earlier directed him to pull behind a Hummer parked on the street. He eased in behind, pulled out his five big ones ready to take possession, and get out of the neighborhood.

The man opened the back of the car, Santa could see the arsenal. The guy grabbed one, brought it back to the car.

"Here's ya big bang. Gotta lotta kick." He took the bills from Santa and stuffed them in his pants.

"I don't see no ammo. What I'm gonna do throw it at 'em. Shiiit!"

"Oh, you want to feed it, too? That, my man, is gonna be another five. He took a step back lifted his arms punctuated with attitude.

Santa reached in his pocket and pulled out the rest of the first grand. "Here's ya five. Now fuckin set me up and let me get the fuck outa here."

"Show respect, motherfucker. You in my streets."

He signaled one of his people to grab the goods. They threw a bag to him. Santa inspected it quickly and left.

As he drove, he planned the hit. "By ten the whole crew'll be there fixin' the new rides. I'll start doin' my thing, step to the car, pull Rambo, and light the place up. I can grab the cash an' blow an' be outa there b'fore they have a chance. Mateo will know it was me. Let it settle a few days, then bam, I'll get the red-head, and it's done, adios."

He went to crash at his mother's for a few hours. When he started to pull onto the block, he saw an unmarked car watching the place. Change of plan, he'd have to drive around, like it or not. While driving, he figured he'd pass by the redhead's house. He was pretty sure there would be another unmarked car.

Paranoia was rampant, keeping him suspicious of everything. He pulled onto the redhead's street. It looked clear. He parked the car a few houses away, managed his way to her driveway. Everything looked the same until he saw the redhead peering from the curtains, looking right at him. With her hand, she formed the shape of a gun pointed directly at him.

He ran as fast as he could to his car and took off. "Fucking playin' with me. That's it. I'm gonna play with her before I kill her. She'll be begging to die. I'll sneak in, wait, then grab her from behind and choke her out. When the bitch wakes, she'll be tied up naked. Oh, I won't fuck her right away. I wanna watch her as she whimpers in terror when she sees the shiny blade and feels the sting of tiny slashes. She's not gonna know what hit her. I wish I could hear her beg for mercy, but with a gag, I'll just have to watch her fits as she tries to twist her way out. Once I done her, they won't even be able to put all the pieces back together. She's gonna die slow and hard." He could feel his pulse quicken with his thoughts, and his breathing became faster. He was sweating. *After all*, he thought, *she was the one that brought it on. She started the game.*

By morning, it was time for things to begin. Santa, wired to the gills on coke, succumbed to the thrill of anticipation.

He pulled up. Tomas started on him.

"You took the Tahoe? Ya think maybe it's on someone's boosted car list? Fuckin' stupid. Get to work on the Navigator."

There were a few faces he didn't recognize. Too bad for them, they did nothing, they knew nothing, but they were gonna be at the wrong place, at the wrong time. In his mind, he began to plan his steps.

After an hour, he couldn't take it anymore. He strolled to the Tahoe as if it were nothing, reached into the back seat. He didn't realize one of the new guys had followed behind him. He turned to spray, but the guy tried to grab the gun. It was too late; down he went, but now everyone was on it.

He knew he'd hit a couple of them, but Tomas fired on him, almost taking him out. It was hard to control the gun. Through the firepower, sirens pierced the air. He jumped in the Tahoe and took off.

He didn't get the money. He didn't get all of them, and he didn't get the drugs. There were too many loose ends. He was fucked. Santa pulled onto the Expressway and crossed the bridge to the Westbank. No one knew him there, and he knew no one.

೧✿೨

After talking with Detective Marse, Rainie and Michael left the police station. "Michael, it's all a jumble, but I'd say, for starters, I'm not going back home. I might as well sell it. I don't think I could ever be comfortable or feel safe there again.

"Shit, I gotta tell Tom, much as I don't want to, and then, there's my parents. That's a conversation I really don't want to have. Mer needs to know because the guy saw where I work. Mer could be in danger.

Gotta find somewhere to live until I can buy or rent— anywhere but uptown or Mid-City." She rambled with agitation and fear.

"Before you do anything, Rainie, breathe," he held her hand. "Yes, you have to call Tom, and you need to tell your parents, they'll give you the best advice. You'll have to call Meredith, and you'll need to take off tomorrow. I'm sure Detective Marse would be more than happy to send a couple of officers to go with you so that you can pack bags for the boys and you. Stay at your parents, at least until they get psycho off the street. For tonight, you'll stay with me if that's okay?"

"I'll call Momma, Mer, and Tom when we get to your place." She was deep in the thought of telling her parents when Michael cleared his throat to get her attention.

"Food?"

"I'm not hungry."

"I don't care. You must eat. What could you tolerate right now?"

"A martini sounds good about now." She stopped. "No, seriously, I could go for a burger, I guess."

"College Inn okay with you? I think you might want to pass on the martini, but I do have a couple of good wines at the house." She shook her head, no. "One would be okay in this circumstance. Think of it as medicinal." He tried to smile.

"I'll go for College Inn with unsweet tea and fries. If I'm gonna be bad, I'm gonna do it right." She weakly smiled at him. He squeezed her hand. "How can you be level headed? Aren't you the least bit freaked out?"

"Of course, I am. I wasn't calm earlier; it's a matter of priority and process. I wish I had been there, but for right now, we have to move on. Rainie, breathe." Even his velvet words couldn't release the tension and apprehension she felt throughout her body.

"I'll try, but I won't promise anything."

At first, she felt sickened by the thought of food, but the story changed when it was before her. The conversation was limited and hushed at dinner. She couldn't help but think, *was it shock or emotional exhaustion?*

The car ride to his place was quiet. He pulled into the parking lot, jumped out, and opened her door. "Michael, thank you."

As they walked to his house, he looked over at her. "Did you know, you and my mother are the only two people on the planet that call me Michael? Everyone else, it's Mike, Mikey, Doctor Mike, but not you. I even refer to myself as Mike. Ever since the first time we met, it's been Michael. Have you ever noticed?" There was a sense of comfort in his eyes.

"You look more like a Michael than a Mike to me."

"It sets our relationship apart." He unlocked the door and stepped aside.

She entered first but turned around, scrunched her nose with a curious look. "Mikey? Really? Who the hell would call you Mikey?"

"That would be my older brother." He smiled broadly, flashing his pearly whites and precious dimples.

"I didn't know you had sibs. I think you've mentioned your parents, maybe once. Are you not close to them?" They walked down the hall.

He grabbed a bottle of water and tossed one for her to catch. She sat on the sofa as he walked to the wall where he had two photos. She hadn't noticed them before. "We talk on the phone a lot. Wendy lives in Washington, DC, with her husband and four kids. She's an attorney for a small firm. Then there's John, don't say it, everyone did when we were kids." She looked confused. "Peter Pan? Wendy, John and –" He sat, turning his body toward hers, pulling her into him.

"Michael, yes, fabulous. Done on purpose or by accident?"

"A story, my love, for another day." He kissed behind her ear. "John is a river pilot. He's a charming big kid."

"I'd love to meet them. I bet your family is awesome."

"They're something for sure, but they're my something. The best." His comment radiated warmth and sincerity.

"Where do Mom and Dad live?" He handed her two photos.

"They live in Baton Rouge. These are my only photos. Here's a formal Mom and Dad, and then candid Wendy, John, and yours truly." She examined the photos.

"You and your brother look a lot alike, and Wendy looks like your mom."

"John and I may look similar but are different in many ways. He's far more outgoing and a real lady's man. John's a year older than me, and Wendy's four years older. We've stayed close."

"I have a hard time believing the charming part." She nudged his ribs.

"You'll meet them. It's been a long day. Make your calls. I'm getting in the shower." He put the pictures back. They walked into his bedroom.

She decided to call Mer first. As expected, Mer expressed concern yet was optimistic. Then she called Tom. She knew it was late, but she had to call him. She could tell she woke him up. He understood the big picture but said he'd call in the morning.

She dialed her parent's number. Being late would alarm them to start with; she had to be quick and gentle. They answered at the same time, each with a phone on their side of the bed. "Mom, Dad, sorry to call so late."

"Is everything all right?" her Dad panicked.

"Yes."

He retorted, "can't be the whole truth, or you wouldn't be calling at this hour."

Her Mom chimed in, "shush, Henry." She could picture the "shame on you" look flashed at her Dad. She could flash it with speed, and there was no mistaking it. The recipient knew they'd been scolded.

"The kids spent the night at Tom's place." Confirming the kids' well-being before divulging the incident. "This evening, Allie caught a man breaking into the house. She hit him with one of the boy's bats, and he ran off. I managed to catch a quick glimpse of him."

There was a brief silence, then her Mom said stoically, "Good thing y'all were there, and Allie had the right mind to hit him with the bat. I guess he'll think again before he goes near your house." She was always good for a "that showed them" kind of thought.

"Suga, you and your boys need to stay with us for a while. Heaven knows we have more than enough room for you and the boys and Allie, too. It's safer here than uptown."

"We'll need to stay a couple of weeks at least. Okay with y'all?"

"Rainie, please. Of course. I know it must've been quite something." Her dad sounded more awake.

"My plan for right now is to get an escort to the house tomorrow, pack bags for the boys and me. You know the basics, plus a few toys, nothing too great."

"Don't forget your good jewelry, my love, leave the play stuff in your jewelry box." Typical Mom.

"I won't. Y'all go back to sleep, and once again, I'm sorry to call you. I didn't want y'all to find out in the police reports or through someone else. Love you."

"Good night, sweetie. Where are you tonight?"

"At Michael's, Momma."

"How nice of him." Her mom was a glass-full kind of lady.

"I will pass on y'all's appreciation. Good night."

She imagined there was probably a bit of a discussion after the phone call, but she sincerely hoped they would be able to go back to sleep.

"I heard the tail end. How'd the Tom call go?" He said as he ruffled a towel in his hair.

"All calls went well. I told them we had an attempted break-in, and Allie hit the guy with a bat, and he fled. 'Bout sums it up, right?"

"You're right, enough info to keep from telling a lie." He shot her a look. "Your turn for the shower. I know you've got to be beat."

"I am, but I have nervous energy like I'm wound up or even high. I don't like it. I'm kinda jittery."

"Take your shower. Digestion will be in full swing. You'll begin to feel tired."

She loved the feel of water on her body. It was calming. She felt like her body; her skin was thirsting for water. Maybe it had been the sterile dryness of the hospital, but whatever. Michael was right. She had started to feel more relaxed and sleepy-ish. The last thing she needed right then was sex, but the thoughts of Pandora consumed her.

Her mind started rolling. *Why'd Michael name it, Pandora? What's worse, why am I thinking about it now? I'm plain twisted.*

She dried and padded to the bed, "Feel better now, perhaps less jittery?" He made room for her next to him. As he pulled her close, he whispered, "Your body seems more relaxed, but I can feel a hum in your thoughts. Can I help? Do you want to talk?"

"No, you need your sleep, and tomorrow is going to be hectic. I'm calming down." Rainie assured.

He held her close and kissed her good night.

She lay there for about an hour with no sign of sleep rather more peaked interest in the upstairs room.

He had a soft purr going, and she could tell he was sound asleep. He seemed peaceful.

She slipped out of bed, took the keys, and made her way out of the house. After fumbling with the keys, she found the shop keys. She turned on a low light and walked around, looking at all the paraphernalia.

She picked up one of the leather straps, one with multiple strands. She slapped her arm with it. No pain. Finding soft tassel restraints, she slipped them over her hands, then went back to the strappy whip, took off her nightshirt, and stood before the mirror naked, running the leather along her torso.

He was right; this could be enthralling. Rainie imagined him with her. Gradually she opened her eyes, still in her euphoria with him until she saw him by the door. She immediately felt embarrassed and started to make a move to put things back.

"Stay right there; don't move a muscle. I want to look at you. Your body is gorgeous. I'm sorry I interrupted you, but when you were not in bed, and the back door was unlocked, I became a little worried until I saw the dim light. Then it was all about curiosity and desire, and there you were in your perfect nakedness with a look of contented arousal. Want me to leave?"

Abruptly turning, she scolded. "No. I don't know what's wrong with me." Arms slack by her side. With a look of shame, she quietly spoke. " I've had this big horrible ordeal, and all I could think of was playing with you up here, how embarrassing. I never was one for self-gratification."

"You mean masturbation?" He grinned.

"What a horrible word. I prefer self-gratification. Either way, it was never my thing." He approached her with his great natural swagger.

"What is your thing? You'd say straight up or vanilla, but I've watched you with only a touch of play, and I can see you amping up and enjoying newfound pleasures." His eyebrows raised.

"Like?" She put her arms around his neck.

He led her to the massive heavy bed. "Trust me?" She nodded, yes. He took four velvet tassels and restrained her hands and feet to each corner post. He had taken the cat o' nine from her and started floating it up and down her body.

It was surprisingly even more stimulating than imagined, but she wanted him. He played and demonstrated a little. He ran his tongue between her breasts down to her navel and then further. The soft flickering kisses started getting harder and deeper. She moaned aloud as if asking for completion. He hit all the right places. Like the first night with him, he held up one of her legs, kissing her toes slowly. Methodically and ever so lightly, he moved up her leg. This time he nipped the inside of her thigh, and the warmth from her body aroused him. He teased her, and her body was more than ready, but he wanted to taste her pleasure. As he sucked and nipped, her body shivered uncontrollably. He sucked with force as he plunged his fingers deep inside her. She rocked into his hand, making his finger hit deeper inside of her.

She cried out, "No, no more, I want you now, right now." He released the other ankle and knelt between her legs. He lifted her hips and began penetration. As he plowed in and out, he continued to touch her, making the sensation even more arousing. He went deeper and harder with each thrust until they were satiated. He rolled alongside her, released her hands, and pulled her to him, wrapping his body around hers.

"You're the most amazing woman. For someone who claims to have only had vanilla experiences, you've brought me unimagined satisfaction. Oh, God, I've wanted you." He sweetly kissed her lips, her forehead, and her neck pulling her close.

Although they had only five hours of sleep, they both woke with a rush of energy, ready to get the day done.

He led her down the stairs and back into the house. He fixed some breakfast while she showered.

When she came out of the bedroom, he was on the phone. " I'll bring her to the station. Two of your men will escort her to her home to pick up some things and collect her car? Please have them follow her to her parent's house in Metairie. I know it's out of your jurisdiction, but I'd appreciate it. Thank you."

He explained the plan of action. "Then join up at your parent's?"

"Absolutely."

❧

As they pulled up to the house, the police radios became a mass of loud squawking and constant chatter, making her heart pound in her chest. Something was very wrong in the city, and after her ordeal, she was nervously edgy. Whatever the incident, it must've been something big. After dropping her off, the officers bolted with lights flashing.

It was good to see her mom and dad. There was a sense of security being with them. Her dad helped haul the suitcases up, and when they came down, the television was covering the latest catastrophe.

"Rainie, come take a look at this. The uptown I knew has gone to hell in a handbasket. There was some big shoot out with machine guns, something you would see in the movies, or maybe expect in New York or Chicago, but certainly not New Orleans."

"Momma, you do know New Orleans is the murder capital of the country?"

"That's what they say, but not like this, Rainie. It looks like a Mafia movie."

"The Mafia exists in New Orleans." It was hard for her to comprehend her mother's naivete.

"Rainie, don't be foolish. We're too set in our ways here to allow Mafia kind of people into our communities," her mom put her hand on her hip and was having none of what Rainie was saying.

No point in arguing with her, she'd learned after years of trying.

She watched the live chaos. The television streamed a loop of an industrial warehouse cordoned off with yellow crime tape and police cars pulling in and out. Then Detective Marse's face came up on the screen.

"Turn it up, please," perhaps she would glean something from his comment.

"Around eleven o'clock this morning, passers-by heard rapid

gunfire coming from this warehouse between Rousseau Street and Tchoupitoulas. Witnesses saw a dark-haired man flee the scene in a green Chevy SUV. There are four dead. He continued, "Two men and a woman were seen leaving on foot. Anyone with any information, please call—"

"That's intense. I hope the police get the thugs soon." Her heart raced; she could feel her palms getting clammy. Fear was taking hold of her body. Rainie looked at the warehouse, wondering if it was the same place from her escapade. She didn't remember seeing a garage door, but she would have come from Tchoupitoulas and only seen the side of the building, which they didn't show on the screen. The car hadn't been green. The SUV she saw was black, no doubt about it. Perhaps, it wasn't even the same creeps – nonetheless, it didn't sit right.

❧

Santa was chomping down a Big Mac when he heard the radio announcer talking about breaking news of a mass shooting around eleven. He listened to the speculations. Was it drug deal gone wrong or Cartel activity?"

Thoughts kept going through his head. He had little money to survive and now a car described in the news. Like the bing of a message, he had an idea to get some fast cash and accomplish all things, including a new ride.

He drove around college town, parked the car, wiped it down, and left the keys. Some fool would steal it. He then started the long walk to the house of the redhead bitch. Sipping on his McDonald's drink, he planned it out. He was sure she had jewelry, lots of things worth pawning, not to mention rich people always had spare cash. Then, he'd steal her car, take any money and her credit cards. The police would assume it was a robbery.

He finally got to the house, but the bitch was gone. The only car in the drive was a cheap Hyundai that looked like it had a lot of miles. He quickly scaled the fence into the backyard and worked on a side window, hoping it wouldn't set off an alarm. Rand watched from an upstairs window. She was getting angrier by the second.

She had learned how to control her energy to move objects but still hadn't been able to touch. There was business at hand, and if ever she could muster the energy, today would be the day. The crazy, horrible man would pay for hurting Allie and planning to hurt her sister.

He made it into the house and started going through drawers and cabinets. There was nothing of value. All he found were a silver stem vase and silverware.

"I don't got nothin' to tie the bitch? I've fucked the whole thing." He tossed drawers, opening cabinets, looking for rope. He stopped rummaging the kitchen drawers, then ran upstairs. He ran up to her bedroom, rifled through her drawers, and came out with one pair of stockings and a few scarves.

"That's it?" He put a pair of her panties in his pocket for a trophy.

He was spooked by a random car using her driveway to turn around, and he scampered behind her bedroom door. Looking through the crack in the door, he saw her.

She ran down the hall into one of the other bedrooms. He ran behind her, but she had vanished. He went into every room, opening the closets, looking under the beds, but he couldn't find her. In a menacing voice, he called out, "I saw you."

Quiet, no response. "Stupid bitch, I'm gonna fuck you then cut you until you beg to die. You'll welcome death when I've finished with you."

Rand was boiling angry; this sicko was pure evil and had pushed it too far. He was coming out of the boy's room, yelling and screaming when she appeared. He scarcely could believe his eyes.

"You fuckin' cunt."

He ran, the knife pointed right at her but went straight through like nothing. In utter bewilderment, he turned and found he was face to face with her. He was rattled and fell as he backed up. "What the fuck?"

He got to his feet. Rand pushed him down. She looked at him with as much hate as she could and, in a cold hollow voice, told him, "you messed with the wrong girl." He backpedaled, tripped, and fell hard down the stairs.

He was banged, bruised, and bleeding, but he was still alive, crawling toward the family room. She followed behind him, threw the picture of her and Rainie in his face. She gave him enough time to put two and two together. He looked up at her. He was petrified. His face blanched, and his body trembled. "Fantasma, no." His voice quaked and became high pitched. He started whimpering, begging, and crying, "No ghost girl. Please. No."

It must have been the combination of fear and drugs, but, whatever, he grabbed his chest. He could hardly breathe and began to pass out.

She watched him. This monster was going to kill her sister. She wished she could kill him, but she couldn't. There he was, dying, all on his own.

She wept.

I Can See Clearly

Tom and Diane brought the boys to her parent's house.

"Congratulations, y'all." She couldn't help but notice Tom didn't seem genuinely pleased, but Diane was giddy.

"Did you tell the boys about the trouble?"

"No, I didn't. I figured you'd want to," Rainie couldn't help but think, *what a coward.*

Tom edged to the door. She could've been a bitch, making him ask her to do his bidding, but she didn't. "I got it. Bye, y'all."

Thomas anxiously spoke as soon as Tom left. "Mom, Dad told us the worst thing." He looked like he was about to cry. "He's getting married to Miss Diane. She can't be our mom. You're our mom."

She hugged him tight, "And I always will be. I hope your daddy is happy with Diane. Just think you guys will have two homes. Y'all are a lot luckier than kids who have no home."

"Mom, you can tell those kids they can move in with Daddy and Miss Diane because I don't want to be around her. She baby talks and only wants Daddy. She doesn't want us around. I even heard her say it. I wanted to puke."

"Puke? That's ugly."

"It's not ugly, Mom; it means throw up. She makes me want to throw up. Henry is really sad, Mom. He cried when Daddy told us. You know Daddy's changed, and he's not very nice, especially when he's with Miss Diane." He hesitated, looking around with a squinched up face. "Why did he bring us to Mimi's?"

"It's a strange story, boo. I think you and Henry could use a cookie or two while I tell you the story." She walked into the kitchen with them. "First, Miss Diane wasn't any nicer to you? I'm sure it was hard for them to tell y'all. Maybe that's what you picked up on. Perhaps she thought baby-talking was a way of being nicer, but to answer your question, we're here because last night we had a stranger break into our house. Allie hit him with your bat, and he ran away. Until the police get finished with all their stuff, we'll be here."

His eyes twinkled. "Way to go, Allie. It was probably the same man that broke into Jarod's house when they were at the movies," his eyes got real wide, "they had a camera. It took pictures of him, and the police know what he looks like. I bet it's the same man cuz they haven't caught him yet, but they will. The police always catch the bad guys, Mom." He said with a mouth full of a chocolate chip cookie.

So far, so good, she thought. "There's another bit of sad news. Allie's in the hospital with a cut on her head."

"I bet Doctor Mike can fix her," Thomas said with confidence.

"He did, but the hospital wanted to keep her."

"Prob'ly a concussion, happens all the time in sports, Mom. Don't worry." He was getting older, and while it was a good thing, she missed her baby boy.

Her phone rang, "Hello to you too. Everything went fine, and we are safely at Momma's. When are you coming over?" The thought of seeing him made her flush from head to toe. "See ya soon."

There was a peacefulness being around her mom and dad that hadn't been there in a long time, and it felt good. Sunday lunches were great but not nearly as intimate as sitting in the kitchen gabbing away.

Her mom called to her after going upstairs. "Suga, can you come help me with a few things?"

Stretching for a pillow on a closet top shelf, she stopped and turned around. "I don't know what arrangement you and Mike have with adult time."

"Don't worry, Mom, Michael doesn't spend the night at my house, and I wouldn't expect him to spend the night here. He doesn't believe in private time when the boys are around. On Tom's weekend with the boys, I do, however, stay at his place." She helped take the extra pillows down.

"I know things are a bit looser now, but Dad is still old fashioned." She hugged one of the pillows in her arms.

"I haven't forgotten how old-fashioned Dad is, and I love him for it. Please have no worries. I appreciate your concern, and if you want me to talk to him about all this—"

"No suga, not necessary. Dad's the one who brought it up to me in the first place. I told him I would get the skinny on the relationship. He's happy to see your friends with Mike. You know, he wasn't a big fan of Tom. Speaking of, his fiancé looks to be very young and immature. Maybe it'll make a good combination for them. Like minds, you know." Her mom gave her a wink nodding her head.

They heard the doorbell ring, then her dad called upstairs. "Your company has arrived, suga."

She trotted down the steps, and to no surprise, it was Michael and Allie. With open arms, she welcomed Allie's embrace.

"I thought you might be happy to see her sweet face," Michael winked at her.

"The boys are going to go ballistic. You're the bomb in Thomas' eyes."

Her mom came down the stairs. "There's our brave girl. Good job, Allie. I bet he'll never show his face again around there. You showed him, good girl. What kind of person does such a thing? Sit, take it easy and rest."

"If you don't mind, I want to go see the boys."

"They're in the yard playing ball." Rainie led her to the sunroom, which had a door out to the grassy play area.

Upon seeing Allie, the boys dropped everything and ran to her.

Henry was the first to speak. "I heard you got stitches. Did it hurt a lot?" He wanted to see under the bandage.

Thomas was quick to chime in, "You're a beast. Mom told me you cracked the bad man with my bat, and it broke. I also heard he ran away like a big coward." He rolled his eyes. "You aren't going to believe this. My dad is getting married to his gross girlfriend, Miss

Diane. They're going to ruin our vacation to Disney World by getting it done there. I don't want to go on vacation anymore. I hate him."

Rainie jumped in, "I don't want to hear you say that again. It's okay to be angry with him, but we don't hate. It's a horrible word. Understand?"

He mumbled under his breath, "so is puke."

"Did you say something, Thomas, something you would like to share?"

"No, ma'am." He said with a sulk.

"I didn't think so. We can talk nicely later about your disappointment." She went back into the house, shaking her head.

"Rainie, the little guy has to be able to unload. People think divorce is hard for kids, but what's even harder is the re-marriage thing. One day you have a mom and dad together at home. The next thing, you have a mom in one place and a dad in another. Then bam! You have two moms or two dads. It's a lot to understand as an adult, let alone being five and seven. I understand. Give him some space and let him vent. I agree hate doesn't have to enter the picture but let him vent."

Crossing her mind was, *what do you know, you don't have kids*. She held back, knowing what he said made sense. "I hear ya."

"Allie wanted to come here first to see you and the boys, but she also wanted to get some of her things from the house. I'll be happy to take y'all over there."

The boys overheard something about going back to the house to pack and were not interested. Henry asked, "Can we stay here with Mimi and Poppy?"

With a nod from her mom, she asked him, "Michael, you sure you don't mind taking us?"

"I'd rather be there with you than have the two of you go by yourselves." *Sage Michael*, she giggled to herself.

Rainie gave the boys parting instructions to behave and listen before she took off with Michael and Allie.

It was good to have Allie out of the hospital. She felt responsible for the attack. She had been the one to open the door for calamity to descend. Had she not had such a checkered past, none of the things would've happened. Marco would probably still be alive. Her poor judgment and carelessness brought a lot of wrath on a lot of people.

Michael and Allie had been chatting away as she had gone into her own reflective world. Michael observed, "you're quiet this evening."

"I guess. All the recent action has consumed my thoughts."

"For sure, but don't become obsessed or self-deprecating. Did you hear Allie talking about her visitor at the hospital?"

"No?"

Allie blushed, "It was nothing. One of the doctors from the emergency room came up to check on me."

"I'm impressed. Usually, once the doc has done their part, you're a done deal."

Michael chuckled, "I get the impression it had little to do with her injury. What doctor comes in and visits for two hours and asks if he can call and maybe meet up once she was feeling better?" He turned to Allie. "He even gave you his schedule for the next few weeks, right? And his number?"

"He did." She giggled.

"How exciting. This man seemed nice?" Rainie went into Mom mode.

"Very."

By the time the conversation was dwindling, they had arrived at the house. He looked over to Rainie. "You okay?"

"I'm fine. I don't want to go in, but I need to get over myself," thinking about what Rand had said. She got out of the car, went to the door, unlocked it, and went inside. For the most part, things seemed the same, but there was a different vibe.

Allie headed to the stairs.

She and Michael went toward the den to gather a few more games. She took two steps into the room, Michael was a couple of paces behind her, and she came to an abrupt stop. "What the—"

Michael passed her, going straight for the body.

"Call 911." He instructed.

Following the call, Rainie picked up the photo of her and Rand.

"This guy was at the drug house, and I bet he killed Ryan's neighbor" She stopped and looked around the room. "I'll tell you what happened here." She started pacing. "I bet he came back for me and Rand showed up, and he thought it was me. In my mind today, I kept getting an image of Rand looking over me. It happens often, but this time she had feathered wings. You can think I'm crazy, but I'm telling you. She's been talking to me a lot."

From upstairs, she heard Allie call in a frightened voice. "Y'all might want to come see this."

There was an obvious pathway created by the encounter. The pictures on the wall were crooked as though hurriedly glanced by a shoulder. "Oh, dear God, he was in the boys' room. Let's go back down and wait. I feel sickened up here." She could feel her chest tighten and found she was holding her breath. Rand was in her head again. "Rainie, like your boyfriend says, breathe. I kicked the bad man's ass. Sorry if you don't like me talking to you. Too bad. Too sad. I can talk to you whenever I want, and there's nothing you can do about it. Ha!" It was like hearing a fourteen-year-old girl childishly argue, but then again, Rand was only fourteen.

Rainie responded silently. "Talk anytime. I miss you."

The paramedics arrived, and they called the Coroner.

Michael sat at the kitchen table with Rainie and Allie, all with the same vacant, blank gaze. So much had happened in such a short period of time; it was overwhelming. "I'm not sure what we should say." He took Rainie's hand while looking into her face.

Rainie answered quickly. "The truth. We came in to get Allie's clothes, and this is what we found. Let them do their investigation. You're welcome to tell them this was the doings of your girlfriend's dead sister or stick to the facts." She shrugged her shoulders. "Up to you."

He dialed Detective Marse. "Michael Landry here again, sir, wanted to let you know we called 911. We found the man called Santa at the Todd's resident. Yes, I've heard the news and imagine you're tied up but wanted to give you a heads up. He's dead. Coroner's office is on the way."

She could hear the detective talking a mile a minute, "No, sir, we haven't touched anything. Thank you." Marse said he'd be in touch.

One of the officers escorted Allie to her room and let her pack up a few items, then Michael, Rainie, and Allie asked to leave the scene.

The first couple of minutes in the car were dead silent, then Michael said, "If I were Tom, I'd watch how I spoke to you and the kids, considering what happens when you piss Rand off."

Whether it was from nerves or because it was funny, Rainie giggled slightly, which broke the ice of silence. The conversation, then, focused on the police and their findings.

In her heart, she knew it was set in motion when she took the ride with Marco. She figured Santa had killed Marco. Anyone that would "slice and dice" someone had to be crazy. She wouldn't have been at all surprised to hear he also was the one responsible for the mass shooting. Even though she couldn't definitively say the place on the television was the drug house, she had a feeling it was.

When they returned to her parents', her Mom had dinner almost ready. "I started to worry about y'all. You've been gone longer than I anticipated, but you needed some time at home, I guess. I'm just glad you're back."

Rainie questioned, "Were the boys a problem?"

"Oh, heavens no, suga. They're good as gold. I was getting nervous for nothing, as Dad pointed out. I'm nervous to a fault, sue me. Mike, I've plenty to eat here. I hope you plan on eating dinner with us."

"Yes, ma'am."

☙

Michael had barely left, and already she was missing him. The boys had gone to bed, Allie was putting things away, she bid good night to her parents. Her mom called her back into the room.

"Come sit by me. Suga', are you doing okay? You've been through an awful lot in such a short time. I know my nerves would be completely frazzled."

"Momma, I'm okay. Can I ask you something?"

"Sure," she looked puzzled.

"Do you dream of Rand very often?"

"Oh, yes, yes, I do. Daddy and I call it our visiting time with Rand. We both have similar dreams on the same nights. I know I sound like a fool, but I think she visits us, and we love it. I wish it happened more."

"Sometimes I have visits, but it's like she lives in my brain and is constantly making comments. Usually fussing about something I've done or said." Instinctively she put her hands on her head. "Michael says he thinks heaven is another dimension and those who believe can communicate with their loved ones. He comes up with interesting thoughts. He's all about faith and God."

"Good to hear. I sometimes had the feeling you pulled away from faith because of Rand's death. I always hoped you would open your heart again."

Rainie sat up straight, almost defensively. "Momma, I can't remember the last time I missed going to church. Why would you worry? I go every Sunday with you and Daddy."

"Anyone can go sit in a church, suga', it's more than going, but I think you're figuring it out. I'm glad this is something you and Michael can share. It's what makes a successful relationship. I know it's why Dad and I are so close."

"Always with good advice. G'night, Momma," she kissed her, "I love you."

As she started to walk out of the room, her mom chimed in, "And Rand's bossiness, hon, hardly surprising." Her mom giggled. "Typical."

Happy Together

Botox Thursday was always balls to the wall with back to back appointments starting at eight.

"You think he knows she's on the books?" Beth, his office manager, questioned.

"Don't know, but I bet it's gonna be a good surprise. I can tell Doc likes her a lot. Did y'all see the way they acted at the party? I'd say, yeah, they're an item, definitely more than friends."

"Good morning Dr. Landry," chimed throughout the office as he entered and meandered back to his desk.

Beth followed him into his private office. As he perused the files, she started her morning dissertation. "You have back to back appointments, starting in a half-hour until lunch, and then right after lunch with your last being at five. Most of the appointments today are regulars, only three new patients, and that's about it. Oh, your last appointment before lunch is Mrs. Todd."

His face lit up, and his attention was off the file in his hand. "Really? When did she schedule?"

"Last week, I think last Monday. Is that okay?"

"Yes, it is, and if that's all, I'm good for now. Thanks."

He picked up the phone and called his round chef friend. "Good morning to you as well, Tony. Is it too late to order delivery for lunch?" He listened. "No, please. I know it's last minute. Is there a private table available? We'll be in and out, so it has to be something quick. We'll be there about twelve-fifteen. Whatever you think would be nice for a light but special lunch. Thanks again."

He looked forward to his eleven forty-five appointment. The organized chaos began.

☙

Things at the office for Rainie were ticking right along. Meredith got the scoop on the events from the day before, all the while nailing décor details down.

"Mer, I have an eleven forty-five Botox appointment. He only takes fifteen minutes tops."

"I bet he's going to take you to lunch. Isn't it convenient the appointment falls right before lunch?" She said with a sarcastic tone as she thumbed through a file.

She glared at Mer, "Only thing available. If it makes you happy, I will turn down any lunch offers and come straight back. I don't even know if he's going to invite me to lunch anyway," she rolled her eyes.

"Like hell, you will. If he invites you, especially after last night, you say yes. You know, I think any other man would have run from your hot mess. Did you recognize Diane? Preggo vibes?" They passed the file.

"I think I've seen her before, dunno. The only thing I know she's a baby. He's going into unchartered territory with her, and since the boys aren't big fans, it's gonna get rough. I've got to break them of the attitude. I don't want anyone thinking I've put them up to it, and you know they will. After meeting her, I get why the boys aren't big fans. She's too young to know how to talk to kids and too old to be a kid. I'm guessing she's early twenties."

Meredith rocked back in her chair in amusement. "You've got to be kidding! Tom is what four years older than you, making him like fourteen years older? I'd say Mr. Todd got caught with his pants down. Poor chic doesn't know she trapped the wrong fellow."

"That's my guess. Tom's big-time attorney status probably enamors Diane and, face it, he is good looking." Rainie shrugged her shoulders.

"I don't find him attractive. Not even the slightest." Meredith's face was deadpan.

Rainie flashed her ice blue eyes at Meredith. "It's because you don't like him."

It seemed as though every day held yet another change. Despite the whirlwind of life, work went on, which would be no different from any other day. They mostly followed up with suppliers, but it was a watch and wait game. The mock-up of the lobby parlor and bar area was almost finished.

"It's time you leave; you don't want to be late. I'm gonna go to the hotel for a quick pop-in."

⁂

It was a quick drive to Michael's office. Just after starting her car, her phone rang.

"Hello?" she asked.

"Ms. Todd, this is Detective Marse with—"

"I know who you are. How can I help you?" She could feel her mouth getting dry and a nervousness causing havoc to her belly.

"Any chance we can talk alone today? Nothing you did, maybe some insight, that's all." She agreed to meet with him after her appointment.

By the time she arrived, there were still a couple of people in the waiting room. By her watch, she was early. She checked in and couldn't help but notice the receptionist was going out of her way to be chatty. Her nerves were disjointed, to say the least, after the phone call, so it was a welcomed distraction.

One by one, the patients came out all with the identical redness over the eyebrows, between the brows and crow's feet. Rainie's turn was coming up along with the other two patients in the waiting room.

The nurse applied the numbing cream, and she, too, seemed chattier than usual. The girls in his office had always been nice, but things were different.

She wondered what they thought. "I imagine Michael has had a hectic day today." She watched as the girl tried to hold back a smile, but her eyes gave it away.

"Dr. Landry has had back to back appointments all morning. After all, it's Botox Thursday. You're his last appointment before we break for lunch."

His smile was dazzling as he walked in. Amid a hug, he said, "Rainie, you don't need this. I think it's a waste. If I thought you needed it, I would tell you. Are you sure you want to do this?"

"Look right here," she turned her head, "See those lines by my eyes? My crow's feet?"

He took her face in his hand, checking her complaint. "Rainie, what you have is ever so slight, and only you see it. I promise. You're the boss, and if you want the injections, I'll do them."

They were standing reasonably close. He smiled at her. "Michael, if I don't, then I've wasted your time. I can't believe I'm letting you talk me out of this. Everyone I know gets it."

"Yes, and they'd give anything to have skin like yours. You're beautiful."

He picked up the syringe, "It's now or never. Your decision."

"Just a teeny tiny bit here and here" He did the injections. "Are you mad at me?"

"No, but I think you're nuts," he laughed. "Okay, I did your injections, now I have—" He turned to the nurse and told her to tell the others they could leave for lunch, and he'd see them at one then looked back into her eyes. "— a request. Will you have lunch with me? It's gotta be quick."

"Am I too red to go out?"

"You're killing me! No, besides, we have a private table."

"C'mon, talk in the car." They went out a different door and headed to the car.

࿔

He opened the car door for her. "You, sweet lady, are a handful, for sure. The Botox thing, you don't need it. You're gorgeous the way you are, but I aim to please. I've been dying to do this since I saw you," he delivered a series of sweet kisses.

He walked around the car, and they took off to the café. Along the way, she shared the conversation with Marse. As soon as they arrived, the maître d' ushered them in as the valet drove off in the car. His chef friend embraced the two of them and walked them to the kitchen, where there was one perfectly set table.

"I've never eaten in a restaurant kitchen before. I know plenty of people who have, and they rave about the excitement and how scrumptious the aromas are." She honed in on the action in the kitchen like a kid in a candy store.

"I knew we didn't have much time; we'll get the fastest and best service in the house." The waiters brought turtle soup. "I told Tony to choose the menu, but it had to be relatively light. I can't be too sleepy injecting my patients." He raised his water glass. "Here's to lunch with my lady."

"Yes, indeed. I have a question. All the fun things you and I have done together, such as this, is this how you entertain everyone? I'm not judging and have no expectation of an answer, only curious," her hands propping up her chin.

"No, everything in our relationship has been new for me, but I have rehearsed in my imagination with you as my leading lady." His smile beamed, igniting glittering twinkles in his eyes. "Whether it's private dining or spending the night together at either of our homes, it's all firsts. Before you, it was a hotel room or my date's place, but rarely for an entire night.

"As the rest of the world dates is how I dated when I went out. Nothing special about any of it. Don't get me wrong, I had fun, and I showed my dates a good time, but what we have is different. I hope you feel it's special. Julia and I were quite close, and as I said, I do think I loved her, just not the in love part. Question answered?" His eyes never left hers except to glance at her tempting lips

She leaned over and kissed him, "Yes. And you think it's okay I meet with Marse?"

"I thought you were off that subject as it's a nothing kinda thing – just a meeting. Marse will probably inquire about what other people may have looked like. Who knows, but it's nothing to worry about, okay?"

She nodded. The lunch was light, perfect, and quick. Before she knew it, they were back in the car, heading to his office. When they arrived, he walked her to her car.

"I know things will be different for a few weeks at your folks, but it'll be good. I look forward to getting to know them better. Now, be careful going back to work and send my regards to Meredith." He opened her door, but before, she gave him a tight hug with a flirty kiss.

"Michael, see you tonight, maybe?"

"Probably," he smiled. Rainie knew he would watch her until she was out of his sight.

She called Meredith, "On my way back. You?"

Mer responded she was still at the job site but would return soon, and Rainie needed to go back to the office. There were a couple of interesting messages, and to start without her.

The next call was to Detective Marse. "Hi. This is—" He cut her off, saying he knew her voice. They agreed to meet late afternoon.

Paul's car was outside when she pulled up. She entered the office and could hear him in the kitchen. "Paul, I didn't want to startle you. Mer said she'd be on her way soon."

He lumbered down the steps.

"Meredith told me you're seeing Mike Landry. We've only spoken a few times. Maybe the four of us can grab dinner sometime."

"Sounds good. The kids and I are staying with my parents right now since the hoopla. I'm assuming you know all about it?" he nodded.

"Terrible. Is it true you're thinking of selling your place?" He sat on the corner of Mer's desk.

"Yep. It's not only the incident, but I've wanted to for a while. There are too many memories, ya know, with Tom. I'm starting a new chapter in my life." The conversation went on for several more minutes, and as he was walking out the office into the hall, she called out. "If Mer is good with it, why don't we plan on going out Saturday night? I'll check with Michael, but I can't see why he would have any objection."

"Talk to the boss. I do as I'm told. I'll be in the office for a few but will poke my head in when I leave."

"Gotcha."

Mer's desk was strewn with papers she had tossed on her way out. Two more people were looking for bids. She wondered if either of them were patients of Michael.

One was for a living-dining room makeover, and the other was for a nursery, which made her think of Tom and a new baby conjuring a snigger.

She made the calls. By the time the last phone call ended, Mer had popped in the door. "I see my hubs is home. Is he okay?"

"Yes, and he's in his study."

"Great," Mer headed in the direction of his study. Rainie could hear muffled talking and a few laughs here and there. As she returned to their office, she said, "I hear we might have a double date this weekend? I'm excited. Since it's Thursday, we better hurry and make reservations for Saturday if everything good isn't already booked up."

"Let me call Michael to firm with him." She dialed his office, and as expected, the receptionist said he was in with a patient, but she would get him to call in between appointments.

"Thank you."

"Anytime, Mrs. Todd, it's always fine."

"Please call me Rainie. I promise I won't be a pain in the butt."

The receptionist giggled, "No problem, call anytime."

Rainie hadn't a doubt that as soon as the phone hung up, the receptionist was informing the rest of the staff about yet another call from Mrs. Todd to Dr. Landry.

She started to go over the files and the upcoming appointments with Mer when her phone rang.

"Aw, you miss me already," he teased.

"I wouldn't get hysterical. I have a question." She flippantly retorted.

He loved her sarcasm, but he could throw it right back, "Another question? You certainly are a curious lady. Always a question. I have only a second. What's up?"

"Would you like to go to dinner with Paul and Meredith on Saturday?"

"Sure, and I knew I had something to ask you at lunch, but got so caught up in you, forgot. Next weekend is Tom's, right?"

"Yes," she was quick to answer.

"Do you want to go with me to Baton Rouge for the weekend? My brother's going to be home. I thought you'd like to go. Who knows when he'll be in again."

With an ear to ear smile and flutters throughout her body, she excitedly answered, "I can't wait. Yes, of course, I want to meet your brother and your parents. Now get to your patient. You don't want to piss her off."

"You sound like Beth, always rushing me. I'll have you know I pride myself on punctuality."

"Goodbye, Michael. See you tonight," and they hung up.

Thoughts dreamily passed through her mind. They had been an item, if that's what it was called, for only a few weeks, and yet it seemed like a lifetime. "Mer, Saturday night is on, and he invited me to Baton Rouge next weekend to meet his river pilot brother and his parents."

She put her pencil down, "I didn't know he had a brother."

"And a sister named Wendy who has four kids and is an attorney in DC. His brother is named John, so it's Wendy, John, and Michael like in—"

"Peter Pan, how awesome! On purpose?" Mer donned a full-on I-told-you-so grin. She relished the thought of Rainie content.

"He said it was a discussion for another day when I asked, but I've seen pictures of them. He and his brother look alike, same height, same weight, different through the eyes, maybe. I can't wait to meet him."

"And I'm looking forward to watching you two for a couple of hours. I'll know for sure where this is going." Meredith playfully raised her eyebrows. "Is it the constant sex, the great dinners, or the whole package, and I don't mean his!" She guffawed.

"Okay, my voyeur friend, you can watch all you want," she opened a file. "The first client is living room dining room before Thanksgiving. Seems nice, might be pushy."

"Colors and prints or furniture too?" Mer was back to business.

"Not sure; we'll find out when we see her. See, this is the shit that will suit Allie. The nursery girl is having twins. It has to be both pink and blue décor, not too girlie and not too boyish. Once again, I don't know if it includes furniture. My notes are right there."

They worked on the hotel mock-up for the next few hours. "Rainie, I'm exhausted. I feel like I've run a marathon. I wonder if I'm getting sick. I think I'll have Paul go pick up food, and then I'm going to bed."

"If you're sick, please keep it to yourself over there," she could feel her stomach tightening and fear trying to push its way into her psyche. Since Rand, anytime anyone complained of feeling poorly, those scary feelings shoved to the forefront.

"You're sympathetic and kind. Not!" She threw a balled-up piece of paper at Rainie.

Turning on fake sad eyes, "Hurt to the core of my being. I'll see your sick ass tomorrow." She picked up her purse, "Seriously, chill, eat, and go to bed. No getting sick, ya hear?"

❦

The early departure from work was perfect, and she agreed to meet Marse at a local coffee shop. He appeared far less stern and menacing. He offered to buy her coffee and began with a cordial conversation. Then he got to the nitty-gritty.

"Ms. Todd, this conversation is basically to quench my curiosity, and you don't have to answer if you so choose. Understand?" Rainie nodded. "Why were you really in the car with Marco, and why did you go to the warehouse with him? Your boyfriend's a good guy, I can tell, and a man with a conscience. I noticed how quickly he came to your side the night I first inquired about Marco. I also speculate the call the evening of the break-in was Dr. Landry's suggestion. Am I right? He wants to take care of you. That's more than obvious. Now that Santana is out of the picture for good, I imagine you and your family will not be threatened by the dope-dealing ring of car thieves. They've moved on, and you're a mere blip on a mistake made by an unstable, now dead, associate. But back to my original question."

Rainie sat looking at him with an internal debate running rampant through her mind. "Answer the man, Rainie. Why play your stupid games with him? What does it matter now? The past is the past." She had her own thoughts. She didn't need Rand to weigh in.

"Detective Marse, I'm pretty sure you're asking a question you already know the answer to. Would I be correct? I'm sure you have looked into my background and found a troubled teenager. No doubt about it, I was troubled. After Rand, my twin sister, died, I went to a dark place. I was angry." He listened intently. "I made some bad choices, but then I started to unravel the spiral, and life became happy again. You sure you want to know?" He nodded with a smile.

Looking into her coffee mug as she twirled the wooden stir stick, she took a deep breath and let it out, and with it was going to be the truth. "After Tom betrayed me, I went off the deep end. Started using drugs, drinking to excess, and having fun escapades with barely legal young men such as Ryan. I was living on the edge per se. The night in question, I was waiting for Ryan. He was late, and his neighbor in the fourplex, Marco, invited me to ride with him in exchange for drugs. I didn't say yes at first but succumbed to the demon inside and took him up on his offer. I went with him; he gave me drugs in exchange for my companionship. I still don't know why he needed me with him and don't care. That's the whole gory truth. I stopped doing drugs around the time Michael and I started getting to be an item. And before you ask, no, it wasn't Michael who changed my ways. It was my sister. How do you like them apples?" She punctuated her last comment with an exaggerated bat of her eyes.

He chuckled, took a long swig of his coffee, and set the cup back. "I'm rarely surprised, but Ms. Todd—"

"Rainie."

"Rainie, good for you that you have changed your ways, and congrats on your decision. I have been perplexed as to why you would be with a Cartel thug. Even though it was one dumb ass thing to do, I have to say I'm happy you were not involved in any of the Moreno enterprises. You didn't seem the part, but that's what would've made you the perfect choice for them. Thank you for answering my question. You didn't have to. One more, if I showed you pictures of some people, do you think you could say whether you saw them or not that night?"

"Maybe. I could try. I'm staying with my parents right now, so coming to the house would not be a good thing. We can meet again. Call me." She looked into her coffee.

"Wait." He stood quickly and went to his car, coming back with a manilla folder. "Any look familiar?" passing the folder.

She glanced at the eight pictures he had in the folder. Of the eight, she recognized two. One was a man and the other a woman. "What a shame. If dressed and polished, she'd be stunning. The man is sleazy looking, and I don't know how well he'd clean up." He tucked them back together like shuffling a deck of cards. "Hope that helped." She smiled at him.

"Thank you. Through the grapevine, I heard Delores and Diego had left the country – apparently not. Again, thanks for your candor."

☙❧

The kids had one more half-day of school. Summer would be upon them and then the stream of day camps, tennis lessons, horseback riding, and the club.

She wondered if Allie had heard from her doctor friend, Eric. It then dawned on her, what if Allie had made plans with her new friend for Saturday? She'd have to ask her parents to babysit. They were never big into babysitting. They loved the kids and spent a lot of time with them, but their social calendar was, and always had been, filled.

As soon as she got back to the house, she touched base with her mom, the kids were playing in the yard, and she found Allie on the phone in her room. She signaled she wanted to talk to her. Allie was free, making Saturday night in the bag.

Rainie strolled into the kitchen as her mom was finishing a phone call. "Wanna sit, Momma?" The chairs were one and a halfers, which made them easy to snuggle up in, and they watched as the boys played in the backyard.

This is the kind of life she wanted for her kids, comfortable, laid back, and dependable. "Here, suga'." Her mom handed her a glass of wine and sat across from her.

"Thanks, Momma," she sat the glass on a table beside her. It was easier to do than to get into the I'm not drinking thing.

"I'm glad you wanted to visit. The boys are heartbroken about Tom's upcoming marriage." Her mom moved into the seat with her.

"I know, Momma." *And what can I do about that?* She thought.

"Maybe if you told Tom."

She looked surprised at her mom, "Like hell, I will. The less I have to deal with him, the better. Besides, I've already told him to get his woman under control when it came to my boys, but if I don't see marked improvement, I'll talk to her myself, and if that doesn't work, I'll talk to my attorney."

" It's not like if you were marrying Mike. The boys love him." Her mom cooed.

She looked directly at her mom with intention in her eyes. "Is this the back-door way of finding out my feelings about Michael? If so, I like him a lot and love him dearly as a friend. I don't think I could love him any more than I do. I'm still quite wounded by the whole marriage thing, but I have thought about it a little." She clasped her mom's hand.

"Of course, suga, and I wasn't going in the back door. If I wanted to ask you about Mike, I'd ask, plain and simple. No, I'm truly concerned about your boys. I know full well your feelings toward Mike, I don't think you do, maybe." It was apparent her mom was concerned.

"The truth is, Momma, I don't think Tom is happy about the whole thing. He's always liked the playboy life, but I think a complication came up, and she trapped him. I don't know for sure, but I suspect."

Her mom took on a contemplative look. "I see, changes the complexion," she sat in silence, looking at the boys playing in the yard. "Do you think you'll ever want another baby?"

"No, my boys are all I need. I had at one time thought it would've been fun to have a girl, but things were already awful with Tom. I wasn't going to bring another child into the misery but had it been different – I think it would be fun to have a daughter. All those fun things like playing dress-up, teas, and then, of course, the proms and sweet—" her voice trailed off.

Her mom patted her leg. "Don't beat yourself up. I think a sweet sixteen party would have been too difficult on all of us, although I had looked forward to it since you two were born. My beautiful reds, so alike, yet different. I could always hug and kiss you and snuggle, like this, whereas Rand was independent, didn't want to be hugged and snuggled, except by you.

"She used to tell me, 'Rainie is so pretty, Mommy. I couldn't help but think, 'Rand, you look just like her,' but she didn't think she looked like you. She knew close enough to fool some people." She wrinkled her brow, "Both of you did. I couldn't believe it when Sister Caire called me. She told me you had been taking Rand's English and she had been taking your Math. She knew what y'all were up to, did you know?"

"No, but now it makes sense. She used to tell us, 'I'm watching you two,'" Rainie laughed.

"And unbeknownst to you two, Dad and I put different laces in your shoes, per Sister Caire. All the teachers were on alert. The school thought it best y'all be in separate classes, but after the discovery of the tomfoolery, they put you two together." Her mom gave her an exaggerated wink with a quirky smile.

"Ah! We were fine as it was, no kidding, huh? It totally screwed me in Math for a couple of months, but I did catch up. Oh my gosh, we thought we were clever," she put her head on her mom's shoulder.

"Thank you for putting up with all our shenanigans, especially mine, for the few years after Rand died." They both sat quietly, savoring the closeness. Rand's presence became strong, which made her smile.

Her dad came home, bellowing, "Leslie, where are you, hot stuff?"

"Hot stuff, Momma?" They both giggled.

"We're in the sunroom." She sounded flirty.

When he came around the corner, he saw them scrunched in the chair, and his face beamed with a big broad smile. "What a flash from the past." He bent over and kissed the top of their heads.

Her phone rang. "Excuse me, y'all."

She went into the other room. "Michael, hi to you too. I was talking to Mom and Dad. You coming over?"

"I was wondering if we could hang out with the boys at my place for a bit tonight? They could swim, we could get po-boys. It might be fun for them to see the street performers. I'll pick you up and bring you back, so you're not driving with them at night."

"How fifties of you. Let me make sure Momma hasn't been cooking today. I don't want to mess up her plans. I'll call you right back."

"Fifties?" he questioned.

"Bye."

After checking with her mom, she called him back and said they would be leaving soon.

"I'm turning onto Northline. Don't tell me I fought traffic only to have you follow me back."

"See you in a second. You're too much, fifties," she sassed.

Rainie primped herself and changed into a cute jean mini. The doorbell rang, and she could hear her dad and Michael talking. Their voices trailed off as they walked to the back of the house. It was a good thing she had thrown swimsuits into the bags when she packed to leave her home.

She trotted down the stairs and met them in the sunroom. "We're all set, and Allie's going to come along."

Her dad and Michael were talking about living in the Quarter. "Do you think you'll always want to live in the French Quarter? I would have to imagine the noise, and drunken fools must drive you crazy. Gracious, it's always a job finding a place to park."

"I think I'll always keep my place, but I have an agent looking for me in the Lakefront area and Old Metairie. I'm pretty specific about what I want."

"You might have to get an old house and renovate Mike," her dad suggested.

Allie came right in time. It was great timing; Rainie was beginning to feel awkward with the whole house thing.

"We're ready. Let's go." Turning back to her parents, "Mom, Dad, we'll see you when we get home."

❧

Michael pulled into the parking lot. "Dr. Mike, you park in a hotel all the time?" There was awe in Henry's voice. Greeting them at the door to his home were Bonnie and Clyde. The boys had a meltdown.

"This is the coolest place, Doctor Mike. Does anyone other than Bonnie and Clyde live here?" Thomas smiled like the Cheshire cat.

"Thanks, glad you like it. Nobody lives here except me and my pups. We keep each other company."

After an hour of swimming Michael suggested dinner. "I think we better get some food. I know I'm starving. Thomas and Henry, y'all are always hungry?"

A stroll through the Quarter gave Rainie, Michael, and the boys a chance to accomplish all necessary tasks – picking out teacher's gifts, po-boys for dinner, and watching the street entertainers. The night ended with beignets and chocolate milk, then a tired ride home.

Allie retired upstairs, which left Rainie and Michael alone for the first time since lunch. "Do you want to stay for a little bit?" She batted her eyes.

They sat in the sunroom. With an arm across his stomach, she snuggled into him. "I had the best time talking with my mom this afternoon. She was concerned the boys were sad about the upcoming wedding, and maybe I could let Tom know. I told her about my hypothesis to the urgent wedding, which prompted her to ask me if I would consider having another child."

"Would you?" he turned his head, so he was looking down into her eyes.

"I don't know. I can't imagine toting a baby around, but I also told her it would be fun to have a girl. There are lots of things girls do that boys don't. There's pretty dresses, more clothes, playing dress-up and house. And then there's the older stuff like sleepovers, dances, and crushes. I think that ship Michael has sailed, and while the thought is fun to think of, it's the practicality.

"I told Momma how I'd felt guilty that I didn't have a sweet sixteen party. After Rand died, I became intolerant, impatient, and extremely moody. My parents and teachers all went out of their way to make life good, but," she sighed, "all for naught."

"You were angry and rightfully so." He squeezed her thigh.

"You have no idea what I put them through, yet they still kept trying. My parents never gave up. At first, they had a hard time punishing me, but that didn't last too long."

With an arched eyebrow and a lopsided smile, he asked. "Back to the question, you think maybe one day you might want another baby? I could always help out," he winked at her.

"As you say, Michael, I'll wait and see what God has planned for me, but right now, I have bigger fish to fry. Like I need to start looking for a place to rent that isn't sky-high. I didn't know you were looking for a house. I thought you would've mentioned it before to me. Lord knows we've talked about everything else," she nudged him in the ribs.

"How about I find a place with an apartment, and you could rent from me. I promise you'd find the rent reasonable," Michael kissed the top of her head.

"I don't think such a house exists where you're looking."

"I happen to know there are a couple in Lakeview. They need reno, but you could advise, Miss Decorator." With his arm around her, he fiddled with her hair.

"Food for thought," she nodded. "What about Old Metairie?"

"There's one only a block or so from here."

"With an apartment, I don't think so," she said confidently.

"No, it's a pool house, but it could be converted. It would be a small apartment, a tiny apartment." He emphasized.

"Probably a shit load of money, Michael. We're putting the cart before the horse, don't you think?"

"No, I don't," he stood firm. "You need somewhere to live. Y'all could live in the main house while the expansion of the pool house took place. Once done, I'd move into the pool house, and you could rent the house." He seemed smug; he had it all figured out.

"And what if our friendship went sideways?" she questioned, squeezing his hand.

"I don't know. I think we'd take everything in stride." He kissed her head again.

"All of this because I told you about my sweet conversation with Mom, but since we are talking hypothetically. Let's say we do decide to tie the knot. I'm not saying we are, just what if? I would want part ownership, like fifty-fifty." She lightly swept the hair on his arm.

"No problem, we could make that happen. When you sell your house, I'm sure you're going to make a pretty penny, and then you'd have money to invest." She heard Rand. 'Ya boy has it all figured out, girlfriend. Stop being so damn pigheaded.'

"Do you have an answer for everything? I'll bite because I don't want to live with my parents forever. I'm used to my own space. Where is this Old Metairie house, and what kind of money are you talking about?" she asked curiously, still sweetly caressing his arm.

"Stella Street, and I think it's one point four."

"Holy shit!" She pinched him and then jumped up. "Uh, I don't think so." Hand on her hip.

"I could probably get it for one point two depending on the appraisal. Think about it. You could probably get eight something for your house, maybe nine." He was calm and methodical in his thinking.

"Yes, but I'd have to divide whatever profit with Tom. We paid five thirty-five, I think. We put down a hundred, so I'd come out with what, two and change, if that? Not much to add to your pot."

"It certainly would take care of the pool house, yes?" He grinned a smug kind of smile.

"Yes, it would, smart ass. My head's swimming. Conversation over," the hand went up. She sat back down and put her head on his shoulder. "I'm not trying to rain on the parade. I'm too tired to think of anything overly deep." They sat quietly with a few tiny kisses.

He seized every opportunity to glance his hand against her breast or slide his hand off her thigh with a whispered touch between her legs.

"Your head stop spinning?" he bit his bottom lip, trying to hold back a playful smile.

Ignoring his titillating, albeit brief mini touches to her body, it revealed the longing with a shiver and well-defined nipples. "Yes, thank you, you naughty boy," she wagged her finger at him. "I'm excited about our dinner Saturday night with Mer and Paul, and two can play at your game, sir." She slid her hand gently passing over the bulge in his pants.

"It should be a good time." His breath was soft and tickling on her neck. "Now, I don't want to be the one to rain on the parade, but I have an early surgery tomorrow. I gotta get."

"I get it. I want you so bad right now, Michael, I ache." She pulled her body close to his.

She walked him to the door. "Just as well, I'm leaving cause it's hell to the no at Mom and Dad's." He kissed her soft full lips and took her hand, putting it on the outside of his jeans. His cock was warmly stiff.

"Hmm? Sweet dreams," she sang sarcastically. He turned beet red and couldn't help but chuckle. She watched as he got into his car with thoughts of a different living arrangement. Maybe he had a good idea.

IMAGINE

Friday morning arrived, and it was a mad dash to get the kids to school. The night before had been a great deal of fun. It evolved naturally. Nothing about it felt forced or uncomfortable—even the conversation of houses, rent, and marriage. Of course, it was all hypothetical.

Could she see it as a possibility? Her answer was a definite possibility, which was one of her favorite thoughts, such a contradiction.

❧

Before getting into the file, Mer was all about hearing the details from the prior evening. "Rainie, I think you're the only one who doesn't see the glow you have whenever you talk about him. Surely you must feel something."

Rainie told her about the idea of renting from him or buying a house together.

"I get you can't move in together because it wouldn't be right with the boys, but if you think of buying a house together as a business transaction, I think you might be more comfortable. It makes perfect sense." She drummed her fingers on her desk.

"Right now, I'm not sure how we would handle buying a house together." The wheels were turning as she noodled the idea. Mer was the perfect one to bounce things off of.

"I would say exactly as you and I did with our biz." Eyebrows thoughtfully furrowed.

"I still don't know how it would work with Michael. I'll cross that bridge when I get to it. Meanwhile, I do need to find an agent for my house." She rocked her chair back.

"Why don't you use the one Michael's using?" Mer asked.

"Starting things with a co-mingle?" She quickly popped her chair forward in protest.

"Rainie, for being smart, you sure can act dumb as shit," Meredith shook her head.

Allie arrived. They brought her up to speed on the new clients. "You can jump on the nursery." Rainie handed her a few magazines and catalogs. "Mark anything you might think would work for a boy and girl."

Her phone rang. It was Michael. "Rai, how's your day going? Boys last day, right? Surgery went well. I'll cut out early if you want, and we can catch a flick with the kiddos. By the way, I gave your number to my real estate agent, and she'll be calling. If you don't want to use her and have someone else in mind, tell her. She's a hustler, but I don't want to get into your stuff.

"You want to do your thing, and I'll do mine?" she asked as a double entendre.

"I don't want to invade your space, at least not like that," he countered. "How's my idea sound about the movies?"

"Fun, yes, the boys will like that, but—"

"But what?" he sounded confused.

"Hang on," she walked outside. "If we always have the boys around us, when are we going to, um? I dig your sneaky touches, but I want to jump your bones and soon."

"I understand the dilemma, but first and foremost, you're a mom, and I'm just your piece on the side for right now." He chuckled. "They get you more than I do, but, make no mistake, when I do have you, I'm going to have all of you from head to toe. There won't be one part of your body I leave unattended."

She could feel the burn of the blush. "Now, how do you expect me to go back inside? I'm tomato red."

"Well, it is kinda hot outside, suga," he was playful, mimicking her parents.

"Okay, fifties!" she teased.

"Would you rather suga or yo bitch?"

He could make her laugh easily. "At least I'm not beet red from your sexy talk, just from your jackass-ness. I love talking to you, being around you. What can I say? You make a girl giddy. What time tonight?"

"I'll close down around three. It's up to you."

"I'll have the boys home by one."

"See you when I get off. Thank you." He broke into a hearty laugh.

"Thank me? For what?" she asked.

"For the big boner, I have to wait out before seeing anyone else. I wouldn't want my patients to get the wrong idea." He whispered, "I love you."

"Right back at you, stud. You crack me up."

She went back into the office. Both Allie and Meredith looked at her, then broke into hysterics, obviously at her expense.

"Whatever, y'all. Michael's funny. I can't help but laugh."

Mer tried to hide the smile, "The neighbors and everyone for a three-block radius is privy to your conversation. Y'all are like dogs in heat, 'right back at cha, stud?' Phone sex in the middle of the day, really?"

She started sputtering. "As if, what, no way, y'all are reading way too much into things. You could've let me know I was talking too loud instead of eavesdropping."

"Are you kidding me? I wouldn't have missed that for anything. I can't wait to tease Doctor Stud on Saturday." By this time, Mer could hardly breathe from laughter. Rainie blushed again. "Great shade of red on you, dearie."

"Bitch." Rainie turned her nose up and walked to her desk.

Allie tried not to crack up, "Y'all are hysterical. I'm sorry, I can't help but laugh. I don't mean to offend you, Rainie, and I tried not to listen, but your voice is—"

Meredith cut her off, "so freakin loud!"

"Is not!" Rainie shot back.

"Do you want me to recite your conversation? If you're going to be all sexy, you need to learn to whisper. I hope y'all don't carry on in front of the boys. Talk about early sex education," Mer ribbed. She wrinkled her nose and squinted her eyes at Meredith. "Your mean face Rainie?" she winked at her, "I'm playing. I love it. You're so in love with him. It makes me happy down to my soul."

Rainie pretended to ignore her. "Did y'all find anything constructive, or did you just nose in my affairs?"

Allie brought over a picture. "It's got the boy-girl theme. Same beds, same theme but different colors, you're thoughts?" Rainie nodded.

"Despite the X-rated thoughts of the day, ladies, I think we have gotten a lot accomplished this morning. I'm going to go eat. I'm starving. You," pointing to Rainie, "need to get your boys and Allie. You're welcome to stay and eat with me or call your man. I'm starting to feel yucky." She got up and went toward the kitchen.

Rainie and Allie picked up the boys from school, then she dropped Allie off at her car and headed home.

"How was the last day, guys? Did your teachers like their presents?" Rainie inquired.

"Where's Allie going?" Thomas asked, sounding a bit miffed. He had almost a pout on his face.

"To see a friend. What's up?" she directed the question to Thomas.

"I asked you about Allie, Mom, because she's on her phone all the time and doesn't play as much with us as she used to before the man broke into the house. I don't think she wants to be with us anymore. I mean, she got him. Why would she still be scared?"

The picture started to become more transparent. "Oh, baby, she loves you as much as she always has, and her being on the phone has nothing to do with the bad man."

"When I get bigger, I could protect her and be her boyfriend." *So that's it,* she thought.

"Boo, interesting thought, but you know she's a lot older than you, and it would be a long time to wait."

"Whatever, Mom," he wasn't interested. They made it home, talked with Mimi, downed a couple of cookies, and then the boys scampered to the back yard.

"Momma, I think we're going to take the kids to the movies this evening and then to dinner." She moved around the kitchen, gathering bread, condiments, and sliced ham.

"Heads up." Her mom tossed her a bag of chips. "Sounds like fun. Mike sure likes those boys. What movie are you going to see?"

"Some sort of superhero movie, I imagine."

"Dad and I might join you guys at the movies. Or, we could meet up with you after for dinner. Would y'all mind?" Her mom asked doe-eyed.

"Of course not, we'd love it." She regaled the Thomas - Allie conversation.

"Suga, it's hardly surprising. Their little world has been topsy-turvy." She watched as Rainie made sandwiches.

"They start camp on Monday. Momma, I need to get your opinion on something, do you mind?"

"Good gravy, no, I'd love it."

"What would you say if I bought a house with Michael? There's a house on Stella it has a pool house. He said he would have it renovated. He would stay at his place until the renovation was complete, and then he'd move in there, bringing Bonnie and Clyde with him. The kids, Allie and I, would live in the house. Am I foolish?"

"Do you know the story behind the house?" Her mom had a taunting smile like that of any secret.

"Not a clue." Plates ready, but she stopped before calling the boys.

"It belonged to a big-time attorney turned politician. Anyway, I forget his name; he was a known ladies' man, if you get my drift. The wife had enough and took up with her pool boy. He, the husband, found out and came in and shot them both. She died. The boy came out okay and testified against the man. The man went to prison. It was quite the story at the time. But the house, they say, is haunted by her spirit. I don't know how much truth there is to any of the rumors, but there have been several owners since then. They never stay longer than a year. I've never bought into the ghost thing, but anything's possible, I guess." She put her hand to her face.

"Wow, what a story, and it would be my luck, a haunted murder house. But let's forget about the house. What do you think about

Michael and me buying together?" She stood flamingo stance with one leg crooked up.

"Rainie, look me in the eyes, and I want the truth, no baloney. Do you think there's an outside chance you're going to marry this man? Don't be coy."

"I don't know." A lump developed in her throat, "Yes, perhaps."

"Suga, I like him and the way he treats you and your boys."

"You know I knew him in college, but I chose Tom, campus royalty. Michael has been in love with me since college, and I ignored him. He's such a great guy, and Tom was a jerk."

"No, I didn't realize the history, but everything happens for a reason. Neither your dad nor I were huge fans of Tom; we said nothing after y'all married. You made your choice, and we were going to abide by it, and then came the boys.

"My love, I see nothing wrong with buying a house with a man you think you'll probably marry. In the worst-case scenario, you go separate ways, sell the house, and take your portion of the profit, but I don't see it not working out. Why would he live in the pool house and not the house with you, Allie, and the boys?" She put the boys' drinks next to their sandwiches and tapped on the window loud enough to get their attention.

"Because he doesn't believe in it. In his words, it wouldn't be right to live under the same roof without being married." She rolled her eyes almost like a teenager,

"I suppose I should respect his thoughts. I know your dad would, but I think it's a bit ridiculous in this day and age."

"Thank you for answering my question. I think we're going to do it. I talked to Mer, and she thought it was a sensible idea, but I don't know about the Stella Street house. I bet Michael doesn't know about the history." She called the boys in for lunch.

"Because of all the shadiness with it, I bet you could get it for a song and dance." She said with an air of nonchalance.

She hugged her mom. "You always make things make sense, but I don't know about the ghost stuff."

Then she thought to herself. *If anyone understood the ghost thing, it should be me.* As long as she communicated with the ghost and told her about how horrible she heard it had been and took her side, surely, they would be on good terms, and she wouldn't scare the shit out of her or Allie or the boys. It was probably a load of crap anyway. They ate lunch.

Not the most graceful of athletes, she tried hard with the boys in the back yard. The next thing she heard was the sound of clapping.

She turned, and Michael was standing at the door with a huge smile.

"Not too shabby, soccer mom." He walked up to her and gave her a quick kiss in front of the boys. "Y'all are teaching Mom a thing or two with the ball?" He took the ball and passed it to Thomas.

"She's getting pretty good for a mom," Thomas retorted.

❧

After taking the boys to the movies, they grabbed a bite to eat at a local Mom and Pop.

The aroma in the small neighborhood restaurant was mouthwatering and perked everyone's appetite. Both boys came to attention, even though still wound tight by the movie when they heard dinner would be at Maria's Café – flame-grilled burgers and cherry Sprite sodas captured their attention.

"On the way here, Leslie tells me y'all are looking to buy the house on Stella. Given the history and sordid story, I bet you could talk them down, that is, if you aren't worried about the rumors." Her dad chuckled.

Michael was amused, "Word travels fast. Regarding Stella, it looks nice from the outside, but I'm not privy to the story behind it. Do tell."

Lowering his voice, her dad said, "Later tonight," nodding in the direction of the boys.

"Later, it is."

"Mike, you want a beer or some wine?"

"No, sir, I'm good with water." He winked at Rainie.

"You don't drink?" her dad asked.

"On occasion, I do, but not for the most part. With my practice, not that I get many calls in the night, I always want to be at the top of my game. I had an extreme case today. Surgery began about six-thirty this morning. I may be hearing from the parents tonight. I wouldn't be the least bit surprised."

"You work on children?" her mom asked.

"This was an unfortunate case. The child was in a house fire and badly burned." He went on to talk about the case.

"That's wonderful to hear," her mom was touched. "I never thought about that aspect of your profession. You know you hear plastic surgeon, and thoughts of big boobs, tummy tucks, facelifts, and the all-powerful Botox come to mind. I never thought about the miracles you could perform with your skills. Admirable." Rainie was utterly relaxed with a smile of contentment.

Thomas and Henry regaled fantastic tales throughout the rest of dinner to the amusement of the adults. The night wound down, and it was mere minutes to the house.

Michael turned down Stella Street on the way to Northline to show her the house.

"When we get back to the house, you need to tell me the story behind the house," he reminded. "The way your parents spoke, it must be a story worth hearing."

"I will, and I assure you'll find it most interesting." *Boy will he*, she thought. She and Michael retired to the sunroom while the boys scampered upstairs. "Fun night, I think, how about you? Do you feel like you know my parents a bit better?"

"I do. Your mom and dad are a lot like mine—in love. I think that's how it should be." They sat on the sofa.

She rested her head on his shoulder. "Me too. They think we have it."

"We, as in the two of us?" He kissed the top of her head.

"Yes," she cuddled closer.

"But, suga, it only matters what you think, right? Now with the sordid story of Stella."

Rainie faced him and told him the story about the man, the murder, and the ghost rumors. She laughed, saying since she was a ghost whisperer, they'd be okay. "It's a shame she's caught in between after all; the husband was the one who killed her. All she did was have get-even sex since her husband was a known womanizer, at least according to Mom. Doesn't seem fair."

"He'll need to repent, but I doubt a man with such arrogance would confess his sins and repent. I've seen murderers and rapists confess and repent, but it's been my experience, those who think they're better than everyone else and entitled don't confess and repent."

"How do you know so much about all this stuff?"

"My journey has been littered with much confession and repentance, unfortunately, but it's been an interesting ride."

"I can't help thinking about Pandora when we start talking religion, and I feel awkward."

"I told you I had already started taking it apart. Do you want to help me take the rest of it apart?"

"I don't think so," she whispered, "Does that make me bad or sinful?"

"Not for the acts themselves, but for the premarital part. Both of us are guilty." He shrugged his shoulders. "Not that its nothing, because it is, but—"

"But I don't want to stop. I love what we do, and it's too soon to get married." Fluttering began in her stomach and landed between her legs like a first real kiss.

He couldn't help the big smile. "Are you saying marriage might be on the table?"

She kissed him, "I suppose." They touched noses.

"You're too romantic, Rainie. 'I suppose,' really?" He drew back with a laugh.

"I promise when the time is right, I'll be the most romantic person ever." *Hopefully*, she thought.

"I cannot wait for that day." He kissed her and quietly whispered, "and tomorrow night, I'm gonna—" he gave her a devilish grin.

She heard the front door open and light footsteps padding their way to the sunroom.

"Rainie?" Allie whispered and rounded the corner, "sorry, I'm late." Her return home was the perfect thing to chill the heat. *Whew, a much-needed distraction*, she laughed inside.

Michael stood. "I'm gonna let you two enjoy your girl talk. What time for dinner tomorrow?"

"We'll talk in the morning," she said as she walked him to the front door. "Do you do that to me on purpose? You're bad and good all at the same time, Michael. I may have to bring you breakfast, my friend. I'll give you—" he put his hand lightly over her lips. "What? Censoring me already, and I haven't even said yes to a proposal, mister. Then we'll have dins with Mer and Paul. After dinner, it'll be sexy play in Pandora." She looked him dead in the eyes.

"Sh. I don't want to wake the boys or have your parents come down with me like this," he gestured toward his crotch.

"Oh, the things I will do to you, and, Michael, I promise." Her laugh was almost sinister.

"Good night, naughty Rainie."

"Good night, sweet Michael," he loved her laugh. *So, this is what happiness feels like. I could melt in a puddle right here.* She pondered this still new feeling.

She watched as he drove off and went back to the sunroom and conversations about Allie's night.

Twirling her hair, she thoughtfully asked, "What do you have going tomorrow?"

"Your mom planned on taking the boys to the club. She asked if I wanted to come along. Your parents make me feel right at home, and I'm like one of the family."

Allie's sweet smile made her get a lump in her throat and tear up. "Because to us, you are family, Allie. The club thing might work out perfectly. I might surprise Michael and bring him breakfast tomorrow morning."

"You better get your rest if you're going to be with him from breakfast through dinner." Rainie wondered what she meant, if she had any clue, or if they had spoken too loudly in the foyer.

"That's a good point. You'll need rest since you're going to be with the boys and my parents the whole day. Talk about exhausting. Let's get our butts to bed." She hugged Allie.

Sleep fell upon her fast and deeply. She woke around nine, jumped in the shower, and was ready in a flash since a nine o'clock wake up put her way behind schedule in her mind.

Allie helped the boys get their club stuff together, and her mom and dad were at the breakfast table sorting through papers. "Meeting Michael, running late. Have fun at the club."

"I have one too many quiches. Please take this one to Mike and tell him I said to enjoy."

"Thanks, Momma." Her dad peered over his glasses.

"Mike's a good guy."

She blew him a kiss.

Questions started flowing through her mind. *What if Michael isn't home? What if he didn't take me seriously?*

She pulled into the Place d'Armes, expecting they may not let her park, but they did and knew her name, as well. She grabbed her bag and the quiche and strolled down to his place. She rang the bell and waited a second before ringing again.

The door opened; Michael was bare-chested with knit lounge pants on. His smile told the whole story. He was pleased, "I'm glad you're home. I started to worry I might be catching you at a bad time, or maybe you were out." She could feel the glow of her face as she blushed.

"Hm. We have to make sure you have a key. Sometimes I'm in the courtyard or the workshop and can't hear the bell, so you'll be able to let yourself in." He bent down and kissed her, taking her bag. "What do we have here?"

"Momma's quiche, she said to make sure you enjoyed."

He dropped her bag in his bedroom and brought the quiche into the kitchen with her following close behind. "I've already eaten and done my morning run and work out. I've been lazy the last few weeks; I've got to get back my rhythm."

"Oh, I see, I'm a bad influence on you." She pouted.

He turned around just in time to see the pucker and quickly stole a kiss. "You have no idea, lady." She playfully pouted, "Life before was pretty freakin boring, way too healthy – work, workouts, church, and more work. My source of pleasure was playing with Bonnie and Clyde. Not saying they aren't fun, but I must say I much rather play with you." He moved in close to her, looking from her eyes to her lips with a twitch at the corners of his mouth.

She took a step into him, their bodies touching. Her heart began to race as her libido soared, making her nipples hard like little beads. "Did you have sweet dreams?" She started backing him into the bedroom.

"I think I know where this is going. After all, you gave me fair warning." His eyes glistened as he bit his bottom lip.

Grinning at him, "yes, I did give you a warning, but I'm also curious if you're going to fulfill your threats, or were they merely idle." She tugged at his pants as she reached up and kissed him. She pulled from the kiss and ran her hands on his chest as she gazed up at his face. Her heart pounded. She pinched his nipples and laughed when he widened his eyes.

So taken by his eyes, she didn't feel him unfastening her shorts. They slid down her legs. He firmly grabbed her ass, turned, and threw her on the bed. "I. Do. Not. Threaten. I. Promise." He succinctly commented with a slight pause between each word.

He devilishly smiled down at her as he straddled across her hips, planting a kiss leading to more and more kisses like make-out parties in high school. His hands wandered to her breasts. Her body beckoned to be kissed, touched. He put her ankles on his shoulders and spread her knees wide. He lowered his body. "Any complaints yet?" He touched his tongue between her legs, hitting all the pleasure points.

This sweet soft play heightened her need for a firmer, almost punishing force. The passion mounted like hurricane waves against the seawall. The flutters gradually turned intense and deep probing. He slid something warm inside of her, which served to turn up the heat even more. He pushed it in deeper, and the deeper it went, the more dutiful he performed—the more intense the performance, the more times she climaxed. Things were so hot she could hardly catch her breath.

She put her hands on herself, which seemed to arouse him even more, raising the bar for her and eliciting soft murmurs of pleasure.

He meandered up her legs, causing her to wrap around him, lifting her body almost off the bed, making his penetration deeper. As promised, he brought her to new places of satisfaction, but before his final moment, she coaxed him onto his back.

It was time to fulfill her threat. Her actions were not sweet, were not delicate or subtle, but were raw with purpose and relentless passion. Her grip was firm, and her strokes determined. She heard him moan then felt his pulse pick up. She lifted up and ran her tongue along his upper thighs all over except the one place she could feel he desired.

He grabbed a handful of her hair, moving her to his hard cock. She looked up toward his face. He had the look she was aiming for, which encouraged her to go down hard, rhythmic, and deep. She kissed him deeply, sharing the fruit of her spoils.

Amidst a most passionate kiss, Michael moved into a sitting position still intertwined in the kiss; he had her straddle him. With no mercy, he plunged inside of her lifting her up and thrusting her down. It was hard, primitive, and nothing but nothing was held back. Rainie had never been handled so roughly, and she liked it. She wanted more until they could take no more discipline, and the moment came with a splendor nothing short of spiritual.

She collapsed next to him, both drenched in sweat and euphoria. After catching his breath, he gasped, "never before anything near. Are you okay?"

"More than okay, maybe a bit sore."

He rolled onto his side, "I hurt you?" His eyes showed concern.

"Hardly, you did not hurt me, just the opposite. I've never had that many orgasms. You most certainly kept your promise," Rainie rolled on her side. "You're soaking wet." His hair was dripping with sweat. She moved it out of his face. "There." She grinned with satisfaction.

"I didn't need a workout today. You gave me more of a workout than anything I can think of, with great benefits. I'm gonna jump in the pool to cool off. Join me?"

"Sounds like a good idea." He picked her up and carried her to the pool, "unnecessary, sir," then he dropped her into the pool. She popped up laughing. "That wasn't very nice."

"Better than a cold shower," he jumped in next to her. "Good thing you're not looking for Mr. Happy because he's now in hiding." He dropped under the water and came back up with a flick of his hair. "You're gorgeous. Tom was such a fool. His loss, my gain, and I couldn't be happier or more thankful. You're not only beautiful and witty with the most incredible laugh, but you're also amazingly great in the sack. Hm." He thoughtfully looked off in the distance, then back at her with a satisfied grin. "Baby, you're the whole entire song, not just a single verse."

ᅟ

"It's a good thing no one can see back here – we're naked." She glided around him in the water. "I've never thought of myself as a sexual person or adventurous in bed, but you've turned on something inside of me I can't explain, but I'm digging the hell out of it!" She splashed him, followed by a kiss. They cuddled and played in the pool, and it was pure with no restriction or restraint. Their relationship was natural and real.

"Are you up for a nap, no, maybe a piece of quiche and then the nap?" He took her hand and walked to the kitchen. "I could use the calories. As I told you, I had already worked out, whew, and then you."

" I'm hungry. I guess I worked up an appetite." She mimicked Michael's sexy-face touching her tongue to her eye tooth amidst a smile of sassiness.

"Here's your fork. We won't dirty any more dishes," he smiled at her.

The conversation was light, the forks cleaned up quickly, and the bed beckoned a nap. Michael was easy to cuddle. She felt safe and loved in his arms. In between his soft purrs, she whispered, "I love you," as she gave into slumber.

They slept for two hours but lounged in bed for another couple of hours, talking about everything under the sun.

"I love watching you, Rainie. With each expression, your eyes flicker with laughter and life. You make me smile just watching you."

"Yeah, buddy, what you see is what you get. So, where did Wendy, John, and Michael come from?"

"Get comfy. It's quite a story." She cuddled closer, tracing his hand with her finger. "My family is a result of kinda two divorces. My bio mother was a conflicted woman and slept with whoever would give her attention. My dad was a river pilot, gone weeks and home weeks; it was convenient for my bio. It's not like she was skanky nasty. I think she didn't do well being the wife of a pilot. She was probably lonely and insecure.

"My dad found out, forgave her, but then she did it again, and he divorced her. I was maybe two – I don't remember any of it. What I know is through stories, mostly weird things John saw and remembered even though he was only three. He's always been perceptive and ahead of the game, even though he comes across more Neanderthal.

"After the divorce, she didn't want anything to do with us and started a new life. Dad had an on two off two schedule, as I said before, so we needed a nanny.

"The nanny he hired had a little girl, Wendy. They lived at the house. Apparently, she was from a well-to-do family, got pregnant out of wedlock, and they disowned her." He shook his head. "I guess it wasn't divorce because she didn't marry, but I've always thought of it as divorce. Mom and Dad fell in love. My dad adopted Wendy. Hence, we all had the same last name. Even before the marriage and adoption, we considered her our sister. Mom is the kindest person you'll ever meet. In many ways, she reminds me of your mom.

"Dad is awesome. He retired a couple years ago and enjoys painting—even sold some. John followed Dad in the family business, but I, being the rebel, wanted to go to med school. I think he would've liked me to be a pilot, but they always left our decisions to us. It wasn't the life for me."

He had her spellbound as she watched him with earnest.

"A fond memory I have is from when I was little, maybe four. Mom was reading to us before bed, and the story was Peter Pan. You can imagine how jazzed we were. The characters in the story were Wendy, John, and Michael. It became a very special story for our family. There's the scoop." He looked at her for a response.

"I cannot wait to meet them." She paused. "Do you think they'll like me?"

"Yes, absolutely, they're going to love you. I'm afraid John might try to be too friendly, but I'm sure you can handle him. If not, I can. You'll meet Wendy at Thanksgiving, but if you don't want to wait that long, we can always go see them. I love D.C. I wouldn't want to live there but I'm into the museums, you?"

"I've been once on a school trip—boring, but I clearly remember the big-ass dinosaur I was a jackass, my poor mom and dad."

"There are so many things to look forward to my beautiful lady. Every day seems brighter with you in my life. Look, the cast of the sun is changing, which means," he quickly drew down the sheet, "we need to get our lazy butts out of bed."

They took their time getting ready, yet they were right on schedule and pulled up at the same time as Paul and Mer. Rainie and Meredith stepped away from the table within the first half-hour and headed for the ladies' room.

"Y'all are perfect together, Rainie, and if you don't follow through with this man, you're a fool. I swear it seems like y'all have been together forever, and yet it has the excitement of new romance." She touched up her lipstick.

Rainie looked at Mer through the mirror as she frosted her lips. "We're perfect together, I agree, and we've started having some serious talks. Oh, and I got the Wendy, John, and Michael story. He's told me about his whole family, and I can't wait to meet them this weekend. Before we can talk seriously about marriage, I have to get my house sold, buy a house, and get moved in, but I suspect between the first and Mardi Gras. I don't know, maybe December would work better because of the decorations everywhere and people are off for the holidays. It's moving fast, maybe too fast. Ya think?" She scrunched her nose in question.

"I can't believe what I'm hearing. I want to scream, and for our age, I don't think y'all are moving too fast. Does Michael know you feel this way because you're good at making plans and not letting the other party in on it? Just saying, he might want to enjoy the feeling of hearing you say you want to get married."

They returned to the table, and the guys were involved in a deep conversation about the most recent politics in New Orleans.

Michael jumped up and pulled out her chair. "I was about to send in the troops."

"Ha, ha, Michael, we had a few things to catch up on, that's all."

Looking at Meredith, he said, "she certainly is spunky tonight."

"She's a pistol, Mike. One never knows what might come out of her mouth. She's been known to create a scene or two," with a grin and wink at Rainie.

"I can only imagine. The lady is quite creative," he raised an eyebrow toward Rainie, "but that can be a good thing, I suppose." The heat began to build inside her gut bringing on a perfect blush.

WE'VE ONLY JUST BEGUN

With camps and work, the week was flying by. Michael made an appointment with an agent to look at the house and a couple of others. They waited outside of the Stella Street house until the agent arrived.

"Do you like the look now you're up close, and it's daylight?" he probed.

She had walked on each side of the house. It was too high to look in the windows, but she thought it was warm and homey from what she could tell. "I like it a lot. I'm anxious to get inside and see if I get a spooky feel," she looked at him and made a ghostly sound.

"Yes, my ghost whisperer!" He hugged her.

The house was perfect and fully met their needs. As far as haunted, she didn't have any ghostly feelings and put it all to rumor.

She told her parents all about the house, and they were most eager to have a look for themselves. The thought of Rainie being right around the corner was an answer to a prayer.

The next day came, and they all met at the Stella Street house. Her mom gushed over the place and thought it was perfect. After a brief spin through the house Michael, her dad, and the boys went to the backyard.

"Poppy, this is the coolest house. There's even a place for my soccer goal, right there," he pointed to the far side of the yard where there was a grassy area. It's close enough to your house I can come see y'all on my bike." He looked up, glancing from his grandad to Mike.

"I don't know if your mom would go for you riding to our house, yet, but in time, pal," patting Thomas on the shoulder.

Rainie and her mom came out of the house just in time to hear Michael talking with the agent. "We want to put in an offer. There are options to consider swapping her home on Nashville Avenue plus some cash. Otherwise, the offer we're prepared to make is nine twenty-five."

The real estate agent balked but said she would verbally present it to the sellers before writing the contract. The agent gave a look of disgust with their cash offer.

"Are there any other offers or people interested in the house?" Michael inquired.

After bidding farewell to her parents and boys, they were off to Baton Rouge.

☙

"Rainie, my parents don't live in Baton Rouge proper. They live outside a distance. It's just easier to say Baton Rouge." He pulled onto the Interstate.

"Your dad is a retired River Pilot? "She asked like she was studying for a test.

"As was his dad and his dad's dad." He quickly glanced at her.

"You broke tradition, bad boy." Both excited and nervous, she became even more animated as she spoke to Michael while she could feel the blood coursing through her with force.

"Yep, I'm the black sheep," he grinned at her.

"I don't think becoming a doctor is too shabby." She turned her body toward him, struggling with the seat belt.

"I love what I do, and it's something I'll be able to do for as long as I want. I don't have to be able to climb up and down on ships. My dad is in great shape, but I still think it was getting dangerous for him. When it came to retiring, he felt like it was time." Michael watched her for a second, totally in love. "He wanted more time with Mom. I can't blame him. She's amazing. You nervous? If so, no need."

They talked about the Stella house for the rest of the ride and their lives growing up, both being children of privilege. He had gone to a Catholic high school and grade school, and she had been at The Academy of the Sacred Heart for her entire school life. The topic of marriage came up; she was concerned his parents would object to him marrying her having the two boys.

"Really?" he glanced her way for a moment. "I told you the story of how my mom and dad came together. They'll eat up Thomas and Henry in a heartbeat. I can tell you. Rainie, I think you should just—"

"Breathe. I know." She sighed.

"Yes. You worry when there's nothing to worry about." He tightly held her hand.

"I can't help it." She knew he could feel the tremble in her hand. *Shit!*

"When do you think you might want to get married?" he asked with a huge smile on his face.

"I think you'll probably be in the pool house," she came back sarcastically, "until December sometime. Everywhere is decorated for the holidays, it would be pretty. You know we can't get married in the Catholic Church. Does it change your desire to marry me?"

"Good try. No."

"Since it's your first, what would you want?"

"Just you, me, Meredith to stand for you, and John to stand for me, am I too boring? I don't have friends to speak of. What would you think of an island wedding or, better yet, in Colorado at a ski resort?"

"Too much to think about right now, Michael, and don't bother with an engagement ring."

"Okay." She saw a bit of a twitch in his lips.

"Do your parents know anything about me?" Her questions were like an auto-pitch machine, he'd answer, and she'd pitch another.

"Lady, they know all about you. I called my mom the first night I met you and told her I had met the girl I was going to marry. Of course, she thought we were dating and wanted to meet you. I explained we were not dating, and you didn't know I existed.

"Throughout the years, we have spoken about you a lot. I think my dad and my brother thought I might be gay," he laughed. "I've never brought anyone to meet them."

"Not ever?" she looked surprised.

"Nope, because I knew it wasn't for keeps. Wendy knows about you and thinks you didn't make the right decision marrying Tom, but she's a protective big sister."

"She's right, but through the marriage came Thomas and Henry, and I would go to hell and back for them. The marriage served a purpose. Besides, I am who I am today because of all I've been through, right?"

"And, Rainie, it was back when you married Tom. As a mom, she would get the mom thing." He glanced between her and the road.

"Wow. Do they know what I look like?" She could hear a slight quiver in her voice and wondered if he detected it.

"Um, from my description, but as I said, my brother and dad didn't buy it. Wendy thought I saw what I wanted to see, and Mom, well, she has a good idea, but it's not like I've shown anyone pictures – I don't have any. You, however, have seen pictures of them, lady."

Country Roads

He pulled up to an ornate iron gate attached to towering brick walls, opened the glove box, and tapped a remote. The gate slowly opened. To either side of the drive were majestic live oaks and clusters of azaleas. Rainie imagined when the azaleas were in bloom. It would be spectacular. She looked from side to side like a little kid at an amusement park, trying to take it all in. When the house appeared, her jaw dropped. At the end of the drive, she could see a home resembling Tara from Gone with the Wind. Off to the side were white wooden corrals and a huge barn complete with an open hayloft. The driveway circled in front with a center fountain. It was the kind of place pictured in old-time war movies.

"Is this where you grew up?" she was a bit shocked.

"Pretty much." Clear and concise.

"Do you ride?" she was still in awe.

"Yes, I do." His smile was warm and unassuming.

"Thomas and Henry would be beside themselves. I told you they're taking riding lessons this summer?" *What the hell, this is freakin' amazing!*

"Yes, you mentioned it. Riding lessons are good. When riding horses, you learn to be confident yet kind, in charge, yet caring. It's good, I think, to possess both qualities."

"This place explains a lot about your calm demeanor. It's elegant and graceful. I can see where it would be a great place to grow up." He stopped the car.

His mom came hurriedly out of the front door, "Michael, I've been waiting. I became so excited when the signal for the gate went off. I knew it was y'all." She took his face in her hands, "Oh, how I've missed you." She circled the car. *Oh, fuck!* "And you must be Rainie. You're as beautiful as Michael described you, welcome, welcome," and she hugged her. "Michael has told me so much about you. It's good to put a face to the name finally. Y'all come in."

Michael grabbed the bags and brought them inside. There was a grand hallway with an elegant staircase, and while it was a massive place, it felt warm and inviting. His mother couldn't have been more gracious, "Can I get you something to drink or eat?"

"No, ma'am, I'm good for right now." *He grew up on a fucking plantation. Holy shit. Breathe.*

"Honey, go put the bags in your room. Rainie and I are gonna sit in the Hearth." He brought the bags upstairs, and his mom led the way to another room.

The house was indeed an old plantation home with old-world touches, making the place ooze with charm and antiquity. They went and sat in the Hearth, which was like an oversized den. A gigantic fireplace, complete with telltale signs of many years of use, was the perfect focal point.

"When Michael told me he was coming home to see John and bringing you home to meet us, I got so excited. To finally have you here with him is a dream come true. You sure you don't want anything?" Her eyes glittered with enthusiasm, almost like a young girl finding the perfect prom dress.

"A glass of water would be lovely. Thank you." His mom jumped up, Rainie following close behind. She wanted to see the kitchen. It was perhaps the most charming kitchen she had ever seen.

All the appliances were top of the line but built into areas that looked a hundred years old. The original wood-burning fireplace made of old chipped and nicked bricks formed an arch housing the stove.

There was a young girl standing watch over a pot. She wasn't what one would call pretty, but she was cute with a small turned-up nose, dark hair, hazel eyes, and she stood maybe five feet tall.

"Mrs. Landry, take a look at da gumbo. Looks to your liking?" She wiped her hands on her jeans and held out her hand. "You mus' be Dr. Landry's Rainie Todd. Girl, we been waitin to meet ya. I'm Dominique. I cook for da Landrys a couple times a week. So nice ta finally meet ya." She spoke with a friendly Cajun dialect.

Dominique looked especially small standing next to Michael's mother, who was maybe five-six with a blonde chin-length bob and pool water blue eyes.

Michael entered the room. He gave her a big hug, "Dominique, I guess you've met Rainie now," he peered into the pot, "smells good."

"Seafood and okra gumbo dats what ya daddy wanted for the weekend, plus since I know you were comin I brought some crawfish pies an' boudin balls, ma boy." She lightly hit Michael in the ribs.

"Rainie, this girl can cook like nobody's business. Someone from her family has cooked here since I can remember." The kitchen was alive with colorful personalities.

Rainie took a sip of the water, "Thank you, Mrs. Landry."

"Please, it's Missy." She grabbed Rainie's hand. *Settle down, breathe, breathe. Oh my God, this is real. I'm talking to his mom.*

"Yes, ma'am," Rainie's stomach was doing flips – happy and a touch of nerves.

Michael came behind her and put his arms around her waist, "I take it nobody's bitten yet, have they? Has Mom tried to feed you? I told you she's very much like your mom." *Is he really pushing his crotch into my back in his mom's kitchen? Dear sweetness.*

"Yes, you're spot on," and she smiled at his mom. "You and my momma seem very much alike." Rainie nodded with a glued-on smile.

"I'm glad he brought you home. Jack will be in soon. He's either in the barn painting or playing with the new foal. Tea?" She was steeping a kettle.

"Mom, where's John?" The squeeze into her back lightened a little.

"He'll be here in the morning." She turned, looking over her shoulder back at him with a smile that began in her eyes right down to her perfectly bowed smile.

"Great. It'll give us a chance to talk to you and Dad alone. Rainie and I found the perfect house. You're gonna love it." Everyone moved into the Hearth.

"I'm sure I will. Do tell." Her voice was raspy like Rainie's.

She took a seat next to Michael on the couch. He whispered, "Rai, chill, she loves you. Breathe." *Some disclosure would've been nice, like 'hey Rai, back on the plantation,' but no, surprise!*

They talked with his mom endlessly about the house. She wanted all the details which Rainie filled in as Michael was describing it to her. "You think Dad won't be in for a while? He had to have seen or at least heard us pulling up. We want to talk to both of you together."

"Sounds important. Give me a hint," his mom prodded, wriggling her eyebrows.

"No hints we've already told you about the house. It's not a done deal yet. Because of some of the circumstances with the house, not saying anything's wrong with it, we told the agent we were not willing to pay anywhere near the asking price. Actually, a bit better than half or Rainie would swap her home on Nashville Avenue for the Metairie house, which is close to her parents and closer, by a little, to the kids' school." Rainie thought, *Oh, yes, and Missy, it's a murder house with a ghost.*

Missy tilted her head to the right with a curious expression. "Good for you. The prices are astronomical now. Michael, one day y'all will have to sell this or keep it in the family and move here. It's going to be a real pain," she pondered the thought. "Rainie, is it hard for you to sell your home?" She watched as she sipped her tea.

"I thought it would be since it was the house my babies came home to from the hospital. They're now five and seven. There are a lot of great memories, but there are also some painful ones, as well. Since I'm starting on a new chapter in my life, I figured it was time to turn the page. Right now, the kids, the nanny, and I are living with my parents, which is kind of moving things along faster than they might have." She could feel the tension leaving her body as the muscles relaxed, letting the blood flow freely. The out-of-body experience was diminishing but filled by Rand's presence. Her voice tumbled through her head, "Get a grip, Rainie, what's wrong with you?"

"Michael told me about the break-in. It must have been terrifying. New Orleans is not the city it used to be, is it?" *Oh my God, she is so Mom in duplicate.*

"No, ma'am, it isn't. The kids can't play in the front yard for fear of being grabbed. There's nowhere for them to ride their bikes. We load them up in the car and take them to the park. Being in Metairie will create a whole new lifestyle, and they can be kids."

Just then, a loud voice came from the direction of the kitchen. "Missy?"

"Jack, we're in the Hearth," she winked at Rainie.

In walked a man that could have been Michael twenty-five years older and maybe twenty pounds heavier. "How's my boy?" he wrapped his arms around Michael and gave him a big bear hug. "Your mom has missed you something terrible, and I guess this is the redhead bombshell that's had you tied up." *Gulp! No, sir, it would be the other way around!*

He had a full belly kind of laugh. He looked at Rainie, who had stood up. "Miss Rainie Todd, it's good to finally meet you. I thought you were a figment of his imagination, and here you are in the flesh. Welcome to our home, kick up your feet. Oh, and, by the way, I'm Jack."

She put her hand out to shake his, which he grabbed and pulled her into a hug, "We do a lot of hugging here. Hope you don't mind."

"I think it's great." Her heart was fluttering a bit like a tap dance recital. Rand again scolded, "get a freaking grip. You're such a weirdo."

"Dad, you want to grab a drink and sit? We wanted to talk to you and Mom together."

His Dad sat, "I think I'd rather sit and hear what you have to say before getting a drink. It sounds important." Jack's face took on a much more somber look.

Michael looked at Rainie with a big smile, "We've decided to get married in December and wanted to share the news with y'all at the same time."

His Mom was ecstatic, "I couldn't hear better news. When did y'all decide?"

"We've been talking around it for some time, and it wasn't concrete until our ride up here. There's been a lot going on with work, the break-in, the move to her parents, and looking for a house, which by the way, Dad, we found. Don't know where the wedding will be or the

exact date or anything other than it's going to be small and intimate."
Fucking hell, things are getting real! Missy turned, glancing at her with
a look of surprise and glistening eyes.

Tears of joy trickled down his mom's cheeks, "Wherever and
whenever, we'll all be there. I look forward to meeting your family,
Rainie." The happiness on her face and in her smile brought tears to
Rainie's eyes.

"I know my parents are going to be excited we'll tell them when
we get back to the city. Y'all are the first to hear officially," she held
Michael's hand.

"It sure sounds good to me. Won't John be surprised when he gets
in? Rainie, John, and I thought you were some made-up person to get the
family to stop pressuring him about a girlfriend," he looked at Michael,
"not that we thought you were a homo." He furrowed his brow.

"Yes, you did, and so did John, don't start lying now. And Dad, it's
gay, not homo," Rainie tried not to laugh.

They sat around talking. Rainie showed pictures of the boys, talked
about her mom and dad, her career, and even spoke about Rand. They
had already heard the story from Michael years ago, but it allowed
them to hear from her about her sister, who she could feel sitting right
beside her. The hour started getting late.

"Missy, let's give these kids some time alone and tuck it in for the
night. Mike, make sure y'all lock your door, you know who comes in
tomorrow morning, and you don't want a first impression to be your
brother jumping in bed with y'all." As he stood, she saw her Michael
somewhere in the future. Jack had more of a gentle giant look, but he
passed on his genes.

"The lock has never stopped him before. Dad, I warned Rainie not
to be too surprised if a man jumped on top of me in the bed around
six in the morning. Still about six?" Michael chuckled. He seemed even
more laid back than usual, and that was saying something.

Almost apologetic, his mom answered, "Six it is. See y'all tomorrow,
and Rainie, welcome to the family. It's been a boys' club around here
for a long time. I'm delighted to have another lady in the midst. Wendy's
gonna be pleased as punch, too. G'night." Both his parents leaned over
with a kiss on the cheek for her and Michael.

She waited for a minute or two, "Michael, you didn't tell me you grew up on a plantation. A warning would've been nice. And, yes, your parents are awesome." With a smile, she cocked her head and asked, "Does your brother really jump on top of you when he comes in?" she snickered.

"Embarrassingly yes, started as a kid, he was an earlier riser than I, and he'd come jump on me, and it hasn't stopped since. I can't wait to see his face when he sees you – he's gonna freak but will probably say something rude. Fair warning. He's a great guy. I've no doubt our families will fit together." He stood and pulled her to her feet, their bodies touching. "Come for a walk?"

It was dark outside, but his steps were sure. Rainie held his hand with total trust. He told her to wait a moment and jogged off. The pool light turned on, "does it remind you of anything?" He asked. Cradling her waist, he hugged her tightly.

In almost a whisper, she answered. "Yes, it looks like the Stella Street pool." Then with slight hesitation, she continued. "You grew up here?" she was still blown away. "I can't get my head around it. I've never known anyone who grew up on a plantation."

"This is home. It smells like home, and when I'm here, I feel its warmth like an embrace. I have never thought about it like anything other than home. I bet John and Wendy would say the same thing." His eyes had the glow of tiny embers.

They strolled hand in hand. "You seem so close to your family. I'd have never guessed it." He gazed off contemplatively, then shrugged his shoulders.

"We are close and have always been. I don't need to talk about my family; they are in my heart, part of me, I guess."

They walked in silence, listening to the sounds of the country at night. It was like a symphony of squeaky crickets, screechy frogs, and the occasional baritone from a bullfrog. The air even smelled different. It was an earthy, musky scent that gave a feeling of rustic purity – a bold contrast to being in the city.

"I know you were only two –"

He interrupted. "My memories are only of my family. Mom bonded with us from the beginning, maybe due to Dad being away.

There might as well have been the proverbial cord. Mom was mom period the end, and she still hasn't let go. She's struggled with Wendy being in D.C., but they visit often. Dad bought her a townhouse, so she felt close to Wen. When John wanted to follow in Dad's footsteps, Mom wasn't happy, not happy at all.

"Dad was somewhat disappointed I didn't follow John and decided on LSU, she was thrilled. Then with Med School, she was cool, but when I moved to New Orleans on a permanent basis, it was like heartbreak hotel. We talk a lot, though. If she had her way, we would all live here. It's the way she is. You'll see when we leave on Sunday how sad she'll be and find any reason to drag out our leaving."

"Michael, that's touching. Does it make it hard on you?" She pulled him to her, wrapping her arms around his waist, head cocked to one side and wholly enchanted in his eyes.

"I'm used to it for the most part. During my darkest times, I'd drive here after work, knowing I would have the long drive back in the morning. She never asked or pried; she just loved me. I talked when I felt like it, and she listened. She's a good listener."

"Hm. That's where you get it from because one of the things I first noticed with you was how engaged you were in our conversations. It wasn't all about you. I felt like you wanted to know me." She crushed in tighter to him.

"I did, I still do," he said. "I want to know what you're thinking and how you feel, but not smother you or invade your privacy. I figure if you want to talk, you will."

She leaned up and kissed the tip of his nose. "Well, sir, I'm not as gracious as you, because I want to know all about you and everything you've done, and where you've been, and how you feel, and I'll drive you to distraction, so I'm told." She lowered her hands and grabbed his butt.

"I love it." He took her hand. "Come, let me show you something," they walked in the stillness of the night.

Every now and then, there would be a whinny from the horses. Michael brought her into the barn, turned on the light, and then proceeded up a spiral staircase.

When they got to the top, it was surprising. There was a huge window overlooking the paddocks. All the walls were adorned with Jack's paintings. Some of them were impressionistic horses in motion, while others featured sights along the river. He had some from when his children were young.

She walked up to a group of paintings of children playing. It was impressionistic, the lines were not clear, and the facial features were fuzzy, but it spoke of happiness and joy. "Are these Wendy's kids?"

"Some and some," he walked around looking at the paintings. "There are many opportunities for trouble around here. We used to play and play hard until we'd hear the ringing. Sometimes Mom would come out and look for us, but usually, she rang the bell. There was no ignoring the bell." He turned and looked at her with a devilish grin.

It was quite a sight, and she was taking it all in. Michael took her hand and led her to the hay area, "This was the magic place. We all learned a few things about life."

"Aren't there rats and mice and snakes? All of you had sex up here?" Her smile was inquisitive.

"The rats, mice, and snakes stay hidden. Besides, I think Dad has four barn cats, at least he did, maybe more or less now.

"Things would happen when he was at work. It's not like we all had sex at the same time, except one time, John had some girl up here. This is shameful, but remember I was young, like fifteen, maybe fourteen. The girl says to John, at least according to him, 'I wish you had a friend here screwing is more fun with another person.'

"All I knew is John came racing in the house told me it was an emergency, and he needed me. I figured one of the horses got out, which happened a lot and to get it back in would take both of us. I went running behind him.

"When he went up the spiral stairs, I asked, 'what's up there'? He said, 'Mikey, get your ass up here.' I got up there, and what do I see but this naked girl waiting on a blanket on the hay. I stopped and didn't know what to say.

"He says, 'do what she says.' We both drop our pants. She instructs John to do her and for me to put one leg here and one leg there. I straddled her head, and while John was going to town, she was doing me. It was my first blow job. I don't know if John ever saw her again, but I didn't, for sure. I didn't find the situation fun."

She looked at him with a "really?" kind of look. "I bet it was pure torture," she laughed.

"I wasn't sure what to do, I knelt there, and she did all the work. When she finished me, John was still going at it.

"I quickly jumped up, put my pants back on, and hauled ass out of there. I could hear John laughing as I ran across the pasture. Yeh, it felt like nothing I'd ever experienced, and it felt good, but the shame and the guilt and the confusion were huge.

"I went to bed and stayed there until I heard John come in. As usual, he ran into my room and jumped on top of me. He said, 'what'd you think? Pretty fuckin cool, huh?'

"I asked him who the girl was and why the hell he needed me. He says, 'she's some weirdo chic, she said too bad I didn't have any friends over, I was like, hell yeah. Mikey's gonna get him some. I don't know why you ran off so fast. Are you still a virgin?' I shook my head, yes. I had played the bases, never the home run, and definitely nothing oral. He told me I 'blew my chance,' then laughed and said, 'well, maybe she blew it for you' and bust a gut laughing.

Rainie watched him closely, he made storytelling an art form, and she could visualize the scene as his eyes widened then squinted as the story spun.

"Once we caught some guy trying to bring Wendy into the hayloft." Michael rubbed his hand over his face. "Shit, he never tried again, best I know. She was furious with us and told us to mind our own business. After the interlude with John, I had some girls, by myself, may I add, in the hayloft."

Rainie teased. "You look like a guilty little boy. What teenage boy wouldn't have been like 'hell, yes?' Did you bring me up here to play?" She tugged at his belt.

"No, they tidied it up. I think my parents figured what our fascination with the barn was about because the blankets disappeared, and the hay was neatly bailed. While the ultimate playhouse was closed for business, we improvised. There are nifty nooks and crannies around here." She looked out the hayloft into the darkness.

"Have you always been hypersexual? "she started to feel flushed.

"Me? I seem to recall most of our playtime has been instigated by you. Yes?"

She laughed. "I'll give you fifty-fifty, but I have never been as adventurous until you," she pointed at him.

"Oh, I've corrupted you? I don't think so. I think I merely provided the opportunity for you to go to those places you had hidden inside. Believe me; I've never had a partner nearly as sensual as you, and, sadly, I've had a lot." He nuzzled next to her.

"I wasn't Miss Goody Two Shoes, but my sexual experiences are lame."

"It wasn't you, believe me, it was your partner. Come on, let's go to bed, it's been a long exciting day, and I desperately want to make love to you."

He held her hand as she went down the spiral staircase, "your dad is a big guy. I can't imagine him going up and down this staircase. It must worry your mom."

"Are you kidding me? Do you know how they get on the ships they navigate? He's like a freakin' monkey. This stairway is nothing." The horses were stirring in their stalls.

There was one standing at the stall door, nodding its head, snorting, and almost prancing. "It's all right, girl. He petted her mane, "Rainie, this is Lightning." She came to live here when she was two, a few years before Elvis, my first horse, died.

He was so alive, and she held onto his every word. "John and I would ride up on the levee. His horse was a fast paint he creatively named Patches." He wrinkled his brow in thought. "When we raced, Patches would smoke them all. Then along came this two-year-old mare with some high-faluten name, Peniraf's Starfire.

"Anyway, we go up to the levee," his look became intense as his hands completed the story with animation. "We were walking along a few trots here and there. Jackass says, 'let's see what she has under the hood,' he took off, and I gently tapped my heels to her sides, and it was the ride of my life. She made Patches look like he was standing still, hence, the name Lightning."

Even though completely consumed with his story, Rainie kept her distance. "Are you afraid? They can sense it. You need to—"

"Breathe?" she squinted her eyes and shot him the bird.

"Yes, and want to make friends. Horses, like dogs, have a lot of personality." They walked out of the barn. "Rainie, look up at the stars. Have you ever seen them as bright and numerous?" As they walked, he pointed toward the right, "can you see the pond over there? I know it's dark, maybe not."

Taking small careful steps, she followed. "I think I see it. I can't wait to look at all these places in the daylight. Why would you ever want to leave here?"

Michael turned and took her in his arms. "Because you grow up and want something of your own. I love coming home, though, and think I always will. Tomorrow we can fish in the pond."

"I don't fish," she said matter-of-factly.

"Have you ever tried it?" She could feel the heat emanating from his body as he brought her closer.

Her breath hitched. "No, when my parents would take us deep sea fishing Rand and I would prance around the boat in our bathing suits and sunbathe on the bow."

"Never just a pole and a pond?" he was bemused.

"Never, but I'll try tomorrow. You fill me full of new experiences." He cupped her butt, pressing himself hard against her.

"I know we're talking about getting married, but I have to ask you one question, and there isn't a right or wrong answer. I expect a truthful answer. Are you in love with me, or is it love me without the in part?"

She buried her face in his chest, putting her arms around his neck, "I wouldn't be marrying you unless I was in love with you. Michael, I love you, I'm in love with you, I like you, and I want to spend the rest of my life with you. I think all these things are necessary."

"You know how I feel, but for the record, I like you, I love you, and I'm in love with you. I've known this for a long time, but some things are out of reach, and I thought a relationship with you might be one of those things. I'm glad it's not. As God is my witness, I promise you I will be a good husband, I will love you, cherish you, defend and protect you, and be the best man I can be for you and your family. You are my everything." He gently kissed her and held her as though there was no tomorrow.

Once in the bedroom, he opened the windows and turned on the fan.

She took her clothes off and then put on a long nightgown.

He looked at her strangely, "I don't think I've ever seen you in a real nightgown. It's usually one of my shirts." He stripped down bare, almost defiant for her touch.

"I wanted to be properly attired in your parents' home." Stepping toward him in a sultry sashay. "Now, after hearing about the early wake-up call, it's for damn sure." She was most emphatic.

With a touch of laughter, he said, "I can't wait to see his reaction. This is gonna be good."

She climbed into bed, and he slid in next to her. He kissed her softly, and unlike most of their interludes, they truly made love, slow, gentle with a melodic feel. "I love you, Michael."

In a soft, whispering voice, he replied, "I love you." She peacefully slept in his arms.

The blissful sleep came to a crashing end when there was a massive thud on the bed. The room was still dark, and all Rainie could see was the silhouette of a person. She whispered, "Hello, John."

The scrambling began, "Holy shit. Wow, I'm sorry. Mikey, why didn't you put a fuckin' note on the door? I guess I've made a great first impression. Who are you?"

"I'm not some girl looking for a threesome." Michael burst into hysteria. She laughed, "Sorry, I had to say it. Hi John, I'm Rainie."

He jumped up and turned on the light. "You exist. Sorry to turn on the light, but I had to take a good look. I always thought you were his imaginary friend to hide his real sexual preference." He looked at Michael, who was still laughing at the situation. "You should have left a fuckin' note. I would've respected your privacy."

"Really?" Michael said, amused, "No, it would've been more of a reason for you to come barreling in. One way or another, you were going to end up in my bed. I told Rainie, she was prepared as anyone could possibly be when woken by a two-hundred-pound man jumping in the bed."

"Am I that much of an asshole?" He sat on the corner of the bed.

"Yes, John, you are, but I'd be disappointed if you didn't harass me and now Rainie."

"I guess I'll see you downstairs. Breakfast is on the stove. I can't believe you told her the hayloft story." He turned his hands up with a what-gives kind of look.

"There isn't much I haven't told her. Besides, you're going to have to arrange to be in town probably mid-December if you're going to be my best man."

"You dirty dog. What did you do to make this lovely lady agree to marry you?" he looked at Rainie. "It better have been good, or I'd reconsider if I were you."

He jumped off the bed and kissed the top of her head. "Congratulations, and by the way, Mikey, she's a lot better looking than you described." They could hear him trotting down the stairs.

"You nailed it, Michael. Y'all both look like your dad, but you can tell John has worked in all kinds of weather. He's all you said and more. I think it's hysterical." She stood and stretched.

"He's a jackass. He has been the same kind of fool since we were kids. I'm sure you'll have your fill of John and Mikey stories." He pulled on a pair of shorts and watched as she slipped into a whimsical romper.

"I can't believe he calls you Mikey. Does he have any idea you're the top plastic surgeon in New Orleans?" She looked at him with eyes wide open.

"I wouldn't go that far but thank you. John's going to call me Mikey until the day I die. Out of his mouth for me, it's a term of endearment. I don't know how I'd feel if he called me anything else. I'm sure you and Rand had some things special to you two and only y'all. Something no one else in the world would understand and might think odd."

"I wish you could have known her. I know she likes you and thought you were the guy for me. She was right, as was Mer and my parents." The smart ass voice of Rand said, "No kidding."

They went downstairs.

"Good morning, you two. Rainie, what can I get you?" *How Leslie of her.*

"If you point me in the general direction, I can fend for myself. You certainly don't have to go out of your way for me. Is there anything I can do to help you?"

"It's all pretty much done. I forgot how nice it is having another woman in the house, but please let me get you something to drink."

"Coffee is just fine, thank you." She surrendered.

His dad asked her if she had a good night's sleep and commented on how different it was from the city. *Awkward!* "Slept great, thank you."

"Did John wake y'all this morning?" He said with a chuckle.

"Yes sir," she said, "but I had fair warning and was ready."

"Dad," John was animated, telling a story in a way similar to Michael. "I go in like usual and dive into the bed then hear, 'Hi John,'" he put on a female voice. "Freaked the crap out of me, and all this pissant could do was laugh. I told him he should have put a note on the door."

Jack leaned back with a belly laugh. "Yeah, and then you would've gone in with a pitcher of water. He knows your game, John. He played, or should I say, she played it beautifully. I bet you were taken back a peg." Hands resting on his midsection looked more like baseball mitts. They were strong and big.

"Yes, sir, but I musta not pissed them off too much because they shared their great news. I guess I'm going to be home almost the whole month of December. Wedding and Christmas."

"Rainie, do you think you'll have the boys?" His mom asked but then looked at his dad. "Jack, do you realize we'll have six grandchildren? I hope they take to us," the sincerity in her voice was reassuring.

"Mom, Thomas, and Henry are the greatest kids. Y'all are going to be over the moon about them, and I think they'll get along fine with Wendy's kids, too." He took his orange juice and plate to the table.

His mom sat with her coffee and watched as her boys interacted. John talked about his last port, offered up the names of people who'd retired or died since they last saw each other. Michael spoke about his latest case of the kid from the fire. He added that his practice was getting to the point he might have to bring on a partner. She listened to the conversation, and when there was a natural break, she commented, "it's beautiful out here. Michael showed me the pool, and there are striking similarities to the Stella Street house. I understand his quick decision to buy. We walked over to the stables, I met Lightning and saw Mr. Landry's—"

His mom interjected. "Please, Rainie, call him Jack and call me Missy. We're laid back around here. The kids call him Poppa Jack or Popjack, and they call me GranMis or just plain Missy."

"He showed me the artwork," she looked at his dad, "I love your paintings. I'd like to show them at the hotel opening."

"Sure, if you want," he was easy-going, they all were.

"I forgot you have an interior decorating firm. Michael has told me a lot about you, and I had a hunch one day y'all would get together. I doubt John will ever settle down, the sea is his mistress, and he has women in every port, I suspect," walking behind John, she stopped and put her arms around his shoulders.

"Rainie, these boys were naughty when they were young. They'd take girls to 'see' the horses and get them in the hayloft." She glanced at Jack raising her brows. "They must've thought we were stupid. Finally, Jack told me to take anything that could make the hay more comfortable out of the stable. I'm sure they found other places. You'll see having two boys. When they hit puberty, it gets wild. Michael wasn't as rambunctious as this one, but he was still a handful, nonetheless."

After his mom and Rainie finished tidying up, Missy asked, "Would you like to see my rose garden?"

As they walked, they talked about the new house. Rainie said she had the perfect place in the yard for a rose garden, but she didn't know the first thing about planting or caring for one. His mom offered to help when she was ready.

"They're gorgeous. I love the garden." Rainie stopped and smelled each rose bush. "I told Michael I couldn't imagine growing up here. They must've had a blast."

Missy pulled a few browning leaves and old blooms like a mother would grooming her child. "They played like kids longer than a lot of their friends. John would get up with the sun, wake Michael, eat breakfast, and head outside playing until dark. Then I'd ring the bell."

"Did Michael tell you our family story?" Rainie nodded.

She whispered, "I had a strange upbringing. No hugs or loves, and then I got pregnant." She sat on a bench by the roses, Rainie sat next to her. "As you can imagine, life as I knew it was over. I was young, nineteen, with no college degree, and possessed zero skills, plus I had a baby on the way. Through God's grace, I managed. I found a job working in a maternity store of all things, but because it was a baby-friendly place, they were so good to me during the pregnancy, delivery, and after the baby was born. Then, the owner became ill and needed to close the store.

"That very day, I went to an employment agency and learned about a nanny position for a single dad of two boys. They told me he was rarely home, and he paid well. The fact I would stay there was an answer to a prayer.

"I think I fell in love with Jack right away. I didn't have a car, so he picked me up. He interviewed me in the car and was so lovely with Wendy. He said I had the job, that his boys could be a handful, but because the house was off the beaten track, he wanted me to see what I was agreeing to, and he understood if I didn't want the position. Driving here, I kept pinching myself. After looking around and seeing our quarters, I told him I wanted the job. Well, I guess you would say the rest is history." She had a dreamy, faraway look in her eyes.

"What a wonderful story. Michael brushed on a few things in telling me, but how awesome. Wendy sounds awesome. I can't wait to meet her." *God, I hope I don't sound like a suck-up.*

"She is. I hope I don't sound too braggadocious. All three did well in school. I was thrilled when Wendy wanted to go to LSU and then to law school, but when she moved to Washington, D.C., my heart broke. It wasn't long before John decided to follow in Jack's footsteps. That was hard. I figured he would do the two weeks on two weeks off like Jack's schedule, but he loved the sea. After he finished all his training and had his commission for the river, he went back to sea. He loved the travel, and he didn't have a special girl, he thought what the heck." Missy's eyes began to tear up. "Hard blow for me but being he and Michael are close in age, I knew I'd have Michael for at least four years.

"He always said he wanted to go to LSU. I figured he'd be around. I was happy he went to Med school; he was such a smart boy. When he joined the practice in Baton Rouge, I thought he'd settle here. I was sad when he moved to New Orleans, but kids have to create their own lives, don't they? I'd love for y'all to go up to Wendy's one weekend with us." She patted Rainie's hand.

Rainie was proud of Michael. "He's dedicated to his patients and his staff." She blushed, "He makes a lot of time for me, I have to admit. I'm sure I've thrown a monkey wrench into his lifestyle. Y'all come to the city often?" She watched Missy admiring her cool, calm, and collectiveness. Michael had acquired her mannerisms.

"We don't come as much as we used to. It seems Michael has been quite busy as of late," his mom smiled. "But we're due for a trip soon. The last two visits we had planned, he called and said he had to take a raincheck. Something had come up. The something was you, and I'm glad. He'd never canceled before, I asked him flat out, Rainie Todd?" Rainie could feel waves of emotion flooding her heart. There was no doubt he had genuinely loved her for a long time.

"Oh, Rainie, I knew he had been on several dates with you, but he told me not to expect anything that y'all were only friends. I told him there wasn't a better way to start a relationship. I knew his heart was happy, and he sounded like he was content, which made me happy." Her eyes filled with tears as she held Rainie's hand.

Rainie looked into Missy's eyes. "When is the next time you're supposed to come in because I can assure you, there'll be no rainchecks. I want you to meet my parents and my friend, Meredith James."

"That's a name I've heard. He has talked about her in reference to you. Y'all have been friends a long time, he tells me." Missy could not have been more accepting of her.

She nodded. "Yes, we have. She and I and my sister Rand were like the three musketeers. She has been with me through it all. If I had taken her advice in the first place, I wouldn't have married Tom, and I would've started dating Michael much earlier." "Don't forget, I told you, too!" Rand reminded.

"But remember, Rainie, you're who you are today because of all you've been through. The boys never asked me about Wendy's dad until they were maybe twelve or so. It was hard for me to tell them I had never been married, and I had been foolish. I also let them know I had no regrets because God gave me Wendy. I was the lady I was because of the hard lessons I had to learn, and they would become the men they were intended to be by the roads they chose." Rainie felt a magnetic draw to Missy. As close as she was with her mom and dad, there were many things she didn't feel like she could broach and thus never did. Was it because Missy had oopsed at nineteen as an unwed mother and had freely acknowledged her vulnerabilities?

"There you are," Michael lumbered up, his face was glowing with contentment. "I didn't know where y'all were but figured it wasn't too far. Shoulda known the rose garden." The sound of laughter echoed through the house as they walked in the kitchen door.

"Michael, next time your parents make plans to come to the city. I want to introduce them to my parents and Mer." Wagging her finger, "No more rainchecks."

"Sure thing, Boss." he smiled.

"Honey, Rainie, and I had a lovely chat in the garden. I told her I'd come help y'all set up a rose garden at your new place, by the way, you keeping your place in the Quarter?" they headed toward the table in the Hearth where Jack and John were jawing.

"Yes, indeed. It'll be great for all the festivals or romantic nights away without having to go away. I love my place." Just the mention of his place in the Quarter brought up instant thoughts of passion, making her breath catch in her throat and her temperature rise.

Rainie took a seat at the table and began speaking to Jack and John while Michael visited with his mom. "Rainie-girl," Jack said. "There's a lot to see around here. You get Mike to show you the whole damn place."

"I think that's the plan, as well as some pole fishing and horseback riding. He thinks he'll make a country girl outta me. Truthfully, I'm not so sure how I'll fair." She chuckled.

"Are you a horse lover?" his dad asked before taking a swig of coffee.

"A lover of your paintings of horses, but I don't ride. As far as riding, my boys are taking riding lessons this summer, but I'm a little afraid of horses. I used to ride as a child, but it's been a while. I've never ridden outside of a fence, like never on a levee, but I think there's a new adventure awaiting me." She said assuredly, punctuated with a giggle.

"We'll put you on a kid horse. We have two for kids, and they're both mellow. You'll feel comfortable. If not, get on the back of Lightning with Mike and hold on." His deep voice bellowed when he said hold on.

"So I heard," she nodded. "Not so sure how I feel about all that." She raised her eyebrows.

Michael came back into the room, "I wouldn't let her go full speed with you holding on. Besides, she's getting a little old for racing now. You're going to have to trust me, but I think you will do fine on Cisco or Dyna. If the little ones can control them, I'm sure you can." He put his hands on her shoulders, rubbing his thumbs into her traps. She could've had him massage her shoulders all day but knew their adventures awaited.

He leaned over, looking at her upside down. "I told you I was going to teach you how to fish, and there's no time like the present. C'mon you, let's get out there." They went through the mudroom. While he was grabbing the fishing stuff, he told her to pick a spot on the pond.

She took in the sights and picked a place. She looked at her reflection, and clear as day; she saw Rand standing next to her. She put her hand out and watched as Rand held it. Rainie felt a comforting warmth at her core, looking at the reflection. She didn't hear Michael come up, but he looked over her shoulder and saw the reflection. "That's extraordinary." His voice was satin-smooth and just barely a whisper. In a ripple, Rand was gone.

"Yeah, I'm surprised she let you see." He handed her a rod making sure to explain avoiding the hook, then pulled out a couple of lures. He stood behind her, both of them holding the rod. "Relax, I'm going to do the work. You can get the feel of casting." His body felt massive as he delicately drew the pole back, his hands guiding hers.

After three casts, she said she could do it on her own. "Go for it but don't be surprised if the line tangles. Be careful of the hook. Michael queued up his rod, ready to hand over to her, and as predicted, the line got caught up.

"Here, take mine, and I'll get this one ready again," she was getting ready to cast, "Did you check the hook and the lure?"

"Not yet, but I will." She examined the line, and dangling from the hook was a ring, "Oh my God, Michael." A lump developed in her throat, and her heart went into overdrive. It was a large sapphire with a carat diamond to each side set in platinum.

He dropped to his knee, "Will you marry me?" Her eyes filled with tears.

"Yes, I will marry you," she said in a choked whisper. Michael slid the ring on her finger. The tears trickled down her cheeks as her smile shone like the sun. "It's gorgeous."

" It was my Grandmother's engagement ring. I'm glad you hadn't cast your line, but I'm even happier I was able to surprise you."

Even though his family had been spying on the proposal, they returned to their seats as though nothing had happened.

Rainie and Michael walked back inside. "It's official now. She said yes," she held out her hand to show the ring.

"It fits you perfectly," Missy hugged her.

John got up. "Well done, beautifully executed." He hugged Michael and looked at Rainie, "were you crazy enough to say yes to this fool?"

"Are you kidding me y'all were watching?" Michael looked at each of them.

"Sweetheart, are you surprised? You shouldn't be." She took Rainie's hand, "it looks beautiful on you."

"Time to call Wendy," he pulled out his phone and paused as the call went through. Wendy picked up right away with curiosity. Michael cut to the chase, "Yes, everything's fine. She said yes."

All could hear Wendy's shrieks of joy and incessant questions. Wendy was beside herself with happiness for Michael. "No set date yet, Wen, but we're thinking mid-December. Yes, we know it's close to Christmas." Another pause, they could hear her talking a mile a minute. "Hold on."

He passed the phone to Rainie, who was still floating from the excitement of it all. She looked at Michael with apprehension. After a half-hour of girly chat, she handed the phone to his mom.

"It certainly is great news." The conversation carried on, and then Michael passed the phone to his father.

"You wanted to see everything?" Michael asked. "Now would be the best time while they're on the phone. They'll be on for at least another hour." He brought her first to the stable to see the horses.

He opened a door, "This is the tackle closet." It was more like a small room. There were saddles and bridles hung on the wall. It had an earthy smell combined with the scent of heavy leather. He started to unzip his shorts. Rainie's eyebrows went up. "Then maybe one of the other sneaky places unless you want to get in with one of the horses, but that can be dicey," he sarcastically advised.

"No, here is fine. I guess I'll be one of many in the tackle closet." She tickled him in the ribs.

"Ouch! Is there somewhere you'd prefer?" His eyes glittered with amusement.

"No. What if someone comes in?" she seemed apprehensive.

"Trust me, please. They'll be on the phone for at least an hour." She undid her shorts and stepped out of them. He backed her against the wall between two saddles. "You should be able to reach the dowels now lift." He helped her pull up "ease down." He had her supported, but the force of gravity enhanced the penetration. He stared into her eyes and watched intently. Whatever he was doing added to the pleasure. Things got faster. She saw his pupils react. *Amazing!* She thought.

He bit into his bottom lip as his thrusts quickened with intensity. She knew the pulsing was imminent as his jaw jutted forward, and his heavy breathing caused his chest to swell. Love radiated from him. He gently let her down. Her legs felt weak as she put her shorts back on.

"I didn't want you to feel excluded, and by the time this weekend is over, we'll have discovered some of the other secret places," he gave a sinister laugh.

They exited the closet, but as they did, she grabbed a riding crop and smacked him on the butt, "you better watch it, buster, or you'll get what's coming to you." She widened her eyes and feigned a gasp, "look how you've made me misbehave." She said with a throaty laugh.

"You're so good when you're bad, or is it the other way around? Bad when you're good? Either way, you got the stuff it takes, lady," he kissed her deeply.

It seemed like they walked endlessly. There was a path leading to three cottages in the back. They were small but precious and inviting. "These are adorable. I guess y'all did have lots of naughty nooks," she peered through one of the windows. I love it."

"This is where the help who worked the plantation lived. While cabins are nice now, they haven't always been."

"So, how long has your dad lived here?" She strolled alongside him.

"His entire life, as did my grandad. If you were to keep on going, there's a road to a guest house. It's a new addition to the property. In saying new, they built it about forty years ago.

"I want to explore," she exhibited excitement like a child.

"C'mon then. Your wish is my command."

FOR ONCE IN MY LIFE

Later in the afternoon, as the sun was a little lower in the sky, Michael suggested they go for a horseback ride. "You can ride on the back with me," he offered.

"I'll ride on my own, thank you." She came back with a feisty, bossy tone.

John came along, got Spot, the successor to Patches, geared up while Michael bridled Cisco for Rainie. He opened Lightning's stall. The horse came behind Michael and nudged him, "okay, girl, give me a minute," he stroked the side of her head.

They could hear Jack walking around upstairs. He yelled up to him, "Dad, we're heading out. Not gonna be too long." Warning Rainie he said, "We're not going to ride too long; riding is more taxing than you'd think." The three started toward the levee down the oak-lined driveway. "Rainie, you okay? Remember nothing to be afraid of. Cisco is the horse I'd probably put Henry on." He doted.

"I'm not afraid, Michael, but no racing off or racing period." Riding on the levee with the breeze on her face gave her such a sense of freedom and independence. "I never understood the need for trail rides or riding on the levee, but I totally get it now. It's completely different than riding around in a circle over and over." She had a grin like finding the prize at the bottom of a Cracker Jacks box.

"Glad you like it, but we're only going to ride for another

twenty minutes. I don't want you to be too sore." He had a caring but controlling tone.

"Mikey, I really got to hear that? Why don't you say, 'don't want you too sore so I can fuck you later?'"

Michael looked at him, "You've got to be kidding me, John. I warned you, Rainie, he was crude, rude, and socially unacceptable."

She looked at John as he clucked to his horse and passed her, "Don't mind him, John, it's not like he hasn't been whispering that in my ear all day long. What can one expect?" John laughed and took off.

"Don't panic. We'll stay at our leisurely pace." John stopped, and they eventually caught up to him. The banter continued throughout the ride, even down the driveway. They cooled the horses, brushed them, and put them up. Michael handed her an apple to give Cisco.

Missy was in the Hearth reading when they came in. She put a finger up, saying to wait a second, and then marked her place and shut the book.

"Dinner tonight?" Her face was a-glow as she smiled at Rainie.

"Let's stay in, Mom. We're gonna take a walk to the field." They headed back outside.

Walking along, they spotted his dad. "Mom's getting dinner together, FYI. We're going to walk out on the fields for a minute and meet back at the house."

"Michael, did you bring girls in the fields?" She held his hand as they walked.

"No, not the fields, too many slithering things, besides huge deadly machinery. They could be on you before you knew it." With every other step, he turned his head toward her, gleaming with contentment.

"What's next on our agenda? We've walked, rode, fished, and—"

"I imagine we'll have dinner, maybe take a moonlit walk on the levee. Tomorrow there's church, then a long Sunday lunch with a two-hour goodbye. I told you my mom has a hard time with goodbyes. John will leave early Monday morning. At least, we aren't the last of the good-byes." Silence crept in as they basked in their peaceful feelings.

A warm surge rolled inside her body, remembering all their adventures from the weekend. She stopped and pulled him close. "I can't wait to bring the boys here. God, my parents would love it, too, but who wouldn't? Michael, there's so much we need to do, like plan a visit to the city with your parents. Oh, and you mentioned going to see Wendy in D.C."

He kissed her forehead and held her tight. "Now my head is swimming, Rainie. Before you, I don't think I had a life. Pretty dang sad. I never had to think about what I was going to do. I worked, worked out, talked to my family on the phone, played with the dogs, or slept. Making plans to go and do is a new thing for me. I'm going to defer to you as the schedule keeper if that's alright." He tenderly kissed her. "You're gonna be my missus. How awesome is that?"

She tapped his nose. "It's fun to plan, something to look forward to. Anticipation counts for a big part of the thrill. You, of all people, should know that, Doctor Feelgood." She leaned in for another kiss.

They walked to the house from the back. She looked at the strange structure on the rear of the house. "I don't get the design." He could see her searching with her eyes.

"Right," He nodded. "I haven't given you a tour of the house." They walked into the house. "You've seen part of downstairs and my, I mean, our room."

He brought her through the formal lounge, the library, and the dining hall, which led to a butler's prep area, the kitchen, then the Hearth, and onto another lounge.

They went up the stairs. Doors were at each end of the hall, both leading to outside porches. One overlooked the oak-lined driveway and levee beyond, and then the other viewed fields from the back. Off the back porch on each of the corners were covered walkways leading to separate quarters.

He explained. "Way back in the day, if a gentleman caller came to court one of the single young women, they were not allowed to sleep in the house. There were separate quarters for them to stay the night.

"My great grandfather had two of these. Most houses only had one. That one," he pointed to the right, "was over the kitchen or area housing for cooking. Because of the risk of fire, the kitchen wasn't attached to the house. The other one is over an old form of storage pantry.

"Remember when I told you not to worry about waking my parents up? It's because their bedroom is in one of the old suitor's quarters. It's more like a suite with a sitting area and a large bath area, as well as the bedroom.

"The other one is what they call a kid's bunk room or Neverland. Throughout the years, they have taken in abandoned, abused, neglected, and runaway boys. It's a cool area. The boy has his own space, there's everything they need, and it's not attached to the house. Until they establish trust, the house is locked at night, but there's a full fridge, bathroom, television, and games for them. They also have an intercom to my parents and the house. Rainie peered in the door.

"If they want to leave and run away in the middle of the night, they can. They're not locked in or anything."

They walked back inside. "This is John's room, then Dad's old bedroom, now his private office, and you know this one well. Across the hall is Wendy's room, then a girl's guest room, and lastly a boy's guest room – grandkid and future grandkid rooms."

They heard the ringing of the bell. "Good Lord, I bet you can hear the bell for a mile," she jumped. "Outstanding."

"Yep, and it means business." He grinned at her amazement.

They could hear doors opening and closing, the shuffling of feet and water running in the mudroom as Jack and John washed up from outside.

When they entered the kitchen, his mom directed them to the Hearth. Each person stood behind a chair at the table. Jack was at one end and Missy to his right. John was standing next to her, and Michael took his place across from John, putting Rainie on the left side of his Dad. Everyone remained standing until his Mom sat. His dad nodded at Rainie, she sat, and then the men sat.

The conversation began with Missy asking Rainie about her thoughts regarding her time there. Had she enjoyed herself?

Rainie's eyes opened wide like saucers. Her excitement was contagious. "There are no words to describe my thoughts. Y'all are gonna think I'm crazy, but I feel as though I've been a part of this forever."

"Not strange at all, dear, but we had the advantage of having heard of you for all these years." Missy stretched her hand across the table toward Rainie. "When someone means a lot to one of your kids, they mean a lot to you, right? Michael loved you. Hence we loved the idea of you before we even met you."

Michael cocked his head to one side. "Rainie, it was not quite as intense as she makes it sound."

"The hell it wasn't, Mikey," John winked at Rainie, "I'm kidding, but we all knew the score, although I deep down thought you were a made-up figment of his desperate imagination."

"Thanks, John. I can't wait until you bring someone around."

Dinner conversation was light, filled with laughter and numerous John and Mikey stories.

"Rainie, ready for a moonlit walk?" On the way out of the door, he grabbed a blanket. His mom called out to Rainie to enjoy the view.

While it was still and void of city sounds, it was noisy as the night before with the sound of crickets and screaming frogs. They were almost deafening when they'd sing. The driveway seemed longer by foot than on the backs of horses. It was all part of the wonderland adventure.

"You were right about John. I think he's more sensitive than he lets on. He comes across gruff, but he's a big teddy bear." She held tightly to his arm.

"Maybe a teddy bear if you're not his younger brother," he coughed up a laugh.

"Was he good to you when you were kids, or was he more like Thomas is with Henry? I get upset because Thomas can bully Henry easily. He's sensitive. Were you more like Henry?"

"You know, it's a pretty good comparison, and that's why I try hard to distract Thomas from being a bully big brother. John has felt a lot of guilt over the years for being such a jerk, and I don't want Thomas to go through the shame. John and I have always been close, but there were times where he was hard on me, harder than he needed to be, but I learned to take care of myself.

"Believe it or not, push came to shove – I guess, when we were around sixteen and seventeen. I beat the pulp out of him. I had my fill. I was much easier-going and wouldn't respond to his smart-ass remarks, but one day he pushed it too far.

"Dad was in town and heard the clamoring and my mom scream, and before I knew it, he was on the two of us like white on rice. He pulled me off him and told John he'd been asking for it for a long time, but then turned to me and said, 'brothers were to love one another, and he expected it would be the last of the fights. We were brothers and better act like it, or we'd deal with him.' The thought of dealing with Dad still makes me shudder. He's powerful as an ox and grew up when the river was a lot tougher than it is now." He put his head back and looked up. *Stars or God?* She mentally debated.

"Y'all play and horse around a lot. I can see where it might lead to heightening emotion and turn quickly especially being guys."

"Not in this house, ever again. We get physical, and it may look menacing, but it's all controlled. We're both masters of emotional control, for the most part. It's a huge thing with Mom. She tolerated the language, to a point, because we were boys, which Wendy found most disturbing.

"Lord help either of us if we laid a hand on Wendy," he started to laugh, "She had a friend John thought was hot. In his inappropriate way made mention she needed to hook them up. Wendy said something like 'gross' or 'no way' and threw a pillow at him.

"He, in turn, threw the pillow back, and out of nowhere came the body block from Dad, and John went flying. Wendy started to cry, John knocked silly, and I was sitting with my mouth agape making mental notes.

Taking on his dad's persona, "Dad says, 'Boy, not even a pillow thrown in her direction.' John yes sir'd him, and Wendy felt so bad she arranged a date for him with the girl. I think she was the only girl John didn't try to snake.

"We had fun growing up, lots of fun, Rainie. He has always been and always will be my best friend. He's a big jokester because he's sensitive."

They made it to the levee, where he spread the blanket out. He laid down, and she sat next to him. He told her to lay back and look at the stars. *He must have been contemplating the stars.* The stars' brilliance was picture book, and he regaled her with his knowledge of the constellations.

"Michael, you know a lot about a lot. It's almost like science class when I'm with you."

"Shit. Sounds horrible. Am I that boring?" he asked with concern.

"No, you're that amazing," she tickled his ribs.

"I don't think you want to go there," he warned.

"Or what?" She challenged.

He had her flat on her back, arms pinned with one hand and legs locked down, and started tickling her with his free hand.

"What do we have here?" He slipped his hand inside her shirt, "so soft, so perfect," he leaned in and put his nose up against her breast. "I love the way you smell."

Like a little girl, she giggled, "Michael, you're cheating."

"Cheating, no ma'am, you started this and challenged me. I warned you." He lifted her shirt and raced his tongue along her stomach. Her giggles were turning into broad belly laughs. "Tell me, where are you feeling my tongue tickle? If you say your stomach, I'm gonna say you're lyin' like a rug. Your body betrays you. I know how much you like it when I," he traced her navel.

"Oh, dear God, you cheat, you cheat." She squirmed even more. "Let go of my hands. At least let me fight back."

"Just say, I let them go. What are you going to do?" Michael let her hands go. She pushed him on his back and tried to hold his arms with one hand. He burst out laughing, "You're hilarious. How are you going to punish me?" he was amused.

"Maybe not here, but I will attack when you're not looking." She squinted her eyes.

He threw his arms out to his side and spread his legs, "I surrender to your wiles."

"Well then, you opened yourself up. You better not complain, mister," she popped his belt open and unzipped his jeans. "Commando? You're too easy, doc." She pulled his pants as wide as they would open.

She looked at him as she grabbed his rock-hard soldier. He gasped. She began working it with a deliberate rhythm inviting the desired outcome. "Tell me what you want. Want it faster, slower, tighter, softer, or deep down my throat?" She could feel his butt tighten, which lifted his hips. She stroked with momentum; she loved the control. His delight was at her mercy.

She worked him harder and faster, gripping him and releasing in a throbbing motion – emulating the throb she wanted him to feel. It was near. Almost. Almost. And then she roughly took him in her mouth and sucked with a pulse, as his quickened.

"Don't stop." He breathed between his clenched teeth. She felt his pelvis tip and then the jolts of release. "Oh, fuck." She continued to try to touch him. He wriggled away, catching his breath. "I give. You win. That was beyond amazing."

"I take it this is the lover's lane of East Bumfuck?"

"For many, but I had too many more private spots. I didn't need to expose myself to the chance of being caught by levee patrol."

"What? Levee patrol?" her eyes widened.

"They pass up and down the levee to make sure teenagers aren't doing the nasty up here."

"You could have told me." He fastened back up, and they laid back in silence, looking up at the stars.

"Are you kidding me? I wasn't stopping you; they would've had to sit and watch. When it's that good, you just don't stop."

About ten minutes passed, and along came the ATV. "Good evening, folks."

"Yes, sir, it's a beautiful night for stargazing," Michael was calm and collected.

"Sure is. Y'all have a good night." The ATV pulled away.

"Michael, ten minutes earlier, could have been very embarrassing."

"So far, I'm the only Landry to escape getting caught with his pants down up here," he laughed.

"John got caught?" She questioned, turning on her side.

"Yeah, John did, but he didn't get in trouble because my dad said it was a rite of passage."

"Your dad must've gotten caught," she laughed loudly. "That's hysterical. He told y'all he got caught?"

"He didn't need to; it was all over his expression. We never spoke about it again."

"Let's get back to the house. I have to pee." She stood and started grabbing the blanket.

"Just cop a squat."

"I don't think so. Let's get back to the house, please." She insisted.

They walked back to the house. "I know I've told you this before, but you're amazing. The intensity of the, um, experience is far beyond anything I've ever felt before. Hubba hubba, thank you. It makes me feel guilty," he confessed.

She smiled, "how so? It empowers me and is invigorating. I climax watching and feeling you. It's a win, win and I feel like the true winner." They were all over each other, playing and laughing.

"Feel free to challenge me anytime at all. You do that, and you'll win hands down every time. You, my dear, are equally as much a control freak as I am. You wanted to control my orgasm, yes?" Michael grabbed her by the waist.

She felt guilty and embarrassed, "I guess."

He took her face in his hands, looking deep into her eyes. "Now, you know how I feel. I love giving you pleasure. Not saying you can't pleasure yourself, but when I bring it to you, it explodes inside of me. It's the biggest thrill there is. It's almost spiritual."

She started fidgeting. "I get it, Michael. I would never have before, but after being with you, I get it. The first night on my sofa when you ran your fingers up my leg, I was like 'holy shit'! You hadn't even touched me, and there I was having an orgasm. I told Mer. It was the most unbelievable thing I'd experienced, but I gotta pee."

He stopped. "You told Meredith? How much have you told her?" He took a step back away from her in disbelief.

"About you, sexually? She's known about every sexual encounter I've had my whole life. She knows what I like, what I hate, what I think is boring, and now she knows I know what real passion is about. She was thrilled for me and said it was about time I had a real lover. Have you told anyone about us?"

"No, I don't have anyone to tell, and I wouldn't even if I did."

"You wouldn't tell John?" she seemed perplexed.

"No. He'd be on your bones like there's no tomorrow. The kind of thrill you bring doesn't happen. It just doesn't."

"It's because you love me, crazy man." She playfully slapped his arm.

"No, it's because you're in touch sensually. You can read my passion levels like no one else." He argued.

"It's because I love you, Michael." She touched his face. "I gotta go!"

"Let me get this? You wouldn't care if I told John about the levee tonight?"

"I wouldn't want him to say anything to me. Mer would never, ever say word one to you. Oh, but Mer doesn't know anything about Pandora. I felt like it was your personal business, and it would be betrayal if I said something."

"Well, I'm glad you didn't. It is personal. What like the other isn't?"

"Are you upset with me?" she seemed sad.

"No, I'm surprised," he allayed her worries.

"I think girls talk more than guys."

He was dead serious, "guys lie and makeup conquests, girls, tell the truth and are way more detailed."

"Michael, forget I ever told you. I promise never to tell her anything again."

"I'm not going to censor you. I won't think about it. Why do you think John was so surprised I told you about the hayloft girl? We don't talk about real stuff."

"Okay so, if I told him I gave you a blow job up on the levee?"

"I would probably keel over, as would he." He laughed.

"What if I told him you told me to grab the dowels, and you lowered me onto your"

"Sweet Rainie, I know what you're doing now. You want to be punished later. I'm going to get the riding crop while you pee and then watch out. Too bad I don't have any of the other pleasure toys. Girl, we'll be going from midnight to sunrise."

"Threats. Idle threats, Michael."

"You kill me. Look what you do." he pointed to his crotch.

She ran into the kitchen and up the stairs. She stripped her clothes off, peed, and jumped in the shower. She had to cool off. There was no way she was going into this, already hot and bothered.

She thought of the house, horseback riding, anything to keep her mind off the things she knew he could do to her and was probably planning on doing. She heard the door open, close, and lock. Naked, he entered the bathroom. "You look like a deer in the headlights. Are you all right?"

"Yeah, I'm fine." She lied.

"You look freaked. I'll make it easy for you, and you can take control. Not saying you had any mercy for me on the levee, may I add. But I don't want to see you nervous, never. We can play or shower and go to bed. You, Rainie, are the boss. Tell me what you want me to do." He stood under the spray, pulling her close.

She looked down. "I can't tell you. You always know what to do. I'm sure whatever is fine. If not, I'll speak up, I promise."

He tipped her head up, and with an ear to ear grin, he said. "I know you don't like talking dirty. I won't do that. What about if I say something and you fill in the blank?"

"What?" she asked.

"Like I say kiss my and you say mouth or breast or..."

"I get the picture" Her eyes twinkled. "How about your wish is my command game?"

"Works too." He raised an eyebrow with a smirk.

"I wish you would take me how you want me," she commanded him.

"Not exactly how it goes, but –"He turned her face against the wall and spread her legs. The rhythm began. One hand on her shoulder and one on her hip, he raised his leg to the seat in the shower, "lean back," he ran the hand on her shoulder down to her breast and the hand on her hip to between her legs. He kept the motion going for a few minutes.

He turned off the water and toweled her. He picked her up and carried her to the bed.

He took everything slow and purposeful, and the touching and foreplay felt like it went on for hours she became overstimulated. He saw her anticipation and need for completion. He obliged. She wrapped her legs tightly around him until she had no more to release and crumbled on her side in peace, "you will sleep well, I promise." He gently kissed her shoulder, "I love you."

The next morning he woke up spry. Everyone was dressed and down for a quick breakfast before church. Her hair was a bit wilder than usual, so up it went. "How'd you two sleep?" his dad inquired.

"Awesome." Michael was chipper.

"Sleeping out here is lovely," she felt like she had to say something.

John whispered to Michael, "you didn't get very much sleep, old man. You've gotten a lot louder as you've aged," he grinned.

They all talked about what a great weekend it had been. Rainie could see his mom starting to get sad looking at her boys. Missy's love flowed freely. "I'm gonna miss you when you go."

"Mom, we're not leaving for a few hours. Let's have a good time and enjoy. Besides, Rainie tells me y'all will be coming to the city in the next couple of weeks, and then we're going to meet in D.C."

"Yes. True." She didn't seem quite as sad.

Rainie asked John when he would be back in. "Still going long runs, but gonna go back to two on two off. The travel has been great, but Mikey here can't be the only one growing up. See Rainie Todd, you have been a good influence, not only on my brother but on me as well." He put his arm around her.

They left for church. John, Michael, and Rainie rode together, "Mikey, you still going to church all the time?"

"Yes. You?"

"No, only when I'm in town to make Mom happy." He glanced in Rainie's direction, "you go?"

"Yes, but it hasn't been until lately that I've gotten anything out of it. I went because I was supposed to and to make my parents happy. It's different now. Michael has been a real spiritual influence."

"I believe it. I bet Mikey's been a big influence in a lot of ways," he chuckled. "The Landry boys got a bad rep early on, Rainie. It wasn't our fault, we had fun, and there were lots of places to have fun at home. I imagine you've seen a few of them on this visit." *His voice sounds like Michael.*

"Hey, bro, heading where you aren't welcome, back off." He looked at him through his rearview mirror.

"Right you are, no insult meant. Good call, Mikey."

"Guys, no insult taken. John, I want you to be comfortable being you."

"Mikey's right. I need to mind better manners, we aren't twenty anymore, and if I want you to find a good lady for me, I better start acting like a good man, right?" She shook her head in response.

Their country church was different than any church she'd experienced. It was a lot less formal. After church, they went to eat at a small restaurant off River Road. The atmosphere was warm and welcoming, big hellos from the spunky server and cashier who looked to be related. The cashier shouted back to the kitchen announcing the Landry's arrival.

Dinner was relaxed, enjoyable, and delicious. His parents firmed up the plans about the upcoming trip to NOLA and tossed around dates for D.C.

"The deciding factor for me, Missy, will be what's going on with the business and what camps and plans we have for the boys, but now you have my number, and I have yours, we can nail it down."

Missy's eyes had already started to tear up, and the sadness on her was evident. As Michael had warned, the parting following dinner was hard.

After several hugs and kisses, Rainie and Michael got in the car and waved goodbye. They pulled out of the driveway and onto River Road. As they went over the Mississippi River, she looked down at the big ships and could only imagine people like Jack and John were navigating the giant vessels through the waters. "I'm glad you didn't choose the river life because I would have never met you."

"I want to hear what you thought of everything and everyone." He briefly looked over at her.

"They're lovely, and I completely understand you now. Your family genuinely cares about people. It's beautiful. At first, I have to admit I was blown away by the place. Please don't get me wrong when I say this.

"I know as a Plastic Surgeon; you make a good living. My dad makes a good living, and I grew up with many well-heeled people. But when I saw the scale on which your parents live, at first, I was like holy shit, but then as I got to know them, I understood a bit more. I saw they took their blessings and blessed others, and it's incredible I didn't leave there thinking, wow, those are some rich people. I left there, feeling those are the most amazing people I have ever met. I know why you are you and why you're so kind and caring, and I understand why you love as you do. It's in your blood.

"Your mom knew, at first sight, she was in love with your dad but never thought he'd marry her. He thought she was the most beautiful thing he'd ever seen with more love than anyone else in the world. Do you realize he trusted her with you two while he was away? He didn't know her from Adam, and yet he knew.

"I hope John can find someone to share all his love with. He's awesome, and if he wants to know if we made love all night long, I don't care because he'd think it was great we were so into each other. There isn't a malicious bone in his body like there isn't one in yours.

"Thank you for loving me and waiting for me, Michael. I love you, and I love your family. By the way, did you get any pictures? Like a fool, I didn't."

He held his eyes to the road. "Mom got plenty. She got a beautiful one of us out on the front porch when we were doing the upstairs tour." She held his hand, petting each finger, and kissing his fingertips.

With the look of a kid getting caught with their hand in the cookie jar, she blushed and said, "I didn't think she knew I was snooping, and I sure as shit didn't see her take any pictures."

"She can be stealthy. Could you feel her happiness in meeting you? She loves you. Meeting you sealed the deal." She was smiling to the point her cheeks were hurting.

LIKE A ROLLING STONE

Eventually, they pulled onto Northline, "When do I get to sleep with you again?"

He passed over the question and went straight to the future excitement. "Let's call and see if the agent knows anything about the swap. The house will be in both of our names no matter what you or I put down, okay?" he wanted to make sure she understood.

"Maybe." She looked into his eyes.

"No maybe. It's a wedding present if we want it," Michael quietly said.

"From who?"

"My family."

"Let's see about the swap. If the sellers go for it, we'll talk about any difference we need to make up. Besides, Tom has his percentage," she reminded him.

"He's already been paid off and signed the house into your name. Your dad told me before we left."

"Ugh. Does anyone consult me on these things?" She clasped her hands tightly with her eyes closed. "Get over it, Rainie," said by a pissed Rand.

"I think a thank you would be more appropriate." He looked at her with a frown.

"The house is outright mine?" she stopped, "and the bank's, but not Tom?" Rand continued to scold, "that's right; don't be a dumbass, Rainie."

"Yes. I was supposed to tell you on the way to Baton Rouge, but I didn't want to start our weekend with you in a pissy." *Pissy, me in a pissy!*

Out came her thoughts. "Have me in a pissy?" She cocked her head. Bubbles were forming in her gut, coming up the back of her throat as her body tensed. Rand screamed in Rainie's thought, "Oh, my God, Rainie, stop it! Yes, you in a pissy, he's right!" The voice echoed in her mind, "he's got you pegged." She thought, *not now, Rand. This is my stuff.*

They opened the doors. The boys came running out, "Mommy, Doctor Mike!" Their little faces gleamed with excitement and tight hugs and kisses.

"I missed you, my babies." Thoughts about the conversation about the house kept circling through her mind. Maybe this wasn't for her after all. She loved their relationship, but she felt steam-rolled, and that wasn't okay.

They walked inside and heard about the weekend with Tom, not too bad, but not too good, either. The boys and her parents were most curious about her weekend. She wasn't sure what to say. She laid down broad strokes.

"Doctor Mike has very nice parents and a very nice big brother. He, his brother, and his sister grew up on a plantation." She saw her mom's eyebrows raise. "They want all of us to stay for a weekend. It's a fun story.

"There's a pond to fish in and horses to ride, and they have a horse named Cisco for you to ride, Henry, and one named Dyna, for you to ride, Thomas. I rode Cisco on the levee."

"But Mommy," Henry worried, "you don't know how to ride."

"She did great, Henry. Y'all would have been proud." Michael chimed in.

"Look what I caught when I fished in the pond," she showed them the ring.

"Wow," escaped from both boys.

"No, actually Michael gave it to me and asked me if we would marry him."

"You said yes, right, Mom?" Thomas' expression was with almost blinding joy. His smile reached from ear to ear.

"I wanted to check with you guys first." She kept thinking. *Maybe this is a mistake. Keeping things from each other, what?*

Henry was spinning around excitedly, "are you kidding me, Mommy?" he looked at Mike.

"When do we get to go to your parents' house? I want to fish and ride horses."

They talked for a while. Her mom more than approved of the ring, and her dad was pleased that she was marrying him. Everyone buzzed around Rainie and Michael as her anxiety went through the roof, but Michael was as giddy and wound up as the boys.

"December sound okay to y'all?" Michael asked.

"We'll be your boys?" Thomas asked.

"Thomas, you'll always be your dad and mom's boys, but if they would, I'd love to share you with them. You'll be two lucky dudes, two moms and two dads, right?" He looked lovingly at the boys.

"Doctor Mike, it's more like one mom and two dads. Diane doesn't want to be our mom. She told us she'd never be our mom and, you know what, it's fine with me cuz I don't want her." Thomas folded his arms with intention.

"Baby, I can't imagine she or anyone saying they didn't want to be your parent, or is that what you think? Did she say those exact words?" Rainie's asked with knitted brows.

"Yep," Henry exclaimed, "it's what she said, and Dad said she was right. She would never be our mom."

Michael's face had a perplexed expression. It was apparent he couldn't comprehend such callous behavior. "Guys, one thing for sure is my parents can't wait to meet y'all and your Mimi, Poppy, and Allie, too." He met their little faces with a loving smile.

"Momma, any word from the real estate agent?" Rainie asked.

"Yes, sweetie, she said she tried to call you."

"Odd I didn't get a call," she looked at Michael, "you?" *Something else you didn't tell me?*

"No. I wonder if the reception wasn't good up there. I'm going to have to let Mom and Dad know they need a booster. Sorry." She watched him skeptically.

"What did she say? Well? Boys, can you go upstairs for a bit, please." Rainie was all ears for the details but still bothered by the withholding of information.

"Suga," her dad spoke, "they want your house and two hundred thousand cash. She's coming by later tonight with the contracts for Nashville and both of you for Stella. I'm sure you and Mike hashed it all out, and I think it's a good idea for both of y'all. I was against it at first, nothing personal, Mike, but after our talk, I felt much better about it." Her dad was always above board, leaving nothing to innuendo.

What the fuck? "I'm sure everyone has my best interest but did it ever cross your mind, Dad, Mom, Michael, I might want a say-so in the matter? Please don't think I'm unappreciative, but I feel like I'm treated like a child sometimes, and I'm anything but a child." She wondered if steam was escaping her ears from her boiling blood. Rand had lost her patience. "God, Rainie, get a grip. Like you say, put your big girl panties on!"

Michael took her hand, looked into her eyes, concerned, "Rainie, no one thinks of you as a child, and nothing was meant to be done behind your back. I don't want you to sign anything you're not one hundred percent comfortable with." His face showed he quickly realized the error of his decision.

"Michael, for the first time I hear Dad has paid off Tom, yay, the house is all mine. Yay, too, I guess. Maybe we don't sell it at all." She turned away from him and walked toward the pantry.

"That's fine, whatever you want." Michael was concerned and appeared to be willing to agree to anything. He followed behind her like a puppy.

"Suga, yes, I got the money together, but it's your money, darlin'. It was from Rand's life insurance policy. When the two of you were born, we took out million-dollar policies on both of you. Rand was the beneficiary of yours and you of hers. I figured paying Tom off was a good reason to invade the money. You still have quite a bit left."

"Why is it I'm hearing this for the first time now?" She turned around. Her eyes squared, and with a look of disgust.

"Because you never needed to know it before," her dad was matter-of-fact and getting a bit annoyed. "This is precisely why I'm not comfortable talking to you about money matters. Rainie, you can be hard-headed, plus it was more for when you were older and didn't work anymore. You've never needed money; you've always had what you wanted." Rand started up again, "You have a real problem, Rainie. Get it together, for once."

She relaxed her anger and spoke with a tad more reverence. "I'm sorry. It has nothing to do with the money. I love you, and it's great y'all want to do things for me." She looked at Michael. "And you too, Michael, but would y'all do it with me and not for me? I want to learn. Please keep me in the loop. I'm excited about selling Nashville and buying Stella." She took a few deep breaths. Her mind was still spinning. *Why is it,* she thought, *everyone always wants to control me? Even you, Rand, so not one more word.*

The conversation seemed surreal, it was going on around her, but she wasn't a part of it. Something had to change; maybe marrying Michael was not the right thing. It was too rushed. There were so many things being pushed through without her say.

"The closing will be quick. Once papers are signed and keys exchanged, I think it's a done deal, and you can start moving in. Am I right, Mr. Williams? Only if it's okay with you, Rai." *Yeah, you know you fucked up!* Rand's voice started scolding," you better straighten your attitude. You're so childish, Rainie."

"Yes, Mike. Papers have to be filed, but given the oddity of the situation, it'll be okay." She could tell she had exhausted everyone in the room.

"When is she going to be here?" Rainie had a curious expression but also a hollowness in her words. *I'm going to join this happy party and deal with it.*

Michael handed her the phone, "You call her."

"Things have happened lightning-fast, and I'm trying to catch up." She directed her comment to him.

"Anyone want a glass of wine because I sure do." Her mom got up and grabbed four wine glasses. Mike took two and put them back. "Y'all not drinking at all anymore? Bully for you." Her parents touched glasses. "Cheers to a happy engagement, a happy marriage, and a happy home."

Michael commented Rainie was a package deal, so he wasn't

marrying only her but pledging to the boys, as well. Not that he was trying to take Tom's place. He'd be the best father figure he could be.

Her dad was candid, "Nothing would please me more than for you to take Tom's place. He isn't the best influence on the boys, but I guess you have deduced that by now."

The agent arrived, and the paperwork went fast. Most real estate hurdles, like financing, didn't exist, given the nature of the sale. All the legal stuff had been taken care of already by her dad. Before long, they were on the way over to the house.

"Mike, the ring is gorgeous." Her mom seemed ecstatic. "You are the answer to a prayer. Our girl has needed someone like you, caring and loving. We were never a real fan of Tom, but you know that." She closed her eyes and nodded as though confirming her statement.

"I'm glad you like the ring. My grandad used it when he proposed to my grandmother. So it's got history." He linked his arm in hers. "I meant what I said about the boys. Your daughter is a package deal. I love those boys like they were my own."

"Grandmother on your Momma's side or your Daddy's?"

"My Dad's. We don't know a whole lot about Mom's parents and grandparents."

"I'm sorry, dear." She patted his arm.

"I'm not. My dad's family was plenty enough for everyone. We're a close-knit unit. I can't wait for y'all to meet. One day when we have time, I'll tell you the story. It's rather amazing." He warmly smiled when he spoke.

"Rainie is beaming over them. I can only imagine they must be something special because our girl doesn't attach well to new relationships."

"Yes, I know, but she did with them." He nodded. "They think she's spectacular because she is." His eyes twinkled when he smiled.

"Mike," her dad put his hand on his shoulder as he came up behind, "speaks volumes."

He could hear her talking non-stop on the phone. He figured it must've been Meredith. "It was great, but I'm not so sure. There's too much to tell tonight. I'll tell you everything, I promise, tomorrow morning. In the morning, it is. Love ya, Mer."

She went over to Michael, "Do you have a heavy caseload tomorrow?"

They drove back to her parents in silence. Once the boys were inside, she stood gazing at him. Even though things emotionally had been dodgy since their return home, she needed his reassurance. She needed him. Was she overreacting? Her gut was saying run, run, run. "Rainie, I'll see you at five-thirty tomorrow on Stella? See if Allie can watch the kiddos, and we can open a bottle on this rare occasion and christen the house." His face dropped with a sad countenance. He pulled her close, looking her in the eyes. "You seem distant, Rainie. Are you okay?"

"Yeah, I'm good." Even to herself, she didn't sound convincing, and it was because she wasn't okay. She was terrified. They kissed good night.

The boys called out to her. She snuggled in the bed with them, "I missed you guys. Everything we did, all I could think of, was how much y'all would like it." She went on and on about the weekend, and before long, they were all asleep.

Morning came, Allie popped in "Kids going to camp today?"

Rainie confirmed the boys and camp and told her to take her time, and she would see her at the office.

She hurried and dressed for the day, continually looking at her ring. "Rainie Landry, Rainie Landry." She wrote her name on the pad by her bedside. The thought of a different name widened the canyon between her and Tom. Her mind was pre-occupied with thoughts of the future, and the ideas were not necessarily good. They were downright scary.

Instead of turning right to Mer's, she went straight, jumped on the interstate, and drove. Her mind drifted all over the place. She heard Rand's voice telling her to turn around and to stop freaking out. Before she knew it, she turned into the Beau Rivage Hotel and Casino on the gulf coast. She checked in, went to the room, and sprawled on the bed. All the old demons in her head started screaming again. She thought about the slumber party, about the loneliness growing up. That's how she felt—lonely and scared and wanting Rand. She cried herself to sleep. Rand whispered to her, "This road, you need to walk by yourself, but remember what you wanted. Go with your heart, Rainie. I know what you want, but do you?"

⊙§

Time went by, Mer found it odd Rainie didn't come over when she said she would. Something didn't feel right. She called Mike's office and left a message. Fifteen minutes passed when Mike returned the call. The alarms started going off in both his and Mer's head. "God, Mike, this is even strange for Rainie. She doesn't just poof disappear. Anything happen last night?"

"I thought all was good, but she seemed somewhat distant. When I asked her, she denied anything being wrong." He went into the conversation between her family and them and the house. He was getting panicked, had he lost her, did he push too hard? Tears formed in his eyes. He asked Mer to call if she heard anything. He got himself together and saw his patients, but his mind was anything but clear. The day was ending, and no one had heard from her. He drove to the house on Stella.

⊙§

Rainie awoke with a start from a myriad of vivid dreams. Sitting on the side of the bed, she started recalling her dreams. She remembered running through the park with Rand. In her usual way, Rand was battering her with questions, mostly about Michael. The dream shifted to their old house where they had lived before Rand died. They couldn't have been more than twelve planning their futures. In the dream, she told Rand that when she grew up, she would marry a doctor and he was going to be handsome and funny and that he would love tickle wars and he'd take care of her forever and ever. It had been a conversation they had while playing the future game all those years ago. Like most dreams, places and times swapped and changed and had no rhyme or reason. From games played by twelve-year-old girls, the setting zoomed to the present. She remembered Rand looked her straight in the face and said, "Well, your dream came true, and now you're running away. Chicken shit. Do something smart and follow your dream, Rai. Wake up!" It had been startling, which made her heart do double-time as her breathing turned into a pant. She needed to go home.

⋙⋘

The phone rang, Mer picked it up, and it was Mike again, "anything?

"No, Mike, I promise I'll call you when I hear from her. She's fine, I'm sure of it. Stop worrying. My guess, she's feeling overwhelmed and has gone somewhere to think and wrap her head around it all." They got off the phone. Truth be told, Mer was feeling a bit nervous, more along the lines of Rainie resorting to some of her old destructive ways, and if that was the case, she wasn't sure how she'd deal with it. Rainie was her best friend, but she couldn't sit by and watch her go through another spiral.

⋙⋘

Rainie drove to the house on Stella. Michael's car was in the driveway. What could she say? He walked from the backyard and watched as she pulled her car next to his. His face was streaked with tears. He was angry, hurt, confused, and scared for her well-being. He didn't know which emotion to begin with.

They spoke simultaneously, apologized, and all he could say was he didn't understand. He put his head down, then looked up at her. "What the fuck, Rainie? You can't do that to me. It's not right. If you need time away, tell me you're going off for a while, don't disappear on me." His lower lip trembled, and the tears trickled down his cheeks. He wiped his eyes and tried to regain composure. "If I fuck up, tell me, just as I'll tell you. I won't up and disappear. I love you, and I think you love me. We can't have it this way."

They sat on the steps going into the kitchen and talked. She told him she felt like her head was swimming, and she was out of control. She didn't purposely intend to hurt anyone, but she felt like she couldn't breathe. "Michael, I was so confused."

"Rainie, we don't have to get married in December. We don't have to get married at all. I love you, and whatever you think is best for you,

I'll roll with it, but don't ever take off on me again. I'm not trying to control you, and if it feels like it, I'm sorry. You ripped my heart out."

"I'm sorry, Michael. I needed time to reconnect with myself. I felt lost, and everyone was planning my life, and I hate that feeling. I love you, Michael, and I want to get married, and December is perfect. We need to make decisions together as a couple." He said he understood, and perhaps his excitement got in the way of being thoughtful. They stood. They held onto each other, neither wanting to let go, both saying they were sorry.

"Rainie, you need to call Meredith. She's pretty upset and worried. Fortunately, your parents were not in this loop." He took her face in his hand and kissed her. "I love you."

She called Meredith. He could hear Meredith expressing her frustration with Rainie calling her immature, selfish, and fucked up.

"I love you too, Mer. I'll see you in the morning, I promise. We can talk then." They unlocked the door and went in.

☙❧

The morning came, and as promised, she made her way to the office. "Good morning, my friend." Rainie put her hand out for Mer to see the ring.

"Let me see. Rai, this is gorgeous. It was a good weekend. I'm assuming? Do you like his parents? His brother? Now about yesterday, what the hell were you thinking?" Mer grabbed her by the shoulders.

"I don't know. I was on the way here, and fear hit me in the face. I had to get away from everything and everyone. I went to the Beau Rivage, got a room. I needed soul searching."

"If you ever get some wild hair up your ass again, let me know. Not cool to do that to people. Thank God your parents didn't know." She sat back at her desk.

"I got it. I promised Michael. Do you still want to hear about the weekend? His mom sent pics in an email. I'll look and see if I got them. It'll be easier to show than tell. How's Paul? I saw his car here?"

Mer called out to Paul, "Rainie's here, and we're in the office."

He came down and hugged Rainie, "I'm glad you're back. Meredith missed you, and all she could talk about was when you'd be home."

Rainie looked over at Mer, concerned, "Is everything okay?"

She burst into tears, "Rai, we're having a baby, and because the heartbeat was exceptionally loud, they think it might be twins. I couldn't wait to tell you, but no, you had to be a jackass and pull your selfish shit."

Rainie hugged her, "Mer, I'm sorry."

"You put Mike and me through hell, which neither of us needed. In saying that, I'm gonna take it easy, at least until I start my second trimester, so a lot is gonna fall on you. You can't be throwing your temper tantrums. Rai, I'm gonna need you. It's your turn to be there for me." Her eyes glistened with ready to fall tears.

"Oh, my friend, I got this. Don't you worry. I imagine we'll move the office to the new house that way you get your home back and can take it easy. If we stayed here, you'd be bopping in and not resting. You and the pregnancy are going to be good. Chill and take care of yourself. When do we find out if you are having twins? I'll be right with you the whole way. How exciting, Mer. What'd the ultrasound look like?"

"Of course, it would be the day the machine went down, but I go back in four weeks, and we'll have pics then. However, I do want to see the new house. We have lots of time to talk about the babies, but right now, I want to see the house."

"You got it, you're sure?" Rainie looked closely at her friend, and there was a tiny pooch in her belly that she hadn't noticed before for some reason. She got up from her computer and put her hand on Mer's belly, and smiled.

"Rai, I hope you don't mind me bailing, especially with—"

"My God, Mer, no. I've thought for the past few weeks you might've been pregnant but didn't want to say anything in case I was wrong. I couldn't be happier. Want to go now or see pics of the weekend first?"

"I gotta see the pics. The house isn't going anywhere." Rainie gave Mer her chair and knelt next to her.

Rainie started fiddling on her computer again and lit up with a smile. Missy had sent a ton of pictures. She carefully went through each one and the significance. "Oh, shit," Missy had managed to get a shot of Michael on his knee, putting the ring on her hand. Both she and Mer teared up.

"It looks gorgeous. Mike never told me he grew up on a plantation, and we've had many heart to hearts." A picture of Jack, John, and Michael came up. "Look at them, they all look alike, but in the looks department, you got the best deal."

"I did get the best one, but they're all similar and gel perfectly. Michael doesn't do Botox or anything. His dad and John are more out in the weather hence the rougher looking skin. They're all down to earth." She told her about the property, the great sex in the horse gear closet.

"The tackle room," Mer corrected.

She told her about his parent's story and the whole Peter Pan thing. "The entire weekend was like something out of a storybook. I was the princess, and he was Prince Charming."

"It's about dang time you're with someone that gets how wonderful you are. I knew it was going to be magical. I had a feeling. When are y'all getting married?"

"December." She took Mer's hand for a squeeze.

"That'll be beautiful, and I understand if you don't want a preggo in the wedding."

"Are you kidding me? You have to be my matron of honor. His brother is gonna be the best man. Please say yes." Rainie had a pleading look in her eyes. They continued looking at picture after picture.

"Can I ever tell you no? Where's it gonna be?"

"No exact date or location yet, but his parents' house would be perfect if it's okay with them. They have three charming guesthouses and oodles of room."

Allie flew in the door, "Sorry, y'all."

"We're getting ready to go to the new house," Mer informed.

"I'm up for seeing it again." Allie was pumped.

❧

Mer 'oo-ed and ahh-ed' about the house, "Your furniture will work perfectly here. You may need to pick up a few pieces but keep it simple. The home is exquisite on its own no need to have your furniture compete. You'll need furniture for the study. That's it."

The new house, the engagement, and the new baby or babies made the morning electrified.

"Since we are officially engaged, I wonder if he'll stay sleeping in the pool house until we get married. I think I know the answer, even before asking." She shook her head. "Moral Michael."

"Talk to him about it," Allie piped in, "let's get back to the office. We can start getting everything arranged for your big move."

"Y'all are gonna have to keep me informed on King's Court. I'll be at the Grand Opening for sure." Mer was glowing. There was a lot to be excited about.

"You need to let it go. You're frying bigger fish right now, and I want to make sure my nieces or nephews get a fair shake from the beginning. Twins can be tricky. Besides, our intern is catching on fast," Rainie was quick to point out.

Allie stepped back, her face in total surprise. "Oh my God, Auntie M is pregnant. Y'all will have to come up with something creative and good because I've always thought Auntie M was the coolest." Her eyes widened as her smile grew.

With life being a massive whirlwind, having Allie was a real blessing. She organized the movers and all the pain in the ass changes of service. Rainie made sure Mer backed away from the business.

Tom scheduled his week trip to Disney for the last week of June. Everything dropped into place. Michael's parents planned to come into town the third weekend in June, which allowed time to get moved into the house and maybe even the office. The D.C. trip was arranged for the weekend of the week when the kids were in Disney.

The only thing not confirmed was the wedding date and the location. Rainie was excited about the wedding and knew the time would fly by. Life was making some massive changes. She figured she'd hold on and enjoy the ride. There was much to be grateful for, and it was a blessing business was crazy. There would be no time for cold feet or nervous jitters. The more stuff going on, the faster the time went. According to Michael, his mom would love to have the wedding at their place. She thought to herself, *just breathe.*

WE ARE FAMILY

It was a day away from the parent weekend, and she was beyond excited. She made sure everyone was going to be at her house for the Landry's arrival.

"Michael, do you think your parents will be okay with us getting married at their place? Mer is going to be eight months by then and can't travel far." She buzzed around the kitchen, chatting as she went.

"I already told you I think it's an awesome idea, and they'll be over the moon about it. You know they got married there. Now, question two?" He sat on the counter, watching her as she went along.

"Do you think we could move your bed out of the pool house and have it a pool house while they're here?" She turned with her hand on her hip.

"Absolutely not. You know my feelings, not with the boys in the house. I'm sticking to my guns." His jaw was set, and he had a determined look about him. There would be no budging him.

She pursed her lips, "Okay. December fifteenth, you know, it's like five months away. You have to be squished in there." She turned on her heel.

"Rainie, I can always stay in the Quarter if it's creating too much of a problem for you."

"No," she answered with a pout over her shoulder.

"Look at your pout," he lowered his voice. "It's not like we haven't been having sex. I don't see where you've suffered, my love. I don't think it's a good message for the boys, and that's what's most important as they grow. I know Diane and Tom live together, but you can tell they don't like it."

"They don't like her. That's the real issue there," Rainie was adamant.

"Whatever, but they have mentioned she sleeps in his bedroom. Kids take note of things more than you think, even at their ages." Changing the subject, "Henry has a birthday coming up in August. We have to see what he wants for his birthday party."

"We do, but right now, for your parent's visit, what kind of food should I have when they get here?" she was pensive regarding the visit.

"Breathe, Rainie. I have to get to work while you, on the other hand, are just steps away from your office," he hopped down, put his arms around her, and kissed the side of her neck. "Don't get your panties in a knot." He whispered in her ear.

"If you think of anything, let me know today so that I can run get it." She was like a long-tailed cat in a room of rocking chairs.

"Will do. I love you. Have a good day." He was utterly relaxed.

"I love you," she ran behind him, "one more kiss."

Allie was already in the office. She touched base on all the projects. Everything had been done and okayed by the baby people. The lady with the living-dining room decorating turned out to be a real pain in the butt as she only wanted Rainie and wouldn't talk to Allie. In the meanwhile, they picked up another client, which Rainie completely turned over to Allie.

Her mom called. "Do you want me to bring anything in particular for the Landry's arrival?"

"Been thinking about what I'm gonna do."

"Do one of your good dips, have nuts, and cheese and fruit. Maybe some salami, better yet, call Langenstein's and get them to put together something. From your first impression of them, I think anything will be fine."

"Thanks, Momma."

The boys were looking forward to meeting Doctor Mike's mom and dad. They had heard stories and seen many pictures. She'd have to remember to take some group shots. She made a list of everything she needed to buy to prepare and to straighten.

Michael got home from work. "How was Botox Thursday?" she kissed him. "Am I in need of some injections before your parents get here?"

"You're insane. Please breathe. You know my parents, and you know how chilled they are about everything."

"What if they don't like my parents?" she worried.

"Crazy lady, you're out of control. Is Allie here?"

"Yes, why?"

"Mom and Dad are staying in my place, and I want to make sure it's freshened up. I could use your help." He pursed his lips.

"Absolutely," she went to change into getting things clean clothes. At the same time, Michael ducked into the pool house to put on more casual togs.

Kids all settled, they took off to his place. When they first walked in, there was a strong pine scent. She walked through the house, inspecting everything, "Michael, you had a cleaning crew come through today, yes?"

He answered from his room, "Yes."

"Then why did you want to come down here? Checking on them? All looks good."

"Nope," he came out of the bedroom, barefoot in only his jeans. "You're way too uptight over this visit. I intend to calm you the fuck down." He took her hand; they went through the kitchen across the courtyard and up to visit Pandora. From a remote, he turned on sexy ethereal music.

He stood silently in front of her. She began to take off her clothes, but he tapped her hand, indicating he would take them off. His eyes were intense. Not soft or loving or friendly. Simply determined. He tied her hair back. "Sit on the side of the bed," he went in a drawer and came out with two things resembling double handcuffs. She had a puzzled look, but they were leather. At least it wouldn't be uncomfortable.

He cuffed one ankle, took her hand, ran it down her side, and cuffed it to her ankle. All the while, he stared into her eyes. "Breathe, Rainie." He took the other ankle and wrist, putting her in a most compromised position, then linked it all together, making her feel hogtied. He stood back and looked at her full-frontal view. *This can't be happening.*

He took a scarf and blindfolded her. "How many times have I told you to calm down. My parents meeting yours is no big deal, but you insist on making it a stress magnet. You need to do as I say. Do you feel exposed? Do you feel vulnerable? I should spank you instead of pleasure you. Why should I be gentle with you when you've ignored my pleas for you to be calm? You must not trust me, and it hurts."

"I trust you, Michael. I don't know if I like this. Your voice is chilling, not loving like usual, but I do. I do trust you. Please let me go and take the scarf off of my eyes." *I don't like this at all. I don't wanna play these games.*

She heard him stirring, and it felt as though he was purposefully ignoring her. A warm spray between her legs was startling. "I know what gets you off, sweet Rainie, and I'll get you there, but first, you have to be obedient and give in to my will, not yours. You must understand I am in control." He lightly pinched her bud. She could feel the blood rushing to her crotch, then a throbbing of want for him began. "No ma'am, not yet. You're holding your breath waiting—give in, I am in control. Dammit, breathe, Rainie. I want to pleasure you, but I won't until you do as I say." She heard him moving away from her. Then as he returned, there was a slight wisp of air across her back accompanied by a soft sting as he struck her with something. "What do I have in my hand Rainie?" He lightly touched it between her legs, wisping it up her body directly below her lips. She could smell the leather.

"You have a riding crop? I can smell the leather." The guessing game took her mind from her compromised situation, and she instinctively began to relax and stopped fighting the fear. How could she possibly hear him smiling, but she knew he was. She could feel it.

"I'm not going to take off the blindfold, but I will take the restraints from your hands. Even though you are able, do not move your legs. I like the view. Open your mouth." She felt him moving toward her mouth. He put himself inside her mouth, sliding in and out. She didn't touch him but created a vacuum with her mouth. "Good girl. You know how to please me. Why is it so hard for you to trust me?" She felt another pinch below and squirmed. "No. Concentrate on my cock." He put a dildo in her hand.

"Use it. Use your imagination." She hesitated. "Right now, Rainie.

Give yourself all to me. Do as I say." She didn't want to and could feel a tear about to spill from her eyes. Who was this Michael? She did as he said. He roughly rolled her nipples between his thumb and forefinger, which somehow made her vaginal muscles relax. She didn't feel as awkward. She concentrated on him in her mouth, and her body began to respond to his pace. He pulled out of her mouth, took the toy from her hand, pushed her back on the bed, and gently slid himself inside her. She was wet, ready, and relaxed. "That's my girl. Give me a good ride." The blindfold heightened her other senses. The waves of passion continued for longer than usual. "For being such a good girl, this is all for you." He pulled out, plunging his tongue inside her. He performed beyond her limits. Just as her body was about to release, he slowed the intensity then pumped her with the toy, and as he did, he sucked and nipped, making her body release.

She threw her head back, every muscle in her body emptying of stress. Even though he had been far more aggressive, he had been right. His command and control made their sexual symphony like a mountain top experience. It was a sensually stimulating encounter unlike any other. There were no distractions. She felt every touch, every wisp of his tongue.

She could feel he was still holding back something. He pivoted his body, never once breaking stride with his most amazing oral skills, and then slid himself into her mouth.

She remembered how rough he liked it on the levee. She grabbed him and pulsed her grasp with his movements. She could tell it wasn't going to take much more for him to explode. She sucked even harder and circled her tongue around him. She heard him moan, which encouraged her to take him deeper down her throat. His body began to jolt, and the finale was momentous. He had brought her over and over, but her encore ensued with his.

He jumped up and began to kiss her as though he would never be able to kiss her again. The toys were strewn all over the bed, and they lay there totally satiated. She ran her hand down the side of his face. She could feel the wetness from sweat, or was it tears?

They lay quiet and still for twenty minutes, then got up without a single word cleaned, and put all things away. Rainie put her clothes on, staring straight into his eyes. He buttoned her shirt without breaking their gaze.

They locked the door behind them and left Pandora. Their more intense episode took their relationship to a new level, and all they needed or wanted was each other. The thrill of the game, which was once mysterious, and erotic had graduated to its climax in one dramatic interlude.

They went into the house. Back in his room, he put shoes and shirt on, and they left.

It wasn't until they were almost halfway home when Michael spoke. He said, "We're growing together, can you feel it? I love you, my beautiful bride-to-be. Thank you for loving me like you do."

"I love you, Michael. I'm not exactly sure what just happened, and I don't know if it's something I want to do again, but I'm definitely relaxed, and the last thing I'm worried about is what anyone wants or doesn't want to eat."

"And hence the point." he was self-assured.

"I'm spent," she smiled at him. "It was intense. You went somewhere in your mind. We came out on a different plane altogether. Agree?"

He kissed her hand and whispered, "agree."

They got home, sweetly kissed good night, and each went to their beds. It was a blissful night of sleep.

When her alarm went off, instead of rushing balls to the wall, she felt no urgency and enjoyed getting dressed and ready for the day. Descending the stairs, she could hear Allie settling the dispute as to who had the best football cards.

Then she heard Michael, "I think the two of you have an equal amount, and they're all good. What you need to do is pull out your Saints cards, figure out which ones you don't have, and we can get them. Then, if you can get along, maybe after y'all get back from Disney, we'll go to one of their training sessions and get some autographs, but only if we can act like gentlemen. Can you do that?"

She had to stop outside the kitchen to hear his loving fatherly advice. Tom would've never engaged. He would have either sided with Thomas or told them to shut up.

She walked into the kitchen, "Did I hear something about a training session? Who's having a training session?"

Henry, with his sweet little voice, filled her in, "No, Mommy, not our training. The Saints training." His eyes were as wide as saucers. "Doctor Mike's going to take us to get autographs."

"Oh, is he now?" she played.

"How did you sleep? You feel good about the day?" he asked her.

"I'm excited about everyone meeting and spending time together. It's gonna be the bomb, yes?"

He gave her a big smile, "Yes, it is. I have half-day today. I'll see you no later than one. You got everything? "

"You still dropping the boys at Mommas? I'm prepared, no sweat. What time are they in again, three-ish?"

"Yes, they're going first to my place, dropping off their bags, and they'll call me from there. You'll have a heads up." She stood by the door as her boys were heading out. A kiss for each, and Michael gently kissed her neck. "I love you."

Allie had the office in check while she had the cooking and preparation for her company, no big shakes. Rainie prepared the dip and cut the vegetables ready to go on the platter. The pasta was nearly finished. She had beer in the fridge for Jack, white wine cooling, and red set to the side, should anyone want it.

Her mom had called three times. The day was ticking by, and all was good.

The house phone rang it was Michael, "hel-lo," she was quite chipper. "Things here couldn't be better. How's your day?"

He hesitated, "Okay."

"But?"

"There's been a bad accident. One of my patients called and asked me to meet her at the hospital. Her son went through the windshield. Evidently, his face is bad, which means I won't be home early. I'm sorry. Pray for this kid."

"Of course, I will, it'll be fine. No worries, you hear?"

"Yeah, I feel like I'm letting you down." His voice sounded sad.

"No, you're being the man I love, go take care of the child. We'll see you when we see you. I love you."

A bit of a hiccup, but she'd get through it without him.

Allie came in.

"What's up?" Rainie turned with a smile.

"Your cell rang, I answered it. Your in-laws are on their way here and will be here in twenty minutes, but probably like fifteen now. You want me in the office or in here? Where's Doctor Mike?"

"He's going to be late." She watched as Allie's face turned to dread. "It's cool, and if it's not, then I'd rather find out now than later, but you're gonna love his parents. Just FYI, they're huggy people."

She grabbed one of her flavored seltzer waters and took a couple of chugs. Allie stood watching. Rainie had the same determined and confident look she had the night she packed Tom up and locked the doors. She was the lady in charge, and there was no mistaking it.

"Grab the colander, strain the pasta, please," she explained about the accident and the boy.

Allie closed her eyes, Rainie guessed she was praying. This whole praying thing was new, and she felt fake, but she was going to err on the side of caution. *Yes, Michael*, she thought, *I'm breathing*.

She finished mixing the sauce with the pasta and put it in the warmer when the doorbell rang. She ran to the door.

"Missy!" she greeted her with open arms. "Jack," and hugged him. He didn't quite bear- hug her like the boys, but it was pretty overpowering. "Welcome. Drink?"

"We're fine, my girl, and the house is as you described. It's gorgeous, and it looks like you and Michael." Missy was as real as it could get.

"Y'all come back and have a seat in the den." Rainie led them to the back room.

Jack looked out the windows. "Look at the back yard, hon. The pool looks like home. Rainie-girl, your yard is cool, and I know someone," he nodded his head toward Missy, "will want to come garden with you."

Missy concerned, "is Michael still at work?"

"He called me a few hours ago to say he was going to be late. There was a bad accident, and a young boy went through a windshield. The parents of the boy asked Michael to meet them at the hospital."

"Mercy me," she took Rainie's hand, "that's horrible, but the child is in good hands with Michael. You know he prays diligently before each of his surgeries?"

" I know. He says God guides his hands. Jack, you want a beer, or soft drink, or water? Anything?"

Jack had a broad smile to go with his unapologetic frankness. "Look here. It's bad enough to have this all the time with Missy, but don't tell me you too?"

Rainie laughed. "Yes, sir, and my Momma as well."

He assured her. "I'll snoop and find what I need. Ladies, you do your thing, don't worry 'bout me."

"Show me around the house. " Both Allie and Rainie walked Missy through the house ending with the master bedroom. "Is it true Michael is sleeping in the pool house?"

"Yes ma'am. He's adamant because of the boys."

"He's his father's son, what can I tell you? They're more alike as time goes by. I think it's a good quality, but I don't have a problem with y'all sleeping together, but what can I say? Michael is Michael."

They finished the tour with her office. "Speaking of, where are the little ones?" Her parents came through the side gate with the boys blasting through just about that time.

"Mommy!"

"Missy, these are the boys, Henry and Thomas, and those are my parents, Leslie and Henry Williams." The introductions went well.

She knew they would get along but didn't think it would be as fast. She glanced to the sky with thanks.

"Suga, where's Mike?"

Jack answered the question. Everyone put on a somber face.

Her dad continued, "Mike is the best in New Orleans, the boy's in good hands. Leslie will tell you. Quite a few of her friends are patients of your son. They rave about him, and as a person, there isn't anyone I know as straight-laced." He whispered to Jack, "he sleeps in the pool house and will until the wedding. You don't find many young men with such a clear head."

"I wasn't sure how long the arrangement was going to last. Mike's a determined person, which is another way of saying hard-headed." Both men laughed.

Thomas and Henry welcomed the thought of another set of grandparents and to finally have cousins. The mothers chatted in the kitchen. Rainie overheard Missy saying how sorry she was to hear about Rand and how hard it must've been on all of them.

It got to be supper time. Rainie was going to have Allie feed the boys. She hadn't heard from Michael and wasn't sure how long to hold off dinner for the adults.

She went with her gut, and dinner was served to everyone right then. It was about a half-hour later Michael called and said he was on the way home. Cleaning up had already started, but the coffee was still dripping by the time he walked in.

He came in looking exhausted. After a kiss and quick whisper that all was well, he turned his attention to his mom.

"Darling," his Mom said, "we were sad to hear about the child. How is he?" She hugged him. "You look tired. Let me fix you some food."

Jack edged in for one of his bear hugs.

Rainie piped in, "Y'all go sit in the dining room and visit. I'll get Michael's dinner and bring out some coffee." Both moms wanted to help. "Missy, go visit with Michael, he's looked forward to seeing you and Jack. Momma, if you could, grab the coffee cups."

She brought the food in and took a count for coffee, calling the number to her mom. Rainie called the kids down. As usual, they smothered Michael with affection. He hugged them longer than his usual quick, tight squeeze. His eyes started to mist.

As her parents were leaving, Rainie confirmed the plans for dinner at the club the following night. Mer and Paul were going to be at dinner, so they'd get to meet Missy and Jack.

The rest of the night was laid back and light chit-chat. Michael sat close to his parents, with Rainie resting on his knees. "Mom, any chance we can have the wedding at y'all's place? It'll be on the fifteenth, and maybe we could get the pastor from your church to officiate the marriage? I know there's enough space. We want something simple."

Jack grinned. "I told your mom y'all might get married at home. Rainie, did Mike tell you Missy and I tied the knot at the house? Y'all end up with a marriage like ours – you'll be blessed."

"Yes, sir, he did. We had talked about maybe the islands or a Colorado ski resort, but my friend Meredith, whom you'll meet tomorrow night, will be eight months pregnant and won't be able to travel. There isn't a more beautiful spot than your house, and with the three cottages, there'll be room for everyone."

Missy told her she could put it together in her sleep not to give it a second thought. About another hour went by, and his parents left, promising to be back for breakfast.

Holding his hand, Rainie commented, "Michael, you look beat. Do you want to go crash?"

"I want to sleep with you tonight if it's okay?" he seemed utterly spent.

"Absolutely, let's go to bed." He stripped to his boxers and undershirt and climbed into bed. She put her nighty on and got in next to him.

He clutched her. She could feel the gentle movement of his body as he cried, "My patient was right around the boys' age. I almost lost it, but I literally had to put his face together again. It could've been one of our boys."

Henry tapped on the door. When he saw Michael, his little head tilted to the side. "Doctor Mike, are you okay?"

Michael wiped his eyes and nodded. "Can I sleep next to you? I had a bad dream." He drew down the covers and patted the bed for Henry to climb in. "Doctor Mike, I heard there was a boy that got hurt, and you had to take care of him. I bet it made you sad. When I'm sad, I come by Mommy, and it all gets better. You did the right thing to sleep by her. Just like you made that boy better, she'll make you better." Michael kissed his forehead.

"Thank you, Henry. It made me sad because I thought of you and Thomas. I consider you two my boys and felt bad for the boy's parents. I pray y'all will always be safe."

"We will be, Doctor Mike. We always wear our seat belts and never ever sit in the front seat." Henry snuggled between them, closed his eyes, and slipped back to sleep.

Morning arrived. Everyone was ready as the day was about to start.

Michael came in the kitchen door with the typical "how'd everyone sleep" series of questions and hoped his parents were comfortable.

Throughout breakfast, they hammered out the plans for D.C., which was only five days from then. The boys would be at Disney, despite their grumblings about Diane and their dad.

Jack talked to them and asked them lots of questions about Disney. They said they loved going to Disney, just not with their dad and Diane.

"Michael, where were you this morning?" his mom inquired.

"To check on the boy and his parents. It did my heart good to see him, and I'm glad I went."

Lightening the atmosphere, Jack whispered, "Boys, the bad thing about coming to New Orleans is there's too much good food, and I don't need more food." He patted his stomach.

The boys gathered around him like bugs to a light. "When can we come to your house and ride Cisco and Dyna? Mom told us all about the horses." Thomas' eyes glittered as he listened and thought of riding horses, fishing, and all the fun stuff Rainie had told them about.

"Y'all are welcome anytime, and you don't have to wait for them," he pointed at Michael and Rainie. "I'll come pick you up."

They spent the early part of the day driving around. They passed Rainie's old house, got sno-balls, and then returned home.

Before going to dinner, everyone gathered at Rainie's parents for a pre-dinner appetizer party. Mer and Paul pulled up as they arrived. They were a nice-looking couple, both polished and perfect, like Barbie and Ken dolls. Mer had an air of sophistication about her. The pre-dinner event flew by, and much of the ladies' chat was about the excitement of new babies, while the men talked about the market swings and then to Louisiana politics, it all jived.

When they got to the club, they were seated at a round table, which brought conversations closer. Both Rainie and Michael observed the interaction between their favorite people. One couldn't have asked for things to be better.

On a brief bathroom run, Rainie pointed Ryan out. She knew he'd probably track her down, and then Mer would finally meet him.

As sure as the sun would come up the next day, Ryan tracked her down, "Hey, babe."

"Hey yourself, how are you? This is my friend, Meredith." He looked good and a bit more together.

"Cool," he shook Mer's hand. The club was wearing off on him in some ways, but not all. "Wow, you're smokin', Rainie. The good life agrees with you. You look happy, really happy."

He looked at Mer, "I used to wonder what was up, she had a look of sad headspace, but it's gone." He looked back at Rainie. "I moved after all the shi..uh, stuff. Got myself a girlfriend kinda, an' I might be able to go back to school," he smiled at her.

He was precious, she thought. "I'm glad you moved, and great you have a girlfriend. I wish you the best of luck in school. You're a sweet guy." She kissed him on the cheek, "you take care."

"I miss you, Rainie. Miss Meredith, it was nice to meet you."

They parted from his company and went to the ladies' room. "Okay, Rai, he's adorable. He does look like he should come out of an Abercrombie ad, but shit, he's young."

"We listened to the Rolling Stones, got high and danced under the sheets, what can I say?" She swiveled with her hand on her hip.

"Watching you and Mike interact, my girl, is something special. I love it when I'm so right. Didn't I tell you?" She winked at her in the mirror.

"It's confirmed the wedding's gonna be at his parent's house December fifteenth. It'll be small – his family, my family, which includes Allie and Eric, and then y'all. I don't know anyone else I would want to invite. He might want to invite his staff, but I doubt it. If so, we'll get a party bus for them. Let's get back before they send the calvary." They touched up the lips and headed back to the table.

When they got back to the table, a few comments were passed about them being like young girls, gossipy in the bathroom. It was all said in a happy tone. "Oh, sorry, Mer and I were talking about the wedding. We came up with the idea of having a party bus for your staff." She looked at Michael, "Possible?"

"I love the idea, and they'll be thrilled to be there. Great idea." The rest of the evening was filled with childhood stories featuring Rainie and Michael, and of course, Mer was right smack in a lot of the girl stuff.

As they had hoped, the families merged as one, and it was a splendid mix. Missy and Jack were flying out the next morning to D.C., and Rainie and Michael would join them on the coming Friday, the boys would still be with Tom.

There were tears as Missy kissed Michael good-bye, "Mom, y'all be careful going back to the Quarter, and we'll see you in D.C."

When they got home, it was last minute packing for the boys' Disney adventure with Tom and Diane. Since her conversation with Tom, things had been better with Diane, but not stellar. It was going to be a work in progress. She understood Diane was young, but anyone with half a brain would know what was okay and what wasn't. Tom's squeeze needed to get with the program. "Y'all love Disney, and I'm sure it's going to be fun if you put your mind to it," Rainie emphasized.

Michael came bounding up the stairs, "where are my two favorite little dudes? Why the sad faces? Don't tell me you don't want to see Mickey, Donald, and Pluto? Oh, and I know, Thomas, you'll love the Princess breakfast." Thomas looked over, shocked.

"Doctor Mike, I'd rather get bitten by rattlesnakes than go to some Princess breakfast. Tell me you're playing. Maybe you confused it with Henry going to the Princess breakfast. He *loves* Ariel."

"Good taste Henry, she's beautiful. I can't say as I blame you."

"Do you think I would go to the Princess thing? I don't care if Ariel is there or not. I'm *not* going. I think we're doing Jedi training. I *am* excited about that." Henry was ecstatic over the Jedi stuff.

Rainie brought the conversation to a close. "Okay, guys, it's bedtime. How about kisses?"

Everyone settled. Rainie and Michael went downstairs, "Michael, you're good with them. I'm a bit worried as to how they'll react to the Disney wedding."

"Not your problem," he kissed her nose. "See you in the morning." She watched from the window as he went into the pool house. She was ready for December to come.

With the boys being in Disney, the week flew by, and she had forgotten since they were gone, she could enjoy company in her bed.

She and Allie put their efforts into winding up what they could before her exciting trip to D.C. Allie and Eric could hold down the fort and take care of Bonnie and Clyde, Michael's labs, while they were away.

☙❧

The bags were packed, and she was antsy to get to the airport. "Breathe, Rainie. We have more than enough time. This is supposed to be fun, not stressful."

"I can't wait to meet Wendy and her family, but what if they don't like me?"

"What if you don't like them?" he gave her a look.

"I'm sure I'm going to like them. I love your parents."

"I'm sure she's going to like you. Every member of the family has given the stamp of approval, and as I told you, we're all pretty much the same. Let's enjoy our time away and—"

"Breathe, I know."

The time came to load up the bags and make their way to the airport. Michael had arranged for a car service to pick them up, which made everything much efficient and worry-free. They checked in, boarded, and were in the air in no time.

They were expecting to be greeted by a car service and brought to the hotel, but Wendy and her four boys were at baggage claim waiting.

"Oh my gosh, Michael, four boys, I didn't realize she had all boys. I thought she had two of each."

"Nope," he grabbed Wendy with a tight hug, "Hey boys, gimme some love." He hugged the whole pack.

Wendy stood looking at Rainie. "I can't believe you're here in front of me. Michael looks happier than I've seen him since he was a kid. It's always been boys in the family, and now Mom and I have another comrade." She reached out to Rainie with a hug.

Rainie felt like she needed to pinch herself. Things in her life had changed and fast. It was head spinning. Her old life was a distant memory.

Michael brought her to a few museums. They ate at excellent restaurants in Georgetown, and yet, were able to spend quality time with Wendy, Dave, and their boys, Matthew, Mark, Luke, and John.

Walking into Wendy's home was like being in a whirlwind of boys and their toys. She could feel the same warmth she felt at his parents' house, but it was far more chaotic. Wendy reminded her of Missy. They looked similar, had the same mannerisms, and sounded identical, although Wendy had lost some of her drawl. It was fun seeing her interact with Michael. The brother-sister relationship warmed her to her soul.

Thanksgiving was going to be interesting with Wendy's four boys and her two. Since it was but a weekend in D.C., it flew by all too fast. There was hug after hug and several good-byes.

Even the boys had warmed up and were excited to have two more boys in the family. Mark was Thomas' age, and Little John was close in age to Henry. Wendy had accepted Rainie with open arms and, like Missy, was full of tears when they left.

Flying back, she rambled on about Wendy and all the boys in their family. The trend started with Michael and John, and then Wendy having four boys. What were the odds?

Michael laughed, "that's one of the reasons she's excited we're getting married, not to mention she was sick of me talking about the girl of my dreams. Can you imagine if we were to have a girl? Can you say spoiled rotten? Girls, as you saw at dinner, are revered in this family."

"Michael, everything I have learned about your family all speaks to who you are, and I love it. I tried to explain it to Mer, but she had to see it for herself. You're something special, Michael Landry, something indeed." It had been a whirlwind of a weekend, and it ended too soon.

❧

Once home and settled, it was back to the grind with the living room-dining room lady who was getting nervous about the holidays coming up. Rainie let her know hers was the first in line for completion. Any add-ons would have to be after the holidays.

The weeks flew by, and with each visit, Mer was blossoming more and more, and, as suspected, Mer was expecting twins – girls at that! She and Rainie cried together. "I wish Rand were here. She'd get a real kick out of me having twin girls. You'll be godmother to one, and I guess his sister or one of mine will be godmother to the other. Being pregnant is harder than people think, or than I thought. I always thought women were playing the femme fatale." She rocked in the chair.

"Hardly. I'm sure some do but imagine putting a twenty-pound weight around your waist and doing all the crap you do every day. Shit, that gets heavy and exhausting fast. I can't even fathom the pressure or heaviness of twins. Make sure you put your feet up every day, or they'll swell like a mother." The twins' nursery was about as pink and white and frilly as a room could get. Rainie walked around looking at all the baby things.

She loved having her time with Mer, and the closer the wedding was getting, the more she found she needed their time together. Rainie never thought of herself as overly emotional, but life was different. Michael had helped to break down the cocoon she'd woven over the years. If they couldn't get in, she couldn't get hurt, but Michael was the slayer of the Rainie wall. Changes could well have been the theme of the year. The contrast was stark. In a blink, school was back in session, Halloween had come and gone. Thanksgiving, while fabulous with Wendy and her crew, seemed to be done way too fast. As anticipated, the kids got along famously and attached quickly.

Tom and Diane's marriage didn't cause issues with the boys, but Tom seemed more unsettled than she'd ever known him to be. As Michael put it, he was a strange duck at the best of times, but he had become even more bizarre. His interaction with the kids continued to shrink, where they would see him every three to four weeks instead of their standard every other weekend. The less, the better was her opinion.

A couple of weeks before the wedding, she received a call saying her dress was ready for pickup. It was a beautiful champagne gold, which was gorgeous with her auburn hair. The front draped in soft billowy tucks, but not too much. Her rather thin body allowed the dress to cascade perfectly. Tucks fanned out gathered on one side, which emphasized her tiny waist, and then it fell straight, no flounce or anything. She felt like it was subtle yet stunning. The seamstress had taken a smidge too much in at the waist. While it didn't show, the waist was a tad pinchy. It would be easy enough to handle—a change in diet from rich foods to salads.

She had told Mer to wear anything she felt comfortable in and deemed appropriate.

Michael insisted on tuxes for him and John and the dads. She felt it was a little dated, but he got to pick them out. After all, he was the groom.

Since much of what they'd done reflected his parent's courtship, she had a ring made for Michael identical to Jack's. He'd get a charge out of it.

The days had seemed to go slow, but before she knew it, they were heading to his parents' house, her mom and dad following right behind.

Missy had it decorated beautifully. As they drove onto the property, her heart filled, bringing a flow of happy tears. Twinkle lights adorned the oaks, and a grand tent blocked the view of the stables. The florist was due first thing the next morning to start decorating the tent poles with floral arrangements. It was going to be quite elegant and dramatic, but intimate. This was the wedding she wanted. Her stomach did flip flops. She couldn't remember a time when she felt so excited.

As was Missy's custom, she came running out to the cars as they went down the drive. Wendy and their crew had arrived earlier, as had John. The scene was complete.

Jack put one of his big arms around her, "Rainie-girl, you nervous? Are those tears?"

"Missy did an amazing job. It's like a fairy tale, and am I okay? Not really. I'm overly excited; I feel like I'm on the biggest, fastest roller coaster ever! Also, I can't wait to finally have him in the house with me like a real family." She rolled her eyes.

"Gotta say I'm amazed he has kept to his word about sleeping in the pool house. He's a man of his word, but he is a man. He loves you more than life itself, Rainie-girl, and your boys."

After showing her parents to their quarters, everyone settled in the hearth. Mer and Paul showed up in time for gumbo, potato salad, crawfish pies, and boudin.

Michael sampled the food, "I didn't see Dominique, but I know she was here. Those are her boudin balls if ever I've tasted them. She's coming to the wedding?"

"Not only her, but her whole family, dear." Missy was in entertaining mode.

"Mom, why was Rainie's stuff was moved into the girl's guest room?"

"Michael, there's a room full of boys next to her. What would it look like if she slept in the bed with her groom before the nuptials? You can't see her at all tomorrow. It'd be bad luck. Dad is taking all the men for the day and will be back a couple of hours before the service. You, son, will be dressing in John's room as yours is off-limits until after the wedding."

"I get it, but I don't want anyone getting drunk and acting like an ass. Will you please mention it to John and Dad? You know how they can get."

"Michael, what's it you're always telling Rainie? Breathe? Take your own advice. Darling, everything's going to be splendid. Have I ever let you down before?"

He held her tightly, "I love you, Mom." He looked in her face, and both were misty-eyed. "You've never let me down, ever."

Toasts began after dinner, which then turned on the tears, and by the end of the celebrating, they were passing the box of Kleenex. The kids didn't get why the adults were crying, but it made them cry as well.

"John, you know I'm sleeping in your room tonight with you?"

"Says who?" He challenged.

"Mom. She said I couldn't see Rainie all day tomorrow and I can't sleep in my bed until after the wedding. My room is off-limits."

"What the fuck? That's jacked up. Where do you think you're going to sleep?"

"The bed." He said matter-of-factly.

"Like hell. I don't want your sweaty body in my sheets."

"What? By far, John, I should be complaining about your bed. Who knows what I'll catch in there."

"Sheets changed, bro, and roll away in the room which I'm taking because I'm the shit. You better go give your girl a big wet kiss and catch a feel cause it's all you're gonna be thinking about tomorrow." He slapped Michael on the back.

Michael looked for Rainie, who was in a conversation with Wendy and Mer about babies and birthing, "I don't want to break up this riveting conversation, but I'd like to kiss my almost wife good-night." Rainie walked away with him. "You know I can't see you tomorrow. I can't even sleep in my own room. I won't see you until you walk down the aisle."

"You better give me one hell of a kiss, buster. FYI, I'll be the girl in the gold dress coming down the aisle." He walked her out into the moonlight. He delivered a romantic kiss but then grabbed her breast with one hand and her ass with the other. She pulled backed with a most surprised look. He gave her his "cat that ate the canary" smile. "Oh, I see how it is, Michael."

"It's all John's fault," he laughed. "He told me I better cop a feel because you would be off-limits tomorrow. I blame John." He kissed her again and again. "Now I need to get upstairs, so I play by the rules."

It was awkward sleeping in another room. Besides being excited, she had a case of the nerves causing a little nausea. "Dang it, too much boudin."

The next morning the guys headed out early. Mer knocked on her door. "You excited? It's only hours now. You told me about the dress, but let's have a look-see." She pulled it out of the garment bag, "it must look better on the bod than on the hanger, sista."

"It's gorgeous." She took off her clothes and slipped on the dress. "Now zip me up." Mer pulled the zipper up, but it stopped. "Don't tell me it's caught the fabric."

"No. Either the alterations girl screwed up, or you've gained weight. This sucker isn't going up, Rainie."

"Do I look like I've gained weight?" She took off the dress and tried the zipper, and up it went. They studied the dress to see if it could be let out, and it was a no go.

"Fuck, what am I gonna do?" Wendy knocked. "C'mon in. I'm having a bit of a meltdown. The dang dress doesn't fit." She was on the verge of tears, from being sad but also because she was angry with herself.

Mer greeted her at the door with warning as to Rainie's temperament at the time. She saw her face and the dress in her hand.

"Oh dear," Wendy gasped.

"What am I going to do?" She plopped on the bed and cried.

"You can try my dress on." Wendy offered. " It's long, and it's pretty, and I'm sure it'll look great on you being taller than me. I'll try this one on, and we can swap. I know it's not optimum but let me grab mine." She brought back her dress. It was a deep evergreen, perfect for the holiday season. Rainie stepped into it with a less than happy expression, "It looks beautiful on you. Such a good color with your hair."

"Look at my stomach. That's not normal. I ate last night but haven't had a bite today. The thought makes me want to hurl."

Meredith looked at Wendy, and Wendy looked back with a funny look.

"What, y'all?" As the tears rolled down her cheeks.

Mer burst out in laughter. "Rai, I think you're pregnant."

"I can't be." She turned up her nose with defiance.

Wendy said she wouldn't have said anything for the world, but she had noticed a small difference since Thanksgiving, which had only been a few weeks.

"No way. I need a test. Isn't this lovely?"

Wendy put her arm around her, "The secret stays in this room. Calm down while I go to the store."

Wendy left, and Mer sat next to her, "You've been using protection?"

"Most of the time."

"From your telling of adventures, you're at it like rabbits. What did you think would happen? It's not the end of the world. Besides, our kids can play together."

"And maybe I just got fat." She had a hard time catching her breath through the sobs.

"Stop it, now. Rainie, you're still thin. You have a little belly you usually don't have, so fuckin what." They sat on the bed talking about the 'what ifs' until Wendy returned.

"I bought two. There was a special. I know it's not first-morning pee but give it a whirl. It'll be negative, but then you can try first thing when you get up."

She went into the bathroom, "You've got to be kidding me. This can't be happening. Pregnant? Me pregnant? I wonder when," as if switching gears, she went back to the dress thing. The pregnancy was not an urgent matter at hand. The dress was another story. "Let me try the gold dress on again. Maybe with the three of us."

They tried to the point where they were sweating. No matter what, it wasn't happening, "Let me try the green dress on again." She looked at herself from all angles. "It is what it is, right? Y'all, secret stays in here until I tell Michael."

It was about an hour until the service was about to start. Rainie looked out the window, everything looked beautiful, and the chairs were filling up, especially since the New Orleans contingency had arrived.

She put the green dress on, which fortunately went well with her gold shoes and the flowers. She came down the stairs. Her mom looked at her and mouthed about the dress. Rainie signaled to drop it.

Missy smiled, "You look beautiful. It's the perfect color for you."

They went to the back where her dad and Jack were waiting with her boys. The music began for the mother of the groom and commenced to the final announcing shrill of the organ. Rainie, her dad, and her boys stepped forward. All eyes were on them, and she noticed Michael watched her every move. The pastor asked who was giving her away, and it began.

Michael whispered, "What about the girl in the gold dress?"

"Later." Her nerves were on edge.

They began the vows with Michael. He presented Thomas and Henry with symbolic rings as a vow to them. Michael was articulate, and with each vow, his eyes became even mistier. The day he had longed for had arrived, and he was marrying that Freshman co-ed he fell in love with, at first sight, many years before. There wasn't a dry eye amongst the guests.

Then the pastor looked toward her "Lorraine Riselle Williams Todd, do you take this man Michael John Landry, as your lawful wedded husband," she could hear herself speaking the vows as though in a dream. It was surreal. The words swirled and echoed in her mind. "If so, say I do...

Let the adventure continue in Half Past Hate, turn the page for a sneak peek...

Quick Peek

The pause was deafening. Michael looked over at her and could tell she was welled up with emotion and was trying to speak. The words were having trouble coming out. He squeezed her hand gently and smiled.

"I do," her eyes said it all. She had never known such happiness. This man standing before her was everything she could have imagined, but more. He was handsome in a real kind of way. His sandy hair had natural gold and warm brown streaks. His eyes were a deep green, emanating love, and it was all hers. Always had been. Somehow, she knew this deep idyllic feeling in her heart was forever, not just for the minute, the hour, or the day, but forever.

The Pastor announced, "I now proclaim you husband and wife, you may now kiss your bride." Michael could barely contain his enthusiasm. What was only a dream at one time was now his reality. Tom's mistake was his gain. Rainie was now his wife, the woman he had always loved.

❧

Diane had been Tom's fun piece of ass. She was more than adventurous, she was his toy to do with as he pleased, but it had changed. He hated her. She had made him hate her. First, she blackmailed him into marriage, and now she wanted a child. No way was he giving in to a child. The girl was delusional. His life was one big screw up. He had to do something to get out of the contrived marriage. He had to face it. Flaunting his infidelity was brazen, and he deserved the ruination of his marriage to Rainie, and for all his despicable acts, he opened himself up for the likes of Diane, a ball-busting, blackmailing bitch. Ultimately Tom screwed himself and good.

❧

Grayson peered over his glasses and looked at his wife for more than three decades. She'd become cold, callous, and calculating. Their perversity had risen to unspeakable heights. At one time, Marguerite had been a pretty, curvy young woman. Now she looked like an aged, embittered lesbian. The soft edges were gone, and the remnants were harsh, almost hateful, but this was his life. Little did he know the hellish web of debauchery he'd created would be damning, leading to the demise of his life, the law firm, and three other marriages.

Many Thanks...

A tremendous thank you goes to the love of my life and husband of thirty-five years. Doug, you were the inspiration. Many years ago, you brought sanity into an otherwise insane world and showed me a different level of love and passion, which burns more brightly with each passing day.

Thanks go to my family, the built-in cheering squad in my moments of doubt.

If not for the stable of editors and coaches–Mark Malatesta, Kate Studer, Toots, and Paige Brannon Gunter—*A Quarter Past Love* would have been a tragedy of run-on sentences and comma splices.

Thanks to Gene Mollica and his team for tying the bow, making this dream a reality with their perfect graphic design for the book cover and to his interior designer, Cyrus Wraith Walker, for his talent in creating a beautiful interior format.

About the Author

Born and raised in the enchanting city of New Orleans, the author lends a flavor of authenticity to her story and the characters that come to life in the drama of love, lust, and murder. Her vivid style of storytelling transports the reader to the very streets of New Orleans with its unique sights, smells, and intoxicating culture. Once masterful event planner, now retired, she has unleashed her creative wiles in the steamy story...*A Quarter Past Love.*